Teenage

waistland

Teenage Waistland

a novel

Lynn Biederman & Lisa Pazer

delacorte press

Copyright © 2010 by Lynn Biederman & Lisa Pazer

All rights reserved. Published in the United States by Delacorte Press, an imprint of Random House Children's Books, a division of Random House, Inc., New York.

Delacorte Press is a registered trademark and the colophon is a trademark of Random House, Inc.

Visit us on the Web! www.randomhouse.com/teens

Educators and librarians, for a variety of teaching tools, visit us at www.randomhouse.com/teachers

Library of Congress Cataloging-in-Publication Data
Biederman, Lynn.
Teenage Waistland / by Lynn Biederman and Lisa Pazer. —1st ed.
p. cm.
Summary: In their separate voices, three morbidly obese New York City teens relate their experiences participating in a clinical trial testing lap-band surgery for teenagers which involves a year of weekly meetings and learning to live healthier lives.
ISBN 978-0-385-73921-4 (alk. paper)
ISBN 978-0-385-90776-7 (lib. bdg.)
ISBN 978-0-375-89722-1 (ebook)
[1. Obesity—Fiction. 2. Clinical trials—Fiction. 3. Self-esteem—Fiction. 4. Family problems—Fiction. 5. New York (State)—New York—Fiction.] I. Pazer, Lisa. II. Title.
PZ7.B4743Tee 2010
[Fic]—dc22
2009049672

The text of this book is set in 12-point Goudy.

Book design by Kenny Holcomb

Printed in the United States of America

10 9 8 7 6 5 4 3 2 1

First Edition

For Eric—for everything
—L.B.

For Mumsy, Shelley Pazer, who never stopped believing
—L.P.

Lisa is grateful to:

Stephanie Lane Elliott, our long-suffering editor at Delacorte Press, whose wisdom and insight pushed us deeper into our characters and lifted our story to creative heights we had no clue we were capable of. How does *anyone* write without you?

Ginger Knowlton, our agent at Curtis Brown, for her tireless efforts and enthusiasm on behalf of *Teenage Waistland*.

My *scrumptious* sons, Jake Sherman and Alex Sherman; Shelley Pazer; Doug Sherman; Sari Sunshine; Sam Sherman; Beth Bradford; Josh and Jamie Bradford; and the rest of my family and friends. You're the best cheering section anyone could ever hope for!

David Bradford, for being my sounding board and impact attenuator throughout the writing process, but mostly for never letting me go without a cooked meal during crunch time.

My sister Dina Bassen; Todd Bassen; James Bassen; Alana Bassen; and Gregory Bassen, for that transformative holiday dinner where your love, support, and brilliant suggestions (go, Alana!) renewed my inspiration and energy for the book, just when I needed it most.

Early readers Chelsea Baken, Gaby Biederman, Lori Snow, Deanne Conrad, and Tami Yellin, for their sage advice and enthusiasm.

And most of all, Lynn "Non-Lynnear" Biederman, my co-author and friend, for one of the best adventures of my life!

Lynn is grateful to:

Superbly talented Stephanie Lane Elliott, senior editor at Delacorte Press, fellow foodie, and friend, for guiding us in your articulate and patient way. Like *Unraveling*, *Teenage Waistland* has benefited from the fine editorial hand that shaped it.

Ginger Knowlton, for her enthusiasm for *Teenage Waistland* right from the start. Years ago, when I heard you say agents and authors are like doubles partners, I knew you were for me.

Brilliant, beautiful daughter, Gabrielle, for her book advice, boundless encouragement, and energy—I mean *really*. Wonderful, special, second-to-none son, Brad; husband and best friend, Eric; brother; parents; aunts, uncles, niece, nephew, cousins, etc.

Rob Newborn, superb friend and Doc, for always coming through, and Dr. Jeff Zitsman for his incredible generosity and expertise.

All my friends, old and new, local and not, Union buds, Ladybugs, and tennis pals for the happiness and true awesomeness they bring to my life. If there was ever a competition for who has the most fabulous circle of friends, I would snap that trophy up easy as pie.

Last, but not in any way least, my coauthor, Lisa Pazer, for relentlessly insisting on making *TW* great, for her relentlessness in general, and yes, for her insistence too, but above all, for her sheer greatness.

Teenage Waistland

I

CattLE CALL

Marcie, 5'4", 288 lbs

Marcie Mandlebaum here: sixteen years old and sporting the collective girth of the Tenafly High cheerleading squad—this according to their captain, my twitorexic stepsister, Liselle. She's too much of a dimwit to master the intricacies of a tape measure, but there's no denying it. Her guesstimate is in the ballpark.

We're crammed into a crummy conference room in the Midtown Sheraton, waiting for some Park Avenue doctor to pitch his clinical trial for Lap-Band weight loss surgery for teens. By we, I mean me; my mother, Abby; and every fat chick within a fifty-mile radius of New York City who could stand to drop *at least* one hundred pounds. A couple of fathers and maybe six fat guys are here, but it's more a female thang—sixty or so heifers being herded around, for the most part, by tiny fat-o-phobic, lipo-sucked mothers like mine. This is *nothing* like SeaWorld, where every baby whale can count on having a bigger mama.

I haven't seen so many fatties together in one place since

our nightmarish visit to Graceland in Memphis last summer. We spent four sweltering hours waiting in a stampede of bulging polyester just to get in. "Ground zero for the world's obesity epidemic." "Welcome home, Moosie," Liselle had snickered. But rather than injecting her usual diplomacy to avert a brawl, Abby seized the reins of Liselle's bandwagon and said, "Of course you're not anywhere near the size of these people, darling, but your weight has been moving in the wrong direction and you need to turn it around." But that was more than sixty pounds ago, so now Abby's dragged me here.

Five rows of metal folding chairs have been halfheartedly arranged in front of the stage, as if the bozos setting up for the event weren't certain this particular audience should sit in them—for me and my tubby brethren, there's a fine line between a chair and a catastrophe. I blow past whatever few empty death traps are left and park myself in one of the open spots against the wall. Abby, hot on my trail, wiggles her way into the three centimeters of breathing space beside me by shoving one blubbery mass into another with an apologetic smile. "Standing room only," she whispers into my ear, ignoring their glares. To Abby, who won't eat in a restaurant that doesn't have a waiting list for an open table, crowds—excluding the one at Graceland—provide indisputable evidence that we're in the right place. The thing is, *we're not.*

Finally, while the groans of stressed metal die down, Dr. Hal Weinstein, the head of the Lap-Band program at Park Avenue Bariatrics, steps to the podium and tests the microphone. This is my signal to pull out my iPod—what *don't* I already know about this surgery? I've been hearing about it blow by blow for over a year. But Abby whacks my hand and flashes her eyes at me—her *behave yourself* glare. "Just listen for a change. You might learn something," Abby hisspers— her standard hiss/whisper combo—and I resign myself to a slow and painful death.

Weinstein leans forward, pauses, and then booms into the mike: "The Lap-Band is *not* the solution to weight loss." My eyes fly open. *WTF?* Has the seminar been hijacked by some fanatical "fat power" fringe group and the real doctor is lying gutted in some back room? My hopes are dashed as he finishes his thought. "The Lap-Band is merely a tool, albeit an effective one if employed in a comprehensive supervised program that addresses the behavioral, nutritional, physio-logical, and psychological aspects of obesity.

"But as a *long-term* weight loss tool, the band is only effective if accompanied by behavioral changes. So while nutritional support and exercise are key aspects of our pro-gram, we place special emphasis on addressing the emotional issues underlying teen obesity. That's why participation in weekly group support sessions is mandatory for the first year after the surgery." I groan and shake my head and Abby nudges me with her elbow.

"The requirements for admission into our clinical trial are documented in your . . ." And then I can stand it no longer, and tune out completely.

To understand the magnitude of this disaster, you have to understand what a clinical trial is—and why, unless you have a terminal illness and nothing better to do with your time left on earth than get poked like a lab rat, it's best to stay away from them. There's a federal agency called the Food and Drug Administration—or FDA, to the literate few— whose job is to ensure that all food, drugs, and medical de-vices (like pacemakers, artificial limbs, and Liselle's future breast implants) sold in the United States are safe and effective. To prove "safety and effectiveness" to the FDA, companies experiment on small groups of carefully selected volunteers in tightly controlled settings.

This Lap-Band thingy is one of these so-called medical devices. It's an inflatable silicone band for super fatties that gets surgically installed around the top of their stomachs. When the band is inflated by injecting saline solution through a port implanted in the abdominal muscles, it contracts. And now you get a tiny stomach pouch into which only the smallest amount of food will fit. So when the aforementioned fatties can't plow through their usual amount of chow, lo and behold, they lose weight. It's a short, simple, *reversible* low-risk operation and you're out of the hospital in less than a day. *And* the Lap-Band has *already* been approved by the FDA! Megatons of weight lost, safety and effectiveness totally proven, et cetera.

But of course, there's a catch. The FDA approved the Lap-Band exclusively for *adults*. So livestock under eighteen can only get their hooves on this miracle of modern medicine in one of two ways: through an FDA-approved clinical trial, like the one Doc here is recruiting for, or, like my best friend, Jen, did, by going to Mexico, where the FDA can't throw its weight around.

For obese American teens who can't get into or afford a Lap-Band clinical trial and have xenophobic parents who won't cross international borders for medical care, there's another surgical option in the United States. It's called gastric bypass, and it's scary stuff—Abby and I looked into it last month. They pretty much slice, dice, and rearrange your entire digestive tract. Something like one to three percent of gastric bypass victims *die* from it, and a large percentage get seriously screwed by pulmonary embolisms, leakage, infection, malnutrition, and other health issues. But because the FDA hasn't approved the Lap-Band for teens yet, far more of us are undergoing gastric dissection than getting banded. Shaken, Abby had marched me right out of that consultation. Her epiphany: Being fat is, in fact, preferable to being disemboweled.

o o o o o o

It's ten p.m. and I'm splayed on my bed, taking a break from ranting.

"Maybe Abby is right and this clinical trial isn't the worst thing," Jen finally pipes up, as if she's had me on call-waiting the whole time and hasn't heard a word. Jen, of all people, should appreciate the epic proportions of this catastrophe; I was at her bedside in Mexico—along with her mom—when she got her Lap-Band done there, the Christmas vacation before last. Besides, we've been inseparable since my first day at Fuller Prep—she flipped off a teacher when he corrected her pronunciation of "antebellum," and even though she was freakishly large, and so sharp and tough that the other kids seemed terrified of her, I knew instantaneously that she was my girl.

"Jen!" I wail. "This clinical trial isn't anything like what you did! For me to even be *considered* for admission, I have to get a million physical exams—bone density, pulmonary function, blood tests—"

"No kidding, genius," she cuts in. "Everyone gets a battery of tests before surgery, no matter where they go."

"But that's only the beginning! There's a mountain of paperwork—doctors' letters, notarized releases, insurance authorizations or evidence of financial ability to—"

"So what? Abby's going to deal with that stuff, Marce, not you. Your insurance probably won't cover it since it's a clinical trial, but Rich Ronny—"

"Hold your fire, Jen. There's more! *Then* I'll be interrogated by their 'fat nazi' shrink to make sure I can commit to the Lap-Band 'lifestyle.' Plus, Abby has her own evaluation, where she's got to sell this shrink on her ability to ride my beached-whale butt into submission—as if Gran doesn't barrage my mother with new starvation plans for me every other day. *Now* what do you think, Ms. In-and-Out-in-Three-Days?"

Jen snorts. "Listen, Ms. Drama Queen. I had the same evaluations. Adults never think teens are equipped to make big decisions, so they just want to be sure everyone involved understands what they're in for. Makes total sense. Can we roll the credits on your daily diatribe now?" "Daily Diatribe" was the name of the hysterically bitter feminist poetry rant series Jen used to post on YouTube.

I snort right back at her. "Nope, saved the best for last. *If* I even get in after all this crap, they're going to make me join a *cult* where I'll have to wax poetic about everything related to my eating—from my 'feelings' to my bowel movements—every week for a whole year!"

"Oh my God—you mean a support group like Alcoholics Anonymous? That really does suck," Jen says in her *horrified by the sheer inanity* voice. Finally, she gets it. "Look, Abby is reasonable. Discuss this with her. Just do it calmly and nicely. She always listens when you're not laying into her."

"I guess I'll give it one last shot. Stay tuned," I sigh, and take off to find Abby.

o o o o o o

"Marcie, I get it. I was there," Abby says wearily the instant I *calmly* embark on my rap about how needlessly annoying and drawn out the clinical-trial admission process is compared with getting the stupid surgery done and over with south of the border. She and Ronny were polishing off a bottle of wine on the porch when I found her, and he politely took off so as not to *intrude*—probably his euphemism for "listen to Marcie gripe." "Just give me your Mexican surgery spiel so that I can go to sleep," Abby says.

I whip out my iPhone with my right hand and Abby's credit card with my left. I really want to fling them at her, but I keep my grip on both items and wave them in her face instead. With the wine and all, she's slow on the uptake and gives me the quizzical variation of her *get to the point already* look. "Mom!" I shriek. "I'm demonstrating the elegant simplicity of the Mexico option. You just need to be able to dial the freaking phone number to set up an appointment and place a deposit. That's it! The exact same surgery! Jen was in and out of the clinic in a single day. No hoops, no groups, no one breathing down her neck for all eternity. Plus, it costs ten thousand dollars—that's less than *one-third* what Park Avenue Bariatrics is charging. We can even upgrade to the all-inclusive Cancún special—the surgery plus five nights at a five-star beachfront resort, a private nurse, and—"

Abby shakes her head, grabs her empty wineglass, and heads inside to the kitchen. "Forget Mexico, Marcie. Money isn't the issue. I want the best for you. You'll be under constant supervision of doctors and nutritionists throughout the entire weight loss process. And the support—"

"Mom! I *can't* sit in a support group listening to a bunch of fat losers ramble on about their stupid little lives. Get me another psychologist—I promise I'll cooperate this time and not spend the session texting with Jen."

Abby slams her glass on the marble countertop. "So that's what you were doing?" she snaps, and storms out. I resist the urge to take her precious crystal wineglass and smash it on the floor. Instead, I just wait to hear her footsteps on the stairs before grabbing a spoon and hitting the freezer.

God, I *hate* my mother. Of course she can afford to put me through this ridiculous and expensive clinical trial now that she's married to Rich Ronny Rescott. The more money Abby can spend on my misery, the more she'll enjoy the ride. Just the *idea* of not getting ripped off sends her running for refuge in the Dolce & Gabbana department at the Short Hills Neiman Marcus. They only make clothes for women size 14 and smaller, and Abby fantasizes about me one day fitting into her beloved D&G the same way competent mothers dream of their girls graduating med school! If Abby had stayed married to my dad, I'd have been banded in Mexico before you could say "burrito grande with extra sour cream." Then again, if my mother hadn't dumped my father and moved me to this soulless suburban hell so she could be with Rich Ronny, I wouldn't need my stomach cordoned off in the first place.

2

BEING MORBID

East, 5'6", 278 lbs

Annie Katia Itou is my given name but I go by "East," a nick-
name arising from "Far East" and my crazy Polish grandmother,
who lived in our sunroom from the time I was a baby until
she died six years ago. Grandma's entire life orbited around
her pills and me, her "little China doll"—yet another term of
endearment that irritated my *Japanese* father. Though he'd
grimace silently in Grandma's presence, he always voiced his
disdain when she wasn't around.

" 'Far East' is an expression used to imply *foreignness* or
exoticness in a derogatory way. Tell her again, write it on her
hand if necessary. Annie is not Chinese, and she's not from
the Far East." One time, Mom tried to gently explain that
while her mother might be uninformed, she wasn't racist.
"Uninformed and racist? They're the same thing!" Dad had
said in the loudest voice I'd ever heard him use. "I won't tol-
erate racism under my roof." Then, in an even louder voice,
Mom shouted, "The woman is in *diapers*, for heaven's sake.
How do you expect her to understand anything I explain
to her?"

Luckily, Dad's moral objections were no match for Grandma's Alzheimer's, and "East" stuck. Had Grandma picked up on "Pacific Rim," the politically correct term for East Asia, she might have nicknamed me Pacific and then the joke in school would be that I swallowed an entire ocean—or that my rear end is as wide as one. You don't ever get used to being called names like "Beast" or "Feast," but after a while, you learn to bear it. Maybe I just don't care about being a reject. That's why I'm not exactly jumping on my best friend Char's latest harebrained scheme.

Char's had us on a zillion different diets and starvation plans over the past few years. Now she's absolutely positive that our solution to weight loss is Lap-Band surgery. She was reading about it online when she saw the advertisement for this clinical trial in the city.

"Totally meant to be," she texted yesterday, along with the hyperlink. "We are so doing this!" Last night, Char called me with more of her latest research. "Asians have a significantly lower rate of obesity than the general population."

"Great. Not only am I an outcast at school," I said, "I'm an outlier among my people. Thanks for the breaking news."

She snorted and probably rolled her amazing blue eyes like she usually does when I exasperate her. Char's fat like me, except she's beautiful.

"You're so negative! I'm gonna have to smack you," Char replied. She's not serious in general, but she's very serious about this. (For the record, I'm negative about this and negative in general.)

Char calls me the Black Shroud. "Hey, Your Shroudness," she'll call, "wanna go shrouding?" That's going clothes shopping with me. She teases me that I could start my own fashion line—Grim Reaper for Girls. Char's always all out there with her big self in her bold colors, and I don't understand how she does it. If it's not black and baggy, I don't feel comfortable.

Looking back, I'm not sure if I grew into East or out of Annie—I just know I'll never be an Annie again. "Annie" sounds too happy and optimistic. Not that I'm always miserable. A shroud is made of fabric, not cement. Sometimes I can completely de-focus on my body, like when Char and I delve into our favorite pig-out—Boylan's black cherry soda and zeppoles from Mario's. The fried dough and flavored soda tangoing on my tongue spins off a warm, happy *all's right with the world* feeling. I exist for this feeling. Or maybe I should say, except for this feeling, I might not feel anything.

Lap-Band surgery would mean no more zeppoles and no more Mickey D's fries washed down with a Friendly's mocha chip Fribble—although there's only a handful of golden sticks left by the time we reach Friendly's, three blocks down. No more cookie dough. No Nacho Cheese or Cool Ranch Doritos—we can inhale a party-sized bag of those every day. If we get banded, we'll probably never have any of that again. Or even if we could, it'll only take a chip or two to fill up the tiny change purse that'll be our new stomachs. You can't cram very much happiness into such a small space. This is what I'm marinating on in this auditorium full of fat kids when Char elbows me.

"Get moving," she orders, standing up. "You're so in outer space."

There's a cute guy wearing a football jersey walking by himself in the direction she's pushing me. Dr. Weinstein is keeping the parents in the main auditorium and the kids are being broken into groups for Q&A sessions in the smaller conference rooms. Through my ballerina flats—the only ballerina anything that could be linked with me these days—I feel the floorboards vibrate and imagine the building crumbling under the weight—all these fat teens wanting to be part of this trial. Or maybe, just part of something.

"Oh, great," I mumble. "I'm already sweating."

"Shut. Up. Shroud," Char says, and pulls me along behind her as she strides toward this smiley nurse holding a clipboard. I groan and shake my elbow from her grip. The nurse says, "Ten," to Hefty Quarterback, and, "Okay, number eleven," to Char. Char whips around and yanks me forward.

"She's twelve."

Twelve is exactly how old I feel when Char speaks for me, which, in fact, she's been doing since the day I turned twelve. Since the day my mother shoved me, my friends—my entire birthday party including the gifts and loot bags—out the front door with Char's mom, Crystal, who piled us all into her minivan and took us to Jan's Ice Cream Parlor. That was the party where I couldn't speak, much less blow out the candles. The party where Crystal sobbed when they sang "Happy Birthday," the party where Char whispered, "East, that's so *you*," as I numbly opened my presents. *So me?* Not that Char meant any harm or could have imagined I'd vomit my ice cream cake all over the table, but that was the moment I realized I had no idea at all who I was. The only thing I knew was that it was my twelfth birthday party, and an hour earlier, I had flung my cardboard party hat at the girl who called it babyish, and ran off to get my Little Miss Briarcliff tiara. I bopped down the drafty stairs to our basement, but never finished looking for the dumb pageant crown. I found my dad—he was supposed to be at work—hanging from a beam instead, his feet dangling above my old wooden rabbit step stool, which lay in pieces on the concrete floor.

If not for Char, I wouldn't still be here. *On earth*, I mean, not just here in Midtown. As I think about this, my annoyance fades. Really, I should kiss her feet for towing me along in her life.

We came here together, all 568 pounds of us; Char is five feet eight, two inches taller and carrying twelve pounds more. If this were an SAT math question, it might be:

Together, two obese girls weigh 568 pounds and want to shed 288 of them. If each of the girls wishes to lose the same amount of weight and still maintain the 12-pound difference, what does each girl hope to weigh?

I'll just tell you. I'm 278 pounds—144 light-years away from my 134-pound target weight. Char weighs 290 pounds and her "so hot" target weight is 146. That's as of yesterday, at least, when Char made me come over for a weigh-in on the digital scale Crystal ran out and bought in the midst of their Lap-Band mania. Char insisted we needed to know our *exact* weight because they'd use it along with our height to calculate our body mass index, and we needed to make sure we have BMIs of 40 or more or else we'd be disqualified. I didn't see how there could be any doubt that we'd be well over the cutoff. But Crystal made it official by waving the calculator and announcing our winning BMI scores, and Char shrieked and stuck her palm in my face for a high five. Char said my high five was lame, but it was the best I could do. It's official, all right. I'm not only morbid, I'm *morbidly* obese.

Crystal's not just on board for Char's latest brainstorm for everlasting happiness, she is, as Char gleefully put it, "scrubbing the deck." When I muttered that *my* mom was going to sink this surgery scheme of hers faster than the iceberg sank the *Titanic*, Char smacked me and said I was awfulizing again. But it's true. How can I possibly dream my mother will help me get this surgery, when she refuses to leave the house for a carton of milk? All she does is eat, sleep, watch TV, shop online, and knit—obsessively. She doesn't notice I never wear her sweaters, and I doubt my brother, Julius, likes them either. He's six years older than me and a junior at Cornell. Less than halfway through his senior year in high school—only two months after my father died—Mom sent him away to prep school in Virginia. It's true, Julius had begun drinking alcohol—during school, even. But he was an A student before everything happened, and was just in a lot of pain. Instead of helping him through it, though, Mom turned her back on him. Julius suddenly was gone, and I can count on one hand the times I've seen him since. He didn't even come home the first Thanksgiving or Christmas after the funeral, and now it's two or three days at most during Christmas vacation—if at all. We used to talk on the phone a little, but even that stopped when Julius moved off campus with his fiancée. Now we just text once in a while. But I don't blame Julius for making a new life without us—Mom's the one who shipped him off to be somebody else's problem. I've always been terrified that if I gave her the slightest bit of trouble, I'd be sent away too, but maybe that would have been the best thing—it's me and Mom who got morbidly obese, not Julius.

Our family of three—fat, almond-skinned Japanese girl with long jet-black hair; even fatter pale and graying blond woman; and lean, dark-haired white boy with big green eyes—would be hard to figure to someone on the outside. Or maybe they'd just think I was adopted.

Mom probably won't attend Julius's graduation next year—or his wedding for that matter. She doesn't seem able to be out of the house and around other people anymore—for any reason. That's why I have to be there for him—so he doesn't feel like he's completely alone in the world. But Julius has no idea how much more weight I've gained since he last saw me—fifty pounds at least. Either Mom hasn't noticed, or she's just not saying anything.

I should be paying attention. That's the look Char's flashing me. Her brow is raised and she's jerking her head in the nurse's direction as if spacing out alone could nix our chances for getting into the trial. The sides of the chair are digging into my hips and I notice I'm not the only one constantly shifting. Suddenly, Hefty Quarterback's huge arm goes up.

"I was wondering—"

"First, please introduce yourself and tell us your age," the nurse says.

"Bobby Konopka, sixteen," Hefty Quarterback says. He's got wavy dark brown hair and gentle blue eyes, and I like his deep voice. His Syosset varsity football jersey is emerald green, probably 4XL, and *Refrigerator* is scrawled in Magic Marker down the right sleeve. A bull among cows. Char raises both her eyebrows at me this time, and I look away so she doesn't detect the heat racing to my cheeks. "Um, where do you lose weight first, and like, how much, how soon?" His voice is unsteady, like mine when I answer a question in class, even when I'm sure I'm right.

"It's different for every person," she says. She's elaborating when Bobby looks up and catches me watching him. I yank my head so fast in the other direction that I feel my neck spasm, but in the split second before I gave myself whiplash, I think he smiled at me! I'm staring at a section of the floor now, fighting the impulse to check if there's any evidence of his smile left or if I imagined it. When the nurse finally finishes talking, a hand shoots up from the side of the room opposite Bobby, and I keep my eyes fixed on it as I slowly raise my head.

A fat girl with short, frizzy brown hair and tiny tortoise shell glasses stands up. She's wearing a lime green New York Philharmonic T-shirt over black stretch pants with gray sneakers.

"Marcie Mandlebaum, sixteen. My question is about the amount of weight you lose with the Lap-Band compared to gastric bypass surgery. I went for a consultation with a bariatric surgeon, and he said that even if I were old enough to get the Lap-Band, he would recommend the gastric bypass because you lose more weight with it."

The nurse is delighted.

"Not so," she says, clapping her hands. "The Lap-Band has only been used in this country since 2001, when the FDA approved it for adults, so up until recently, we didn't have enough data to compare it with gastric bypass. The small pouch created with bypass surgery is a permanent physio-logical alteration that can stretch, so that over time people can regain some or all of their weight back—"

"Like Randy Jackson on *Idol*," someone calls from behind Char and me.

"He's one example," the nurse says. "Weight loss is cer-tainly slower with the Lap-Band, but after two years, overall weight loss is about the same. We believe the Lap-Band is superior to gastric bypass because it's much less risky, it's reversible, and it's adjustable—we can tighten or loosen the band to adjust your food intake.

"How long will it take to lose weight with it, though?" another girl cuts in.

"It's individual," the nurse says again. "Teens have faster metabolisms, so you could lose one hundred pounds or more in a year. But you have to eat right, because it's easy to cheat the band. Liquids go right down, so if you eat ice cream, milk shakes, candy, or anything that melts or starts digesting in your mouth, it's not happening."

One hundred pounds in one year. My mind is shifting back and forth between imagining being thin and forfeiting Fribbles.

o o o o o o

"It'll be horrible when school starts," I tell Char on our way home. "I mean, two fat girls in the cafeteria sharing a four-ounce container of plain yogurt. What's that gonna look like?"

Char sighs and rolls her eyes. "We barely eat at school anyway, so it's going to look exactly like what it looks like now—two high school girls on a diet. The only thing different will be all the *after*-school eating we won't be doing, like Mario's. So stop awfulizing, Shroud. The crazy stuff you worry about so never amounts to anything."

"I'm trying to imagine our lives without food, that's all."

"East. Imagine your life with a boyfriend. That's all *I'm* saying."

I don't tell her I already am. Or that the boyfriend already has a name—Bobby, the Refrigerator. "I guess," I just mumble, twisting my hair back into a bun. As if any guy could ever like me.

"I mean, girl, we so could be bopping. Strutting—like, check us out." She's shimmying her big melons. "Check us." I don't point out how they could deflate, become tangerine-sized by Christmas. "Happy! East, we could be *really* happy."

It's then that I realize that this might be what I'm afraid of most.

3

moobies

Bobby, 6'2", 335 lbs

I don't feel like talking. I just want her to get me into this trial thing and not tell her friends.

"Bobby, sweetheart? Bobby?" It's normally an eight-minute ride from here, but the GPS shows arrival at home in twelve. Either way, I'll probably miss the whole first inning.

"Bobby, *slow* down!"

"I'm going fifty-five."

"Fifty-eight! *Slow down now!*"

Syosset is the next exit. Mom flicks off the radio so we can talk. That's a lot of talking time.

"My phone's buzzing. Bet it's Dad."

"Leave it. You're driving. So, did you talk to anyone in the Q and A session? What did the other kids seem like?"

"Fat."

"No." She makes that clicking sound with her tongue. "You know, do they all want to be in the trial?"

"I don't know."

"I spoke with a few of the mothers. Park Avenue

Bariatrics has a good reputation. That Dr. Weinstein is one of the top laparoscopic surgeons in the country."

I nod. "Can I put the game back on?"

"This is not a small decision, Bobby."

"Yeah," I mutter.

"Did you ask about, y'know?" She's waving her hand across her chest. It's bad enough having *moobies*—man boobies—but that they're anything remotely similar to my mom's makes me want to crash the car into the guardrail.

Even with my big pipes, I'm a fat slob. But the worst is the damn breast meat. Me and MT are the only virgins in our crew—eight of us in the group since middle school, five on varsity football together, six done the deed. One, me, not even coming close. The guys have been busting on me. At parties, *they're* always hanging with hotties, but they push me toward the fugly girls or the Coke-bottle-glasses type— the ones they think are the charity cases. Zoolow's pretty big too, and he, like every guy on first-string varsity football, has no problem getting girls. Every guy on varsity except for me.

This twig at the Massapequa party said, "Whoa. You need a mansiere, like a *bra*ssiere, but for men. Ha-ha." I'd have strangled her with *her* padded brassiere except she's dating one of the guys on the team. "Shut up, Boney" was all I said. But since then, it's been out there—that skinny girl's laughter in my head. Even when it's not in the locker room, or the halls, or at other parties, it, her, the whole moobie thing— it's always there.

"Bobby?"

"Uh-huh."

"So you don't know about—?" She's pointing again. I gotta look straight ahead.

"I'm driving. Sorry."

"Honey, I think you should try to be part of it. I know how unhappy and self-conscious your weight makes you feel. Plus, it's just not healthy for you."

"Yeah."

"There were only a few boys there, so you have a good chance of getting in. I'm excited for you, Bobby. You too, right?"

Exciting is being starting offensive lineman and creating a huge hole for the running back. Leveling guys—that's exciting. Having girl surgery to get rid of girl boobs—no. Surgery because girl diets don't work—no. Not exciting.

"Yeah. I'm excited, Mom."

"I have a good feeling." She sighs and does her deep breath thing. "You should tell Dad how strongly you feel about this when we get home. Don't be afraid to express how being heavy bothers you—you *aren't* your father and his feelings don't have to be yours. Get it off your chest, Bobby. Did you hear what I said?"

"Yeah."

"No pun intended," she says, and pokes me. "Seriously, you need to talk this over with Dad."

I feel more tightening in the pit of my stomach.

"Don't worry. I explained to him how your self-esteem is more important than, well, anything else, and he said he'll try to be open to the idea." Mom, as usual, reads my mind. It's funny. My dad is like my best bud, but Mom keys in on things he doesn't. Like me missing junior prom. But I probably couldn't fit into any tuxedo. And I don't dance. Zoo and Craighead hounded me to come, even without a date.

"I know a few girls going stag. I'll set you up, Refrigerator-Man," Zoo had said. "Maybe you'll get lucky, lose your V-card."

"I don't need anyone to fix me up," I lied.

Prom night, I stayed home and watched TV with Dad and a box of Krispy Kremes. It was fine. But Mom pulled this ad for the Lap-Band trial out of the paper, so I guess I'm not the only one who knows everything is not all good.

o o o o o o

"Refrigerator-Man. Buddy," Dad calls. "You're late. I tried to call you in the car. Get over here. Beckett's on the mound."

"What's the score?" I plunk down on the couch.

"Bottom of the second. One nothing."

"Nice." I'm shoveling onion dip with a Ruffles potato chip.

"Forget that. Here." Dad passes me large containers of lo mein, fried dumplings, and greasy spareribs. "Just delivered. Hot. Egg rolls too." He motions with his chin. Sundaes will be later, after dinner. More tradition.

I grab the plate and chopsticks Dad set out for me.

"Thanks," I say, emptying the lo mein carton. "Did you see that?" Dad's playing it back even after the replay and we cannot believe the call.

I'm ripping into the spareribs when Mom enters the den. Shaking her head at the two of us slobbering down the food and screaming at the TV, she kneels to pick up some stray kernels of fried rice on the carpet.

"There'll be no more of this if he gets into the trial."

"Shhh. Watching," Dad says, pointing his slimy finger at the TV. Mom frowns again and sighs deeply.

"Fine. I'm off to yoga, and then to close up the store," she finally says, and bolts. Except, two seconds later, right when Jeter is sliding into second, she strides back in all huffy and slaps down the paperwork from the bariatric place on the coffee table. Dad pushes it aside so he can get to the duck sauce packets. Mom pushes it back.

"He wants this, Rob. He needs this. Tell him, Bobby," she says. I act like I don't hear her. "Bobby?"

"Game'll probably be over around six. Wanna just pick up some meatball subs for dinner on your way back?" Dad says, his eyes fixed on the screen. "And make sure the back gate to the lumberyard is double-locked this time."

"No, I've got chicken marinating in the fridge." She throws me a meaningful look and takes off, muttering something about the mess.

"Bye, Mom," I yell.

It sucks that I'm making her do all the pushing. I get that. I might not be as hyper about it as she is, but really, I want this as much as she wants it for me. I just don't know how to explain it to Dad, and Mom can talk to him better anyway. When the Energizer Bunny comes on at commercial, I lean over to pick up the brochure with the Lap-Banded-stomach drawing on the front, and then look at my plate. With that little pouch, I'd only be able to cram down one fried dumpling. Dad pulls the brochure out of my hand.

"So? You want to do this liposuction?"

"It's not like that."

"It's horse manure, is what it is. Did she convince you?"

"No, it's my decision. . . . I mean, if you'll let me."

"If I'll *let* you? This isn't even you talking—it's your mother. What about football, son?"

"What about it?"

"*What about it?* For God's sake, kid. Do you think they need a ninty-eight-pound weakling on the front line to *trip* the other players?"

"No way. I'll stay strong. I'm gonna stay all-state, Dad; what, are you kidding?"

He's leafing through the forms and papers. Dad was all-state too. Offensive lineman, same position as me. In his Syosset High yearbook stuff like *Robert Konopka, you gorgeous hunk, remember me,* and *I love you* was written in curly girl handwriting surrounded by little hearts. I saw it in the basement with his college football stuff. Memorabilia. It sucked seeing those words next to my name under a picture of a guy looking exactly like me—minus the moobies. We don't do the senior/junior thing. My dad and me are both Robert Konopka. For a while, people would say Little Bobby and Big Bobby. When I shot up to six feet two and went from 275 to 335 pounds, though, Big Bobby wasn't the big Bobby anymore.

"Says here that for the first six weeks, you'll be on liquids and pureed foods and less than a thousand calories. That's nowhere near the amount of energy you'll need for football. And what week in August does practice start? Says here you'll need six weeks to heal before you're able to do any strenuous exercise."

Damn. Forgot about the recovery period. It'll be close. "Dad, I promise. I'll be fine by the time I go back. I'll make sure of it."

"You promise? You won't have your strength, not sipping water and eating baby food, not at a thousand or even two thousand calories a day." Dad's looking at me now. He hasn't even noticed the game's back on.

"I've got plenty of excess energy. I'm wearing it." *On my chest.*

"And Coach? What does he say about it? He thinks his top lineman needs to slim down too?"

I grab the fried-rice container, but it's empty, so I toss it back on the table. "Dad, please let me deal with Coach, okay? It'll be fine."

"Not so fast. Watch who you're talking to. You and your mother just don't get this. And this thing's the price of a car."

"Obviously, I'm working at the store this summer, so if the money—"

"Hey. Listen. *Our* store. *Your* store one day. And then your son's store, when you're too old for it. And it's not the money." He's shaking his head. "You're big. So what? You're big—we're big, Bobby. You, me, Grandpa. It's who we Konopkas are. That's no good anymore? You're the top all-state lineman in the league. That's no good either?"

"No. All-state is like everything to me. I'm proud—"

"Certainly made me proud. My son holding up our family tradition."

"I'm not gonna even be *as* good. I'm gonna be *better.* I swear."

Dad studies my eyes until I look away. "I don't think so, Bobby. I just don't see how," he finally says, and turns his attention back to the game. A-Rod is at bat and he cracks the ball past Lowell.

"That guy's a force," Dad says, pushing the table away so he can stretch out his legs. I watch how excited he gets at some stranger's talent and it occurs to me how kids at my school and people around town—even kids in rival schools—all know my name. I hear them on the field.

"Ree-fri-ger-ay-tor!" I need to stay all-state, he's right—it's who I am. And glancing at Dad's expression when the next batter strikes out, I know there's another Robert Konopka who really needs this too.

"A-Rod's so strong, it's ridiculous," I say.

"Got nothing on my boy," Dad says. He leans toward me and swats my leg with the rolled up Lap-Band booklet in his hand.

4

the cheat sheet

East

"Lemme see that." Before I can even release the top button on my jeans and find a comfortable position on her carpet, Char grabs my questionnaire for the psych appointment from my backpack and starts riffling through it. "Are you crazy? You can't say this. Your Lady of Shroudness, this is so not the kind of answer that's gonna get you selected." She's tapping at the question that reads *I can't have fun when I have to watch what I eat. Evaluate this statement as it relates to you.*

"What's wrong with what I wrote?" I say. "If we enjoyed life without food, we wouldn't be morbidly humongous."

Her nails are digging into the papers as she's examining them. "Don't you get it? You can't be honest!"

"Well—"

"No. No. No." She's reading and shaking her head, and when she looks up at me, it's as if she's detected a foul smell. "You checked off 'emotional eater' and 'use food to self-medicate.' Are you kidding, East?"

"No. It's true. Eating always makes us feel better."

"How are you possibly on high honor roll? If you were a cutter, would you tell them that too?"

"If *you* were listening to the nurse, you would have heard her say how important it is to be honest about our eating behaviors."

Char takes a deep breath and loudly blows it out toward the ceiling. "Okay, let me spell it out for you. This surgery requires us to make drastic lifestyle changes. The purpose of this questionnaire is to help them evaluate our ability to make these changes. The only correct answers are the ones that make us look like excellent candidates. So save the honesty for your diary." She yanks a stack of papers from her desk and waves them in my face.

"Stop," I say, batting them away. "What is all that?"

"The keys to the kingdom," Char announces with a bow.

I must still be staring blankly, because she tosses my questionnaire onto her chair and smacks her desk.

"I downloaded this booklet from the American Society of Bariatric Physicians website. It's a cheat sheet, East—the answer key! It contains the *official* guidelines that doctors use to make their psychological assessments. Exactly what we need to say to get in! I pretty much cribbed the whole thing for my questionnaire."

"You did not! Let me see."

"It's already done and gone, girlfriend. My mom mailed it yesterday."

I pull myself up off the carpet and sit on her bed without taking my eyes off her. Why wouldn't we mail them together? And since when has she—have we—gotten so desperate? Finally, I say, "This is still *surgery*, Char. Even if it is laparoscopic and they're only cutting tiny holes instead of completely opening us up. We need to be hon—"

"You're still so not getting this, East. We can't risk not getting in! Next year, all this could be gone!" Char grabs a handful of her stomach and punches her hip. She stares at me for a moment for emphasis and then sits next to me on the bed. "Seriously, East—one year from now—think of a place you'd like to be, looking all thin and fab."

The picture flashing through my mind is Bobby with his arm around me at my junior prom, but Char's always suggesting we take a bus up to Cornell to visit Julius so we can meet some "hot college men." "How about Julius's graduation?" I say.

"Bingo!" Char yells, bouncing back to her feet. "Imagine you and me showing up together in Ithaca next spring looking all hot and sexy—think about how excited Julius would be to see you thin again!" She's strutting around in a circle with her chest out and tossing her hair.

"What? Ugh, gross. Who wants to look hot for Julius?" I laugh, making a face like I just drank sour milk. Char stops mid-strut, grabs the guideline sheets off her bed, and thrusts them at me. Then she retrieves my questionnaire from her chair and goes back to studying my answers.

"See? Another wrong answer. You can't say that you turn to food to deal with negative moods, stress, and depression. According to the guidelines, psychos, depressives, and mental cases in general are bad candidates because they're less *capable* of sticking with the program. A whiff of mental illness and you're so out," she snaps.

"I'm just being honest about my 'relationship with food,' okay?" I mutter. When you can count your important relationships on two fingers, should you really give one up?

"Fine, do it your way." Char sighs. "Keep on sounding like your miserable Shroud self so they skip over you and pick a jollier kid."

"Fine," I growl. "We'll do it *your* way."

Char erases huge portions of my answers and then tosses my questionnaire back at me. "Oh, before I forget—under dieting history, make sure to list at least ten different diets so they see how much serious effort you've put in without results."

"*Ten* diets?" I wail. "I can't think of ten."

"Pfft. Sure you can. We've been on at least a hundred. Here, off the top of my head, in alphabetical order: Atkins, the Blood Type diet, the cabbage soup diet, Fat Loss for Idiots, the *French Women Don't Get Fat* diet, the grapefruit diet, the Hollywood Diet, the Negative Calories diet, Nutrisystem, Weight Watchers, and the Zone." She crosses her arms smugly and smiles. My best friend, the Rain Man of diets.

"Uh, what about the No-Fad Diet diet?" I ask, and Char throws a pillow at me. "Okay, 'Describe yourself how you think family and friends would,' " I read aloud. *Friends. N/A* I write in the air and say, "Not applicable in the plural sense."

Char snatches her pillow back like she's going to need to throw it at me again. "What about Friday night?"

"Mary and Diane probably invited me only because you asked them to."

Char shrugs. "We still had fun, and it's important not to sound like a loner."

I sigh. "Is it okay if I put that *people* would describe me as smart, maybe a little too serious, and shy."

"Yes, good," Char says. "Forget the 'shy' and 'serious,' though. And add that you're a good daughter, sister, and friend. Wait, forget 'good' and put in 'reliable.' 'Reliable' sounds better."

"It sounds canned."

Char rolls her eyes. "It *sounds* like you're responsible and dependable—a good little girl who'll change her eating habits, be positive, and do what she's told, no questions asked. Except for the part about you being positive, we wouldn't even be lying. Seriously, you always do what you're supposed to do. And I promise—the minute we're accepted into the trial, you can go right back to catastrophizing the hell out of everything."

"That's a relief," I mutter.

"Okay, now." She's reading the next question over my shoulder. " 'When did your weight seem to become an issue and was it tied to any specific event?' "

Char and I hardly ever talk about my dad, but I know we're both thinking that was when I—we—started gaining. "I've got this one," I say.

"Good, cause I gotta pee," Char says. I watch her walk out and then return to the questionnaire.

Up next, Weight History. I skim the annual checkup reports my pediatrician's office faxed for the bad news. *Age: 12, weight: 115; 13, 165; 14, 220; 15, 268.*

Fighting tears, I flip back to finish off the Eating Behaviors section.

What generally signals you to stop eating?
A. I feel satisfied and full.
B. I feel uncomfortably full.
C. I am disgusted with myself.
D. I never really feel full.

I circle C several times and then erase it and circle D to bypass another tiff with Char. This is like those quizzes in *Seventeen* magazine. I'll tally my points and turn to the answer key, only to discover there's no hope for me.

"My mom said to remind you to take the leftovers from tonight's chicken. It's on the counter wrapped in aluminum foil," Char says as she bounds back into the room. I smile and shake my head.

"How is there anything left over after what we ate?" I try to joke, but the last part gets caught in my throat. Crystal always makes extra food so that I can have something homemade to eat the next day. Every time she does it, though, her feeling sorry for me makes me feel sorrier for myself. "Okay, I'm done with this stupid thing, I think."

"Really? The first page too? The family background part?"

"Right," I mumble, rustling the sheets back to page one. "That part. Guess I saved the best for last. Ugh."

"Ah, yes, definitely time for some—ta-da—M&M'S," Char says, producing a fresh king-sized bag from under her bed and tossing it to me. I tear it open and cram a large handful straight into my mouth to get the chocolate running through my veins as quickly as possible. Then I pour more into my hand and pass the bag to Char. She puts it on her bed without taking any. Then she sits on the floor, next to me, and starts pulling on the carpet fibers. "Things sometimes run in families," she finally says.

I shake my head. "My mother wasn't always like this and you know that." Char half shrugs and keeps pulling on the carpet. "It's not my mom you're talking about, is it?" I say.

"I'm thinking you'd better keep what happened private," she says softly. "If— When anyone asks—and they will, you know—it's part of your family medical history, just make it like your dad had, I don't know, a heart attack or something."

"Heart attack, check," I say. "I'll just fill this part out when I get home."

"That's fine," she says, her voice still soft. "But um, your mom . . . I think we should probably come up with a backup plan."

"Oh, I see. You're not a hundred percent confident anymore about your 'get her a nice outfit so she'll feel better about attending the parent part of the psych evaluation' plan?"

Char's back to the carpet fibers. "It's true—I'm worried about her meeting the shrink, but actually, it's not the getting her out of the house part as much as the family supportiveness thing that worries me," she says even more softly.

"What—" I start, but Char jerks up her head and looks straight at me.

"I'll just come out and say it," she says in her regular voice. "I'm, um, not sure your mom showing up in her present condition is such a good move—the appearance of having a supportive family is key, so I think we should get Park Avenue Bariatrics to deal with your mom solely over the phone, not in person."

I can feel the tears brimming. I throw up my hands and scatter the questionnaire sheets all over the floor. "What's the point of any of this? First you convince me I can get her out of the house with a Gap velour sweat suit. *Now* you're saying that if I pull that miracle off, I'll still be screwed. This is a massive waste of time!" I bury my face in my hands and wait for the usual Char shoulder or neck rub, but she smacks me on the arm instead.

"Feeling sorry for yourself is the big waste of time! You're awfulizing again. We just need to focus on the no-show plan. It's not a big deal, Shroud. If anything, this will *help* get your mother agree to the surgery. And the frosting on the cake is that our worst-case scenario—that she won't leave the house—now becomes the best-case scenario." I'm still trying to make sense of what Char's talking about when she announces, "Check this. Problem solved. Your mom is really sick at home with something, like Lyme. Wait, better. She has swine flu! Yes, swine flu! That's why she can't leave the house."

I stifle a groan. "Your swine-flu story will *ensure* they reschedule the evaluation, not do it by phone. They'll want to make sure my 'family support system' hasn't died before letting me into the trial."

"Good point. Forget swine. Okay. She has a nasty, oozing MRSA infection. You know, those infections that can't be cured with antibiotics and people are like deathly afraid of catching them. Oh my God!" Char screams, and jumps up. "I'm a genius!"

"Genius?" I say. "MRSA has the same problem as swine flu, only worse. It's more fatal. And I don't like the idea of giving her a real illness. How about bedsores?"

Char scoffs and sits back down. "Bedsores heal when the patient gets out of bed—it's so the opposite of a good reason for your mom to be bedridden and do the interviews by phone," she snaps. I'm waiting for her next brainstorm to hit, but she's got her chin in her hand now and I'm surprised at the panic that starts rising when Char's run out of solutions. Murphy, the family Persian, enters the room and curls into Char's lap, and that's my signal to leave before I start sneezing. Char absently strokes him while she watches me get up and gather my papers. Suddenly, she flings the cat off her lap, jumps to her feet, and cries "Bingo!"

"Yes, Char?" I say dully as I swing my backpack over my shoulder and head to the door.

"Allergies! Nonfatal, not contagious, not a family medical issue, but definitely a good reason not to leave the house! And, since no one's going to bother predicting future pollen counts, a severe seasonal allergy is a good reason not to reschedule."

I feel a smile spread across my face. How much of a lie would it really be? Mom would probably be allergic to *something* as soon as she stepped foot out of the house anyway. Char's waving her hand for a high five, and I give her one. "Worst-case scenario," I warn. "If she hates the sweat-suit idea and won't leave the house."

"Done! What do you say we run over to Mario's for a couple of pastries to celebrate? In a few weeks, those cream claws could be hist-oh-ree!" Char says, doing her strut thing around the room again.

"Um, Char? *Nothing's* going to be history if I don't convince my mother. I'd better talk to her immediately, before I come to my senses."

○ ○ ○ ○ ○ ○

It's nine-thirty p.m. and I hear the muffled sounds of Mom's TV. Two empty family-sized mac and cheese tins and her coffee mug from yesterday are on the counter. From the din of Char's chattering parents and the afterglow of Crystal's chicken cacciatore, I've crossed into a twilight zone of stale air and dim lighting. The only sound of life in here comes from the TV, and I follow it to Mom's room.

She's in bed, her hair all messy and greasy. She doesn't go to the beauty parlor anymore, so she keeps getting grayer.

"Hi, Mom." She props herself up and moves a large pile of yarn to make room for me to sit. Her eyes are fixed on the TV, though, as I come toward her. "Can I turn it off?"

"Oh," she says, and hits the Mute button on the remote. That remote control is her lifeline. Once, about six months after Dad died, Mom finally left the house to go shopping. I thought she'd finished grieving and would return to cooking meals, making lunches, and driving me around, and to her part-time interior decorating job. My heart sank when I looked in the grocery bag. She had purchased, like, every AAA battery the store had in stock. Never mind milk, but the batteries for her remote . . .

"I have something to discuss with you, Mom," I say. "Can I turn on the lights?" I sit on the edge of her bed and block her view.

"Here." She turns on the lamp on her night table. Her arms have gotten huge. For every pound I've gained, she's packed on two.

"I've been reading about this program for obese teens and I really want to do it," I blurt. I hand her the Park Avenue Bariatrics "Qualifications for Teen Lap-Band Surgery Clinical Trial" information sheet and the application form, along with her reading glasses, which are permanently filmed over. Her dresser is coated in dust, and the housekeeper can't get into her room half the time.

Mom takes one glance at the cover sheet and puts the packet down. "What's this, East, surgery? *Experimental* surgery? Isn't that what 'clinical trial' means?"

"No. It's not experimental at all. It's been proven safe and effective on adults. And it's more like a procedure than surgery. It's just that it hasn't been officially approved for teens yet, so it's called a clinical trial. Park Avenue Bariatrics has FDA approval to do Lap-Bands on teens."

"It says for *obese* kids. You're hardly heavy enough to qualify, are you?"

I close my eyes and focus on not crying, or, worse, screaming. "I do qualify, Mom. I more than qualify. And I need the help. If I get this, I won't be able to eat as much and then I can finally lose weight. And there's more than enough money in my college fund to pay for it and the entire cost of college, even NYU." I say the last part fast—despite the fact that my father's late mother left us money, the thought of her could get Mom hysterical and blow the whole thing.

"If you want to lose weight, why not just lose it on your own?"

Why? I don't bother mentioning the countless diets I've tried that she's been oblivious to, or how there's never a single prepared meal here, and that, at my current rate of expansion, I'll be as big as her in no time. In fact, I don't answer her at all.

"Surgery is dangerous." She says it more like a plea than a statement. But then her voice hardens. "*That girl's* put you up to this, hasn't she?"

"Mom, for me, *not* having this surgery is dangerous," I say loudly, ignoring the Char crack. Ever since Mom stopped talking to Crystal, everything that has to do with Char threatens my well-being. If I tell her Char and I are taking the train into Manhattan, she acts like I'm jumping the Grand Canyon on a motorcycle. That's Char's analogy, but it's true.

"You'll need anesthesia, and they're going to cut you

open. I saw it on *Oprah*. Very scary." She's holding the information packet away from her, as if getting it too close to her body could cause harm.

"There's barely any cutting. It's laparoscopic, Mom. They make tiny incisions through a tiny scope. And *you'll* be with me." I'm praying that my needing her, something I haven't in a long time, will replace her fear. Instead, I've dropped a bomb. Her face goes the color of the dingy white curtains that haven't been cleaned since Dad. Or opened.

"I don't know. I don't think—"

I cut her off before she says it's not a good idea. Any time she voices a fear, it takes on a life of its own in her mind and is that much more likely to come true. "I need the sur—the Lap-Band. And yes, Char's doing it, and Crystal has totally checked it out." Mom and Crystal stopped talking a few months after Dad died, and by then, Crystal wasn't just her oldest, best friend, she was her only friend left. Dad's death was like this irresistible force—whoever Mom didn't push out of her life eventually pulled away.

"Crystal's been in on all this?" Mom says, harshness seeping into her voice. My heart starts racing as I try to calculate the source of her anger and respond in a way to defuse it. I take a deep breath and choose my words carefully.

"Well, of course Crystal had the exact same response as you when Char first told her about it—she knows how impulsive Char can be better than anyone. But after Crystal read the materials, researched it online, and talked with Char's physician, she became completely convinced that this sur—program is the only way to ensure that her *daughter* live a long, happy, and healthy life." I can't help that my voice cracks on this last part.

There's no longer any trace of anger on Mom's face, but her eyes are darting back and forth. Like she's thinking . . .

"There's paperwork I need signed just to qualify for the *procedure*, and I'll need a few routine medical tests and a psychological evaluation so that they can see how responsible I am. Then there's one more evaluation session to get in to the trial—the first part is with the teen, and the second is a private consultation with the parent alone. Mom, there's a really beautiful outfit I planned to buy you for your birthday anyway, so you could wear it to the meeting—or I bet I can even get them to interview you over the phone and then you won't have to—to go all the way into the city and deal with parking and stuff. And then Char can be with me at the hospital, and you wouldn't even have to come—"

"East, please stop," Mom begs. "You're talking a mile a minute."

"I know it's a lot. But like I said, it's safe and you won't have to do—" My voice is cracking again when she cuts me off.

"Honey, stop. I'll read the brochure, okay? And if everything's as you say, then I guess letting you get this surgery is the least I can do for you." She takes a deep breath, but her eyes begin to water and when she starts speaking again, her voice is shaking. "F-forget about phone interviews and having Char with you at the hospital. I'll do what you need me to, and *I'll* be with you at the hospital too. I'm going to be with *my* daughter every step of the way. If we're going to do this, we'll do it right."

We? It's like a wave of bright light sweeps through the room. I jump to my feet completely stunned for a moment, then fling myself into my mother's arms—something I haven't done in years. She's holding me tightly right back, stroking my hair and sobbing at the same time. Suddenly this surgery is bigger and more important than I realized. Maybe it could even save us both.

5

EVALUATING PSYCHOS

Marcie

If there's one thing that has gotten me in trouble throughout my entire life, it's my mouth. What goes into it, but even worse, what comes out. *Your mouth is your own worst enemy, Marcie. When in doubt, keep it shut,* Abby always says. Dad says I'm sometimes too honest for my own good, and Ronny thinks I'm *spirited,* surely his euphemism for "loudmouthed, opinionated brat." Whatever I am, it can't be helped. Normal people are born with a flap that prevents everything on their minds from spewing uncontrollably out of their mouths. I have a genetic defect—no flap whatsoever. That's why, on the three-block trek from the parking garage to the Park Avenue Bariatrics office, Abby is harassing me for my big interview: the "psychosocial evaluation."

"Just watch your mouth and be polite," Abby warns. "No wisecracks or snide remarks. And for God's sake—do not insult anyone."

"Are you saying I *shouldn't* mention that recurring dream of mine—where Liselle and her whole shallow crew of size-zero bimbos get wiped off the face of the earth in one fell swoop of my butt?" My laugh comes out more like a wheeze as I struggle to maintain her pace. But Abby halts in the middle of the sidewalk and I plow right into her. She spins around and squeezes my arm.

"Let's get something straight. If you don't make it into this clinical trial, don't think for a minute I'm taking you to Mexico. Your surgery gets done here or it doesn't get done at all. Do I make myself clear?" I yank my arm from her grip. WTF?

"What if *I* say all the right things, but I don't get in because after talking to *you*, the shrink decides that my living environment sucks and that that homeless fellow living in an old dishwasher carton on Forty-second Street would provide a more supportive family environment than chez Rescott? Wouldn't you take me to Mexico *then?*"

Abby glares at me through watery eyes for a moment, then pivots and resumes walking.

"Mom—wait! I'm sorry," I call, lumbering after her. Abby speeds up, but I catch up with her at the crosswalk. She gives me her back as she dabs at her eyes with a Kleenex, and I step around to face her. "Listen," I say softly. "What I said back there was really wrong. I'm like ninety-eight point three percent positive that I'd get *less* support from that guy in the box, okay?" Abby tries to suppress a smile, but when I raise my eyebrows—the *c'mon, I know you wanna* look—she finally lets it out.

"Okay. But stop giving me such a hard time."

"Mom," I try in the sugary voice that always works for Liselle, "don't you see how you're the one who gave *me* the hard time?" Abby's face tightens, but she doesn't turn away, even though the light has changed. *It's not what you say, it's how you say it*, Abby says, so I soften my voice even more. "I know you just wanted me to be with you, but that's meant I've had to give up everything else I care about—Dad, my best friend—hell, *all* my friends. I haven't made *any* since we moved here, which isn't my fault. You're the one who agreed to push me up to eleventh grade—they'd have kept me in tenth even with my test scores if you asked them to—and now I fit in even less."

Abby looks straight ahead without blinking, but she hasn't budged. I keep it soft.

"Mom, I fit in at Fuller. Everyone but like two people voted for me for class vice president. Here, I'd be satisfied with being invisible. But I'm not. I'm a joke—Liselle Rescott's 'new' sister. *I didn't know Liselle was a quintuplet. Why did Liselle bring her house to school today? What's her name again? Moosie?* Do you have any idea how many times a day I hear that stuff?"

"How many?" Abby sighs, checking her watch. And that's when I lose it.

"Damn it, Mom! I want to go home. Just let me go home. Please. I'm miserable here."

"You *are* home," she snaps. "And I know you're unhappy, Marcie. Believe me, I know. That's why we're here, okay? Please, let's just go while we still have the light."

o o o o o o

A huge woman with mammoth hips is waiting in front of the elevator when it opens. "Excuse me," Abby says, though she could easily slip right past her. The woman apologizes profusely and steps to the side. I follow Abby out, and the woman smiles conspiratorially at me. As if all fat people belong to a secret club. I don't smile back and catch up with Abby as she beelines down the hall, scanning the suite numbers for the right door. She stops in front of one and waits for me to catch up.

While Abby goes to the receptionist's window, I survey the waiting room with relief. Long green pleather-upholstered benches line the walls. All-you-can-eat seating—no armrests to signal where your buttocks must end so others may begin. There's nothing more terrifying than entering a waiting room, or a classroom, and trying to find a seat while others are watching.

A few Saturdays ago, my worst seating disaster ever . . . It was at a special creative writing seminar at the community center. I had been so excited—only two kids from my school were selected, and the presenter was one of my favorite authors. By the time I arrived, she was already speaking and only middle seats were available. It was bad enough the kids had to grab their notebooks off their desks and lean away to make room for me to get through the aisle, but the desks—the kind with tops that lift up like tray tables on airplanes—were like freaking doll furniture. The desktop just wouldn't clear my stomach on the way down, no matter how hard I pushed. I had to sit with the table up for the whole morning, mortified and barely processing a word. Then, at lunchtime, I tore out of the building and frantically dialed Abby on my cell phone from behind a tree, imploring her to come pick me up. I never even got my book signed.

o o o o o o

I'm beached on a sagging, rust-colored corduroy couch in Dr. Glass's brown-paneled office, waiting for the inquisition to get under way. The springs are completely shot in this old sofa—not surprising, given the clientele—so my butt is basically on the floor. Her walls are plastered with framed certificates. Master's in Social Work. PhD in Clinical Psychology. Big deal. My dad, the top lit professor at Fuller Prep, has *two* PhDs—one in literature and one in education. He turned down a position at Tufts so that I could go to Fuller. Now he's stuck in a crummy apartment in Cambridge, Massachusetts, all by himself, and I'm living in a ten-thousand-square-foot McMansion in New Jersey with my mother, Rich Ronny, and brain-dead Liselle.

My parents met in a classics seminar at Harvard, and Dad would always go on about how clever and resourceful my mom is. But that was before she dropped thirty pounds and started spending late nights with her editor at *Inc.* magazine. Then, while I was away in Mexico with Jen, Abby announced that she was going to marry the cover boy of the November issue—Ronny Rescott—and asked my father for a divorce.

It didn't occur to me that Abby planned to take me with her. Fuller is one of the country's best schools, and with my top ranking and assistant editorship at the *Review*—a huge accomplishment for a ninth grader (though a few jerks suggested Dad pulled strings)—I could have been a shoo-in for Harvard. But Abby said that Tenafly High is one of the best public schools in the entire country and that I could always come back to Boston for college. Even then, I wasn't too worried. There was no way my father was going to let me go. Except he did.

I shouldn't blame the divorce entirely on my mother; the

academic life just isn't in her gene pool, and there's no fighting DNA. My father hails from a long line of rabbis and scholars; my mother, bulimics and anorexics. I know there was a time in history when food was scarce and being a cow was de rigueur. But as far back as my great-grandmother, whom I knew only from photos, the Lipsky women were cramming themselves into girdles; starving themselves before weddings, bat mitzvahs, and vacations; and disappearing into bathrooms after meals.

With that sludge clogging her gene pool, Abby's addiction to diet pills, liposuction, and dudes with cash isn't much of a shock, but *her* mother totally takes the cake (and most assuredly pukes it up later). To Gran, being thin, gracious, gorgeous, and perfectly coiffed in order to get a rich man to marry you is the entire meaning of life. That's it. Women are bait and men are prey, and the concept of growth and self-discovery involves nothing more than identifying the exact shade of shadow that brings out your eyes. The only time this woman probably ever even picked up a book was to put it on her head and practice walking around the room for good posture.

I was most likely still in utero when Gran began feeding me the program—according to Abby, I was a big kicker from the time she was six months pregnant with me, and I haven't stopped kicking since. When Gran's hospitalizations started becoming more frequent last year, I tried one more time to communicate with her—to let her know that my sights in life were set much higher than on landing a man and that she should just accept that.

Gran was so busy showing wallet photos of herself in younger days to the doctor reviewing her chart that I stood in her hospital room doorway for about ten minutes before she even noticed I was there. But once he squeezed past me, she got all excited and patted the space next to her on the bed. I took the armchair instead—Gran was thin and pale and I was afraid to mess with all the tubes. I nodded dumbly as she carried on about how handsome her doctor was and how she bet he spent more time with her than anybody. When she finally stopped for air, I took a deep breath and began.

"Gran, what would you say is your greatest accomplishment in life?"

"Why, all the men who've loved me, my darling," she rasped—without even pausing for thought.

"But *why* did so many men love you?" I said calmly, as though this was a perfectly reasonable response.

"Because Gran is beautiful," she replied, *straight-faced*.

"But Gran, what if *I* want to be loved for something more than how I look?" Again, not even a pause. Her certainty was maddening.

"Marcie, imagine you're having a romantic dinner with a man, and you're going on about your books and big ideas. He's going to take one look at your hands and say to himself, 'If this woman is so smart, why didn't she get a manicure?' " Rage welled up inside me and that was it—I was done with her for good. I got up, mumbled something about seeing what was taking Mom so long at the coffee machine, and sat fuming in the waiting room until Abby was done with their visit. And I'm not visiting her again, no matter how freaked Abby gets about it.

My weight has gotten so dire that on the rare occasions I'm trapped in the same room with her, Gran is too horrified to even mention it anymore. It's like standing in an elevator with a hideously scarred burn victim. You smile politely and pretend they're just like everyone else. But now that she's laid off me about my weight, she's doing double time on Abby—even when she knows I'm within earshot. "Darling, you really have to get that poor girl on a diet. I don't care how brilliant she is. She's never going to find happiness in her condition."

Abby tries to defend me, but only with lame crap like, "Marcie will lose her weight when she's ready." How about this, Mom? *Marcie's just fine how she is. Now, thank you and shut up.*

o o o o o o

Jen is texting on about how glorious it is to finally be able to cram herself into size 4 jeans when Dr. Glass makes her entrance. Suddenly, I start to panic—this woman is less than half my size, and without a "polite" or "compliant" chromosome in my DNA, I'm going to say something to screw this evaluation up.

"Marcie Mandlebaum, right?" she says, coming over to me and putting out her hand. I take her tiny hand in my fleshy paw and I'm afraid to squeeze too hard—it seems so fragile.

"Nice to meet you, Dr. Glass," I stammer.

Dr. Glass smiles and moves toward her side of the desk. She's wearing a close-fitting *white* skirt, and it occurs to me that it's not quite Memorial Day yet. An "unspeakable" fashion faux pas like this would provide Gran with enough idiot conversation fodder to last her a year. *Clamp it, Marcie.*

"Please call me Betsy," Dr. Glass says. She sits pertly in

her nine-hundred-dollar Herman Miller Aeron Chair (Ronny has one). Wouldn't that money be better spent on a new couch? I somehow manage to clamp down on this thought too before it comes flying out, but my own worst enemy is hell-bent on sabotaging me.

"I guess you hear 'Bitsy' a lot," it blurts. I freeze in horror, but, thankfully, Bitsy laughs.

"I wasn't always this small, Marcie, so I kind of like it. Feel free."

I let out a deep breath and relax. She's not so bad. Maybe I can get through this without blowing it after all.

6

taking out the queen

tuesday, june 2, 2009

Bobby

"Betsy Glass. Nice to meet you, Bobby." She holds out her hand but my palm is disgustingly sweaty, so I shake just her fingertips. They feel cool even though her office is boiling.

"Hi," I say, fumbling toward the oversized chair by the open window, but she says, "Right there is good," and directs me to the couch opposite her desk. She'd better not want me to lie on it.

She sits down behind her desk and picks up this stapled packet, holding it level with her boobs.

"Nice handwriting," she says. "Did you fill this out?"

"My mom did. They're completely my answers, though."

"That's fine."

"We just went over them together."

Betsy smiles. "Bobby, that's fine. Tell me about—" She looks up from the paperwork and catches me staring. My eyes fly over to this football in a plastic display case on a shelf behind her, and she raises an eyebrow and swivels around.

"Oh. That's my son's from high school. They won the sectionals in 2006 and he was MVP."

"Nice. What position?" I say as coolly as possible, but my balls are sweating and I'm already worried I've nuked my chances to get into this trial.

"Running back."

He's probably lean and mean like Craighead.

"He's at Michigan State now."

Probably getting laid all the time. I cross my arms over myself.

"I'm thinking about applying early decision to Notre Dame," I mumble. Football is my best shot at a great school. Last year, a Notre Dame scout handed me his card in the locker room. Dad was pumped.

"What position do you play?" She's facing me again, so I start examining the mesh patterns on the bottom of my jersey.

"Offensive lineman—right guard."

Betsy frowns. "So your job is . . ." She stops and waits for me to finish her sentence.

"I create holes for the running play and protect the quarterback from tackles so he can make the pass," I explain.

"Right. My son's tried for years to get me to understand the game." Betsy smiles. "I think about the quarterback as like the king in chess. The other players can't let anyone get to him."

"Yeah, sort of."

"So, as the lineman, you're sort of like the queen."

"Ye—no." I say, but it comes out like a growl. *The queen is the only piece in chess with boobs.* I clear my throat. "I mean, I guess the pawns set the offensive line, but it's not too much like chess."

"Okay, the analogy doesn't fit." She smiles again. But I'm thinking that queen part does fit actually, which is what really sucks my king-sized ass.

Betsy purses her lips and scrunches her eyebrows a little, the same way Mom does when she's trying to get at something. "The offensive line requires major contact. Don't you have to be a certain size to block?"

"Um, not necessarily." Sweat's beading up on my forehead and I wipe it away with my sleeve. I stink. The papers on her desk are flapping around from the breeze. How the hell am I so hot?

"No?" Her face crinkles more. "My understanding is that size is the most important attribute for an offensive lineman."

"Size is important, yeah. But strength also. And height and arm length."

Betsy stares at me for a few moments, her lips still in a tight line. Then she takes a deep breath.

"Bobby, if getting this surgery meant you would no longer have the bulk to play for a Division One school, like Notre Dame, would you still want it?"

"Definitely," I say way too quickly. "Yeah. I mean, I know it'll be tough, but I'm also sure I can build enough muscle to stay big and strong." *Big in the right places.*

Betsy sighs. "I'm not sure you're thinking about this realistically."

I shift to make myself more comfortable. "I get it. I do. Really."

She picks my questionnaire up off her desk again, still shaking her head. "Bobby, high school football is one thing, but college is another. When a lineman slips below three hundred pounds, he's usually not allowed to play. If you have this surgery, by the time you go to college next year, you'll be closer to two hundred pounds than three hundred. I need to know you understand that this surgery *will* put any college football career you're thinking about in jeopardy. At least as a lineman."

"Yeah," I mutter, nodding down at my filthy fingernails. My dad and I have the same ink-black freckle below the nail of the forefinger on our right hand.

"Bobby?" I look back up at her. "That means having this surgery is likely to affect the colleges you'll be accepted to, and that will affect other things down the road. Your decision will ripple throughout your life, present and future."

I nod and keep eye contact this time. I don't know what to say to convince her.

Betsy shakes her head again. "Bobby, I need to hear you say it. I need to hear that you understand what I'm saying, and I need to hear that you mean it. Is this surgery important enough to you that you're willing to give up football and everything it means to your future?"

Rivers of sweat feel like they're pouring out of my forehead, but I don't even try to wipe them away. "Yes! I want it—this surgery. And if—and *yes*, I'm willing to give up football and everything it means in order to get it," I practically shout. And the certainty I hear in my own voice is so startling, I almost believe it.

Betsy stares at me hard, but I keep my eyes stuck on hers like my life depends on it. "Okay," she finally says, looking down to rustle through her papers. "Let's bring in your parents—okay, just your mom is here—and talk about the lifestyle changes this surgery requires."

7

UNDER COVER

East

"Mom. *Mooom.*" I'm knocking on her door for the third time this morning, listening for sounds of movement while I finish getting ready. "We should try to leave by two-thirty, the latest," I say. I'm careful. If I open her door, if I rattle her cage, I'll blow this. But our appointment with Dr. Glass is at three-thirty and it takes a good forty-five minutes to drive into the city and find parking. I have to get her up now or we won't make it. "I'm wearing a sweatshirt and jeans. You could wear that maroon terry zip-up," I call in again. Nothing. "You know, the one Julius sent you at Christmas?" Nothing still. I head back down the hall, then stop and raise my voice a bit. "I'm making us an early lunch, okay?"

When I reach the kitchen, I hear shuffling overhead. She's finally moving. I purposely didn't mention that Char and Crystal have the appointment before ours. Mom can't bear anyone seeing her like this, and the possibility of running into her ex–best friend is sure to keep her burrowed under the covers for life. I'm scanning the refrigerator shelves, looking for something to ease Mom's stress, when I hear her bedroom door open.

"East?" she moans, as if my name takes too much energy to say. I slam the fridge and race upstairs. Her door is open, but she's back in bed and her room looks like a tornado churned through her closet and flung everything out.

"But—but you promised. . . ."

Mom rolls onto her side with a moan and pulls the blankets up so I can't see her face. "Please. I'm sorry. I just can't. Not today."

I pick up this fraying, stretched-out gray sweater thing. "Here. Put this on. You'll look good in this," I try. But she doesn't even lower the blanket to look.

"I'm so sorry, East. Please just reschedule. I'll do it another day, I promise. I feel too awful to get out of bed." She's whimpering into her pillow and I just stand there unable to feel my limbs. Finally, I manage to back out of the room and close the door behind me before I burst into tears. I'm an idiot to think anything could ever change, that anything good could ever really happen. What's the point of even trying?

Five seconds later, I'm curled in a ball beneath my covers, sobbing. My arm has just enough life in it to fish around my night table for some Reese's Pieces—and to send my alarm clock crashing to the floor. I sit up. Sunshine is streaming in through my lace curtains and here I am in bed just like my mother. I fling myself out of the bed and pick up the clock—it's noon! I spin around to grab my phone and speed-dial Char's home line.

"Char!" I blurt into the phone. "Thank God I caught you."

○ ○ ○ ○ ○ ○

"It's okay. It'll all be okay. You so need to de-Shroud," Char is saying as my fingers twirl the hair in my ponytail into knots in the Park Avenue Bariatrics waiting room.

"I'm going to vomit."

"Stop. It's three-twenty-five already. Betsy and my mom will be finished any minute. You have to get your act together. Get back into that psyched-up state. C'mon." I nod glumly and dig through my bag for a comb and another Jujube bear.

"She shouldn't have blown you off. You're so right. But—"

"Shhh," I say. "Everyone can hear you."

Char lowers her voice. "Look. She promised to stay awake and wait for your call. You told her about her allergies, right?"

I freeze.

"Quick, call her now," Char whispers loudly enough for the receptionist on the other side of the glass partition to hear, and then we're huddled over my phone listening to it ring and go to the answering machine.

"Mom!" I plead. "Please get up. Dr. Glass and I will be calling soon. You have allergies, okay? That's why you're not here. *Allergies.* Please remember. And please pick up when we call."

There's a worried expression on Char's face when I snap my phone shut, but she stows it away quickly. "This can still work, East. It really can. Just stay cool. Your mom has allergies, that's it. Nothing terrible. Just play it the way we planned."

I shake my head. "Even if Dr. Glass will do the interview by phone, my mother'll be zoned out. How can she convince anyone I have a supportive family environment?" *Supportive family environment*. Just that phrase has my eyes filling up again.

Char leans over and rubs my arm. "The interview isn't a big deal. Betsy talks about the postsurgery eating and exercise program and asks some general questions. That's it. Your mom can so handle it. And if she sounds zoned, you'll tell Betsy it's the allergy medication. We need to get this right. Right?"

We. Char and me. That's the only *we* I can count on. "Right," I whisper as the receptionist calls out my name. I take a deep breath. "Right," I say again as I stand up. Even though my knees feel like they'll buckle.

○ ○ ○ ○ ○ ○

Crystal squeezes my shoulder as we pass each other in the narrow hallway to Dr. Glass's office, but her smile is tight and her eyes a little glassy, and any panic that Char managed to soothe in the waiting room is back.

"How are you, East?" Dr. Glass says warmly as she opens her door.

"Great. Very well," I chirp, but immediately recognize how fake my cheerfulness sounds. My vocal cords just can't hit those "la-la happy" keys the way Char's can.

"Your mom?" Dr. Glass says, glancing down the empty hallway as I step into her office.

"Um, actually, she's not coming. She tried to—she really wanted to—she, uh, she just felt too awful." I push myself to move toward the two chairs set up in front of her desk even though Dr. Glass is still standing by the open door. *Stick to the plan.*

"Oh, your mom's ill?" Dr. Glass says. "Nothing serious, I hope?"

I shrug involuntarily while I'm shaking my head and visualize Char whacking me for it. "Just allergies. My mom gets them bad this time of year. She didn't realize she wasn't up to it until this afternoon, and well, um, I didn't want to cancel last minute."

"Oh, not a problem," Dr. Glass says as she walks to her desk and flips open her appointment book. "When do you think she'll be able to come in? Or, better—just have her call and reschedule. . . ."

I feel my mac and cheese lunch rising, along with a fresh wave of terror, and I slump into a chair. What about not being able to forecast pollen levels? But I hear Char in my head again. *We need to get this right. We.* I take a deep breath. "Dr. Glass—"

"Betsy," she says.

"Betsy, please—is there any way that we, um, that we can do the interviews with my mom over the phone? She's just— it's her allergies. It's hard to say when they'll strike, so I don't know. . . ." My voice trails off. Dr. Glass closes her appointment book and walks over to shut the door.

I glance down at my chewed-up nails as Betsy takes the empty chair next to me. She folds her hands in her lap and looks into my eyes.

"My mom feels awful today," I say again. *That* isn't a lie. She does feel awful. *Too awful to get out of bed.*

"I like to meet with the patient and at least one parent

together because parental involvement is key. As I mentioned in our last session, your mom's support is critical, especially since it's just the two of you."

"I know. And my mom is totally on board with me doing this," I nearly stammer. Right. Support has always been a one-way street on Forty-one Green Lane. My throat is swelling like I'm the one having an allergic reaction. Betsy is nice and I've just lied right to her face. Literally two feet from her face.

"East?" Betsy cocks her head slightly—the same way she did when she first brought up Dad's death in the last session. "What happened? Was he ill?" she'd asked. I had just nodded. Like Char said, suicide equals mental *illness*. My answer wasn't really false.

"Yes?" I finish yanking the cuticle off my thumb and close my fingers around it to hide the blood.

Betsy takes a deep breath. "Your brother isn't living at home, and with your dad passed on and no other close relatives nearby, your mom isn't *part* of your family support system. She's *it*."

I nod.

"There's a strong correlation between family support and patient outcomes—I can't emphasize this enough. This isn't an easy journey for anyone, let alone someone dealing with a terrible loss."

Make that plural, I'm thinking, but I just nod and dig my fingers into my leg.

"Love never dies," Betsy says softly, placing her hand on my knee. I stick my nails in deeper. *Oh, but it does.*

"I'm fine," I say loudly and Betsy removes her hand. "My mom and I discussed everything. She's going to help me.

Every step of the way." I attempt a smile for emphasis—my jaw is so sore from all the teeth clenching, though, I have no idea what it came out like.

Betsy sits silently for a moment and then gets up and walks around to the far side of her desk. "Okay, why don't we call her and see if she's feeling well enough to talk. This contact number on your application?"

Right. I suppress a laugh. That's my cell phone. "Let me give you the number to the phone that rings in her room, since she's probably still in bed. Not feeling well and all," I say. I give Betsy our home number and she taps the buttons.

"It's ringing," Betsy says. But her smile begins to fade.

"No answer?" I say. Betsy shakes her head. *Six rings*, she mouths. *Seven*. When she reaches what I figure must be the ninth ring, she makes a "yikes" face and hangs up.

"We get a lot of telemarketers," I say. "Let me just call her quickly from my phone so that she recognizes the number." *Telemarketers*, right. Char *is* a big influence. What if white lies are a gateway drug?

"Hold off—I hit redial," Betsy says. "It's ringing again." When she glances in the direction of my nails digging into my thigh, she hits the speakerphone button. "Don't worry— we'll reach her."

"Hello?" Mom finally answers but it sounds like "huh-low," like she's already sedated. *Please have listened to my phone message.*

"Mrs. Itou?"

"Yes, speaking."

"This is Dr. Betsy Glass calling from Park Avenue Bariatrics. I have East with me."

"Hi, Mom," I say with a ridiculous amount of cheer.

"You're on speakerphone, so turn off the TV or we won't hear you." I laugh. It sounds more forced than if I were really being forced to laugh.

"Oh, East. You're in the city already?"

"Yes, Mom. Char picked me up almost three hours ago. You must have dozed off."

"Char?" she says dully. I laugh heartily.

"Funny, Mom. Crystal drove. I explained to Dr. Glass you weren't feeling well enough to come in, and she was kind enough to do this interview on the telephone."

"I hope you're feeling better, Mrs. Itou," Betsy interjects.

"Oh. I see. I'm on speakerphone. Yes, better. Thank you," Mom sputters from her haze. I'm terrified that Betsy will ask her what day of the week it is.

"I'd like to discuss some of the postsurgery lifestyle changes with both of you, and then, Mrs. Itou, you and I can reschedule our parent interview for here, in my office. When you're feeling better, of course," Betsy adds. My mind races. Sure, they'll set up an appointment, but Mom won't show up again, and then my chances for getting into this trial will go from slim to none.

"Well—" Mom starts, but I cut her off.

"Maybe Dr. Glass would be willing to have the private interview with you on the phone *today* after I leave so that my application won't get held up."

There's a moment of silence on both ends of the phone, and then Betsy finally says, "Mrs. Itou, we usually don't conduct parent interviews on the telephone. And typically parents like to meet the team their children will be working with. But if you think your allergies might prevent you from coming in within the next couple of weeks and you can talk on the phone today, I do have this time carved out for you. . . ." For a second, I imagine Char whooping and high-fiving that I've miraculously managed to pull off the whole "phone interview with Mom" plan. But Betsy's tapping her pen against her arm and she's looking at the ceiling. She smells something.

"Let me sit up," Mom says. There's a sound of bedcovers rustling and something shattering on the floor. She clears her throat. "It would be easier if we could do this on the phone. East says it's not surgery. No cutting, but there's anesthesia."

"Well, that's not entirely correct, but I can review the medical details with you after East leaves," Betsy says. "Right now I'd like to discuss the support East will need before, during, and after the procedure if she's accepted into the trial."

My mom starts sneezing.

"God bless you," Dr. Glass says. *God, thank you*, I think.

"Thank you," Mom finally says. "You were saying?"

"East told me it's been just the two of you for—"

"Almost four years now," I jump in.

"I'm so sorry, Mrs. Itou."

When my mom doesn't respond, Betsy looks at me. All I can think is, *Please do not ask about Dad.*

"I don't mean to bring up a difficult subject. I just need to get a clearer picture of whether East is a good candidate for our trial."

"East is a good girl. She does everything she's told." I try not to cringe. Betsy's pen is tapping against her arm faster now.

"I was explaining to East that you are her most important support partner and there will be a lot to manage. She will have an exercise program and a very limited diet, especially in the beginning," Betsy says.

Silence on the other end of the phone.

"East, did you explain to your mom how she'll want to keep trigger foods out of the house and how your diet will consist of liquids and pureed and soft foods for a full six weeks after the surgery?"

"Yes. And Mom also read through the paperwork very closely," I say, praying my mother will come back with a coherent response.

"The company we, er, order groceries from has a large selection of baby foods." Mom finally says.

"Mom, *we're* going to cook healthy at home," I say with faux enthusiasm. This is the closest I can come to giving Betsy the impression that Mom and I are psyched for all the time we'll be spending together trying out low-calorie recipes without losing it.

"Do you cook a lot, Mrs. Itou?" My mother is painfully silent. Is she cooking up a good lie for Betsy, or did she just fall asleep?

"Not—uh, sometimes." Mom sort of croaks this out after a few long moments, and I feel the old anger rising. *Never. The correct answer is* never, I'm thinking. *But thank you for at least not saying it.*

"Mrs. Itou," Betsy says, "if East gets the Lap-Band, it will dramatically change her lifestyle. Her ability to consume solid foods will be greatly curtailed, so it is imperative for her continued growth and development that the calories she does consume come from high-quality protein and fresh fruits and vegetables. Foods containing processed sugar and flour, rice, potatoes, and pasta are off-limits. They have minimal nutritional value and are high in calories. She'll need to keep a food diary, and even after the first few months, she won't be eating more than a few ounces of food per meal."

"East is a good girl. She will do—" My mom interrupts herself with a loud yawn. I imagine Char shrieking, *Whisper it's her medication!* But it's like I'm in one of those nightmares where I try to cry out for help but can't make a sound.

"Mrs. Itou, I think I may have caught you at a bad time," Betsy says with a frown. "I appreciate you taking the call and I certainly hope you feel better. East, do you want to say goodbye to your mom?"

"I'll call you from the car," I mumble into the speaker-phone. Betsy abruptly disconnects the call and starts scribbling away on a sheet in my paperwork folder. *Catatonic mother*, she's probably writing. I've got to get to Mom before Betsy does and plead with her to at least try to sound a little interested.

"Okay, East," Betsy says. She rises to her feet and removes her blazer from the back of her chair. "Thank you for coming in again. I'll walk you out."

"But aren't you going to call my mom back?" I say. I'm afraid that if I stand, my knees will really buckle this time.

Betsy comes around from her desk and slowly lowers herself into the chair next to mine again. "East, I don't think your mom's quite up to it. And it sounds like something more than a seasonal allergy. Perhaps we'll get another opportunity to talk in the future, okay?"

The future? I lean over to make the sharp cramp in my stomach go away.

Betsy touches my shoulder. "You are a wonderful, responsible young lady, but I'm not convinced you have a strong enough support system right now to be a good candidate for surgery. It doesn't mean that—"

"I need to do this. Please let me in," I blurt, and the levee holding back my tears finally crumbles. Betsy leans over to retrieve the tissue box from her desk. When she hands me one, my eyes meet hers and the pity in them makes me cry harder. She puts her hand on my arm, but that makes it even more impossible for me to stop, so I shake it away.

"I'm really independent. I take care of myself. I'm my own support system. And I have Char! Please," I plead between sniffles.

"You take care of your mom too, don't you?" Betsy says softly.

I shrug. "It's hard for her to do things. She's even more overweight than I am. A lot more. And she's . . ." I can't say it.

"She's depressed," Betsy says.

"Yes," I whimper. A new wave of sobs takes over my body.

"I know. It's in her voice."

"But, it's worse!" I blubber. "She doesn't leave the house."

Betsy shakes her head while she studies her hands. "It must be terribly hard for you. Has your mom tried to get professional help?"

I shake my head.

"Has anyone tried to get professional help for her?" she asks more softly. I cry harder into my tissue.

"East," Betsy murmurs, "I'm so sorry—"

"No—please don't say you're sorry. Please. Just give me a chance," I sob. "Look at me. I'm going to be just like her! I'll get bigger and bigger and one day, I won't be able to leave the house either. I promise, Dr. Glass. I promise. I'll do everything right. I'll prove it to you! My dad didn't just die from some illness—he killed himself and I'm the one who found him. But I got straight As that semester anyway, and every year since. I arrange for the gardener and the house-keeper and the plumbers—everyone who has to come to the house. And all the bills too! I've never paid one bill late. I cook for myself and my mother. Don't you see? Compared with everything I already do, complying with the clinical trial will be easy for me. I'll have the most detailed food and exercise diary you've ever seen—I'll be the most dedicated motivated teenager you've ever had. Really. I promise."

Betsy stands up and takes my hand. She's got tears in her eyes. "You are a very strong young woman. You should be very proud of yourself." She puts her hand on my back as I get up, and gently guides me toward the door.

I stop and turn to face her just before she opens it. "Please," I beg. "Please don't make me turn out just like her."

8

EVERYBODY IN THE POOL

wednesday, June 24, 2009

Marcie

Abby is waiting in the pickup line at Tenafly High with a huge grin on her face, and she's waving frantically through the open passenger-side window for me to hurry up. On principle, I won't jiggle down the pavement for anyone's amusement, so I keep a steady stride as I make my way to the car. There's screeching and whooping as kids pile out of school and horse around until their rides come. God forbid these little debutantes, who aren't yet driving their own luxury car, take the bus or walk. Instead, it's like a damn mommy fest every day—the circular drive packed with Mercedes, BMWs, and Hummers, and the mommies out in clusters gabbing about this one's botoxed brows or that one's new double-D implants and whatever other minutiae is making the rounds.

Alpine, New Jersey, the zip code with the highest income per capita in the country and the exclusive enclave of my personal hell, is too small to have its own high school, so it feeds into Tenafly's—the next town over. I'm a proponent of bussing—it was a big deal in Boston when mostly black kids got bussed into more-affluent white areas. Diversity is great for building tolerance, but here it's just one overprivileged school district merging into another. The only diversity in this population is Asians and fat people. And I represent 50 percent of the latter.

I used to ride the bus. I insisted on it—I'm no prima donna. But when my butt got so ginormous that there was no room for anyone to sit next to me, some little bulimic in Juicy said, "Could you move over, please—you're taking up the whole seat." I couldn't move over unless I climbed out the window and she knew it. But she kept insisting and soon the whole bus was chanting, "Move it on over." I called Abby crying from the bathroom before first bell, and never took the bus again.

Liselle kisses up to Abby by occasionally offering to drive me to school in the new red Beemer convertible Ronny bought her when she passed her driving test (on the fourth try). My mom won't hear of it. "That's sweet of you, honey, but it's your senior year, and driving to school with your friends is part of the fun." In fact, Abby won over Liselle instantaneously by making it clear on day one that our moving in wouldn't, in any way, screw up her glamorous little life. The truth is, Liselle is the spaciest imbecile that ever got behind a wheel, and I'd sooner get into a car with Lindsay Lohan on crack than with her and her band of giggling morons—most of whom wouldn't fit if I were along anyway.

By the time I reach Abby, she's practically halfway out the car window. I chuck my backpack into the backseat and climb into the front. I know the "cat that ate the canary" expression is cliché, but there it is, spread all over her face.

"You can't be so happy because it's my last day of school, right?" I say as we pull away from the curb.

"Of course, there's that," Abby chirps. "And, I get to look at your smiling face all summer."

"No you don't," I mutter. "I'm going up to Dad's just as soon as I can pack. Jen and I are probably going to look for internships in Boston together."

"You have much bigger plans here," Abby singsongs. She turns to me and grins madly.

"Wait? The trial? Mom, no way? I'm in?"

"*Way*, my darling. We got the go-ahead in today's mail. You are going to be T-H-I-N before you know it!"

I cover my face with my hands. I hate phonies, wannabes, skinny imbeciles who think they have the world coming to them, and everyone who thinks physical appearance makes a lick of difference to who someone is. Nevertheless, I'm bawling like crazy. Abby starts crying too, and neither of us give a rat's sphincter that we're blocking the school exit and half of Tenafly's finest are beeping and flipping us the bird.

o o o o o o

Bobby

I'm walking home after swimming at Zoolow's—our annual last-day-of-school pool party. My shorts are still wet and sticking, but I threw on a dry T-shirt the second I got out of the pool, so nothing's showing up top. The guys didn't rag on me about having brought an extra shirt this time. Last time, when MT asked where my hat and coat were after I jumped in the pool wearing a shirt, I held him underwater until he turned blue.

Zoolow's mom offered me a ride, but I needed to take off.

A bunch of girls were heading over and I didn't want to be wet in front of them. Or the only guy not in the pool.

I'm pretending I'm Curtis Martin rushing for a fifty-yard dash, fourth-quarter, game-winning touchdown. I cradle my backpack in my arms, do a quick check to see there's no one around, and start running it. *And there's Konopka, all-stater back in his high school days. He's got the ball! This guy's as quick and powerful as any of the league's top running backs—look at him go! Konopka's weaving his way straight to the end zone! He's at midfield! He sees an opening, he's at the 40, at the 30, 20. They can't touch him! The crowd is going wild!* "Bobby, Bobby!" *He could go all the way! Yes! Touchdown! Can you believe they once called this guy Refrigerator? Man, the only name for him now is Six-pack.* "Bob-bee, Bob-bee!" *This crowd is out of control! They've got him in the air! Look at those cheerleaders clawing at him!*

I'm holding my backpack above my head with both hands—*I am the man. I went all the* . . . A car beeps loudly behind me—I hadn't even heard it coming. I hop onto the curb and turn to see Dad, on his way home from the store.

"Hey, buddy—hop in."

"Hey, you're home early," I say, to change the subject of me being caught with my backpack over my head. I quickly pull the towel out of my backpack and spread it over the front seat to spare his leather my damp, chlorinated butt.

"You coming from Zoo's?" he asks. "When's everybody leaving for the summer?"

"Most of them tomorrow and Sunday," I say, seriously bumming about the ghost town this place will be when everyone's off on their teen tours and stuff while I'm "tooling around"—stupid family joke—at Konopka & Son Lumber.

"The summer flies," Dad says, like that's consolation. He pulls into our driveway and backs up to the garage at the side of the house. I hop out of the car quick to answer the call of nature, but Dad's calling louder.

"Whoa, Bobby. Give me a hand unloading."

I toss my backpack onto the ground and go around to the trunk. He zaps the Unlock button, and I lift the door. The SUV is packed with cartons splashed with stickers of totally jacked bodybuilders.

"Dad—are these weights?" I feel a rush of excitement.

"You bet. You can throw your old dumbbells in the basement. Got a four-hundred-seventy-pound Olympic free weight set, new barbells and dumbbells."

"*Niiice.*"

"And a Smith machine squat rack. Your old bench is still good. This should be all you need to build mountains of mass."

The whole thing doesn't click for me until Mom sprints out through the side door. She's smiling wide and nodding her head. Big eyes. *Oh man.*

"The letter came? I'm in?" I yell. She's nodding harder. I spin around to give Dad a high five. He hands me the barbell instead.

"Oh yeah, kid. Letter from Coach also arrived today. Practice starts second week in August. If you're dead set on having this stupid surgery, you'd better get cracking."

o o o o o o

East

I still haven't replaced the bulb in the lantern outside the front door. And, another mental note—I have to get a repairman to fix the lamppost next to our rusty mailbox. It could topple any day. And, I need to speak to the creepy gardener. Weeds are choking off what's left of the lawn, and he's got to get rid of the dead rosebushes lining the driveway. These plants aren't coming back.

Not that anyone but Char and service and delivery people come over, but still. If not for the TV's bluish glow in my mother's bedroom window, this place would look completely abandoned. Or haunted. Dad would be upset if he could see what's happened to our house. Though, as I walk up our crumbling concrete walkway with the rest of the mail, I can't remember the place looking much better while he was alive. Except maybe the time Mom threw him a surprise thirty-fifth birthday party. Months before, Julius dug out flower beds and I helped Mom plant bulbs and then, magically, our flowers bloomed the day of the barbecue. I was so proud showing them off to everyone. Dad twirled me around that day, calling me his flower goddess. The next time we had that many flowers was a year and three months later, at his funeral.

○ ○ ○ ○ ○ ○

Char's acceptance letter was in her mailbox this afternoon, so she dragged me the two blocks over here to find out what came in my mail.

"What's the rush?" I groan as my house comes into view. "It's clear I'm not getting in."

"Shroud, positive energy," Char says pulling open my rusty mailbox. "East!" she screams when she spots the Park Avenue Bariatrics return address among the flyers and bills. "It's thick. It must have forms!" I grab the envelope and back away from her. I read the acceptance letter twice to myself before Char grabs it from my hand.

"Shroud baby, you so did it!" she yells, alternating between high-fiving and hugging me and doing the Char-strut back and forth in the street, waving the acceptance letters over her head and shouting like a lunatic. But I'm more stunned than anything and, as tears run down my face, all I can think is *Thank you, Betsy, thank you. You won't be sorry. You'll see. I'll make you prouder than you've ever been of anyone.*

"Shush already." I wipe my face and laugh.

"So stop with that, Shroud! Just run inside and give your mother the good news so we can hit Mario's and celebrate!" Char shrieks, breaking into another strut.

I shake my head and start walking in the direction of the restaurant. "C'mon, Char. She's probably still sleeping. I'll tell her tonight."

o o o o o o

Later, when I open the door of the darkened house and hear the muffled sounds of the TV, I pull the acceptance envelope out of the mail pile and shove it into my purse. I don't want Mom to get nervous and frightened about the surgery all over again. Not, at least, until I send in the check.

"Hi, Mom," I call. "I'm home. Do you want to see the mail?"

9

FOODAHOLICS ANONYMOUS

FRIDAY, JUNE 26, 2009

Marcie (−0 lbs)

"I'm Marcie Mandelbaum, I'm from Alpine, New Jersey, and I'm not a joiner." I announce this at my first and, if I had it my way, last meeting of the Teen Bandsters support group. It's my turn to do the usual introductory rap and I'm standing in a circle of fat kids on bridge chairs, feeling ridiculous.

"What do you mean you're not a joiner?" Bitsy asks.

I look around. One girl pouring off her seat in a big red sweatshirt is smiling vacantly out into space; another, with a thick gold lip ring and multiple nose rings, is scrutinizing me with such intensity, it's as if all the ringed creatures on Planet Pierce are expecting a full report. Most of the other kids, though, appear to be in one of the various stages of sleep.

"I don't join things—group things," I say. "I join book clubs—like the kind where you get three books for free and then are required to buy a new one every few months. Not the kind where you sit in a circle and spill your guts to complete freaking strangers with nothing in common." I shrug. "Except for being fat." A couple of snickers around the room.

I plop down hard in my seat to punctuate being done and check my iPhone for messages behind the handouts Bitsy passed around earlier—Jen's supposed to stay riveted to her cell for support during this humiliating enterprise. *I'm a hit with the Twinkie squad*, I type, but Jen's not texting back.

Bitsy clears her throat—that special kind of prolonged phlegming grown-ups do when they really want to say, "I know you're texting. Put that damn thing *away*."

"You're wrong about being overweight being the only thing you have in common, Marcie," Bitsy announces loudly, like it's her ace in the hole.

A jolly blonde spilling out of a low-cut white T-shirt with a black bra underneath—from Victoria's Big Fat Freaking Secret, no doubt—quips, "I guess we're all also buying our clothes from Omar's Tent Emporium," and I swear the floor is shaking from the acres of flesh rumbling with laughter. *Goody, it's stupid fat-joke time*, I text. *JEN!* She's still missing in action, but I'm relieved the attention is off me.

Bitsy does one of those phony smiles where the sides of her lips go up but her eyes don't crinkle. "Firstly, Charlotte—"

"Char, remember? I prefer to be called Char," Jolly Blonde says loudly. This sumo wrestler girl, who's sitting so close to Char it's like they're attached, puts her head in her hands.

"Firstly, *Char*," Bitsy says crisply, "this room is a haven where we discuss our problems without ridiculing them. Please don't degrade yourself and others. And please don't call out." Bitsy stands up and walks the interior of the circle peering at each of us intently, as if we're playing Duck, Duck, Goose and someone is going to get whacked on the head at any time. "Secondly," she finally says, eyeing *me*, "you all indeed have something very important—and very wrong—in common." The room is finally completely silent.

"You all believe that weight is your only problem—and that once it's gone, your lives will be magically fixed." She's pacing the circle again, searching our eyes for reaction. All's deathly still except for the vibrations from my phone.

> **Sorry, Marce! Tony P from lit last year JUST texted. He wants to hang out Sat, but UGH—have to ditch Stephen to do it. Maybe I should switch Stephen to tonight.**

Tony? Stephen? WTF? To my horror, my worst enemy digests Jen's text and lets out a tremendous snort—the kind with both nose and mouth involvement that sounds like a fart. Silence broken and all eyes are back on me. Bitsy swirls around like an animal that has spotted its prey.

"Marcie, can I take it that you disagree with me—that you *don't* think your life will be magically fixed once you lose weight?" she challenges.

"Oh no," I cannot resist saying. "I couldn't agree with you more. My best friend was banded in Mexico like a year and a half ago, and she's lost like a gazillion pounds. It's totally *crazy* how many problems she suddenly has. *Boyfriend problems*, that is." I hate cracking up at my own wiseassedness, but thankfully everyone else is laughing too, and even Bitsy's smiling.

"You've raised a great point, Marcie," she says brightly, totally ignoring the fact that she's been spanked. "Dramatic weight loss brings with it a whole new set of experiences, both positive and negative. Would you mind telling us a little about your friend, Marcie? About her experience before and after the surgery?"

I oblige by whipping out my phone. "How about a show-and-tell?" I say. "Pictures being worth a thousand words and all." I hand it to Bitsy and show her how to flip back and forth through the photos. The first one is of Jen and me up in Cambridge at a poetry reading three years ago. She's slumped in her seat holding her fingers to her temple as if she wants to blow her brains out—we both have this aversion to bad verse. But at 255-plus pounds, the girl is all over the place, even with half her left arm and leg cut out of the frame. I'm standing beside her in the center of the picture, my hand resting on Jen's shoulder; I'm dressed in my beloved I SEE DUMB PEOPLE T-shirt and my favorite Abercrombie destroyed jeans (size 9 in juniors, thank you)—and I'm *laughing*. I doubt anyone in the group will recognize that girl because I certainly don't. The second shot is of Jen in a black minidress at the spring sophomore formal. She's posing with my dad, who's got his arm around her little waist, and I get a quick pang thinking about all the dinner-table debates Jen and I would get into with my dad—they sometimes even went on until the wee hours of the morning. Ever since our friendship began, Dad's been like Jen's second father—or maybe even her first given that hers is hardly ever around.

Bitsy gets the hang of the photo flipping and says, "Okay everyone, come take a look. Marcie's got some excellent before-and-after pictures of—" She looks at me.

"Jen," I say. "Jennifer Redding. My best friend from home." The kids are crowding around Bitsy and oohing and ahhing. Even sullen sumo girl is beaming, and jolly Char is fist-bumping everyone in the room, saying, "We have so seen the future, and it's smokin'." A hulking silent mass of flesh in a Syosset High football jersey—the guy from the info session—springs from his coma and grunts, "Wow," to no one in particular. The only other guy in the room is a freak with a thick red unibrow and no neck, but even with his disability, he's still managing to bob his head up and down in approval.

Everyone drifts back to their places and Bitsy hands me my phone. "We like to bring teen success stories into group to share their weight loss experiences with the Lap-Band, and Jen certainly seems to be one," Bitsy says. "Do you think she'd be willing to come in and talk to us?"

"Most definitely!" I exclaim. "Jen's been torturing me with instant updates on, like, every ounce she's lost, hour by hour, every day for a year and a half. I'd be more than happy to share the wealth."

"She should just Tweet," Football Jersey Boy mutters.

I lean forward and give him my *you don't know the can of worms you just opened* raised-eyebrow look. "Lap-Band Dancer on Twitter, My Big Fat Mexican Lap-Band on Google blogs, Feminist Pilates on YouTube—need I go on?" I lean back in my chair and watch my fellow Bandsters crack up.

Bitsy stands and claps her hands for silence. "Thank you, Marcie. Please ask Jennifer about our invitation *later*. Put your phone away now." I raise my hand. "Yes, Marcie, what is it?" Bitsy says.

"Um, Jen said yes already. She's coming to the city for next week's session."

Bitsy interrupts the new round of laughter. "Your texting speed is impressive, Marcie, thank you. Now, everyone, the rule here is when you walk into this room, your phones get turned off. Not on mute, not on vibrate. *Off*." She watches as I slip my phone into my bag under the chair, then she takes her seat again in the circle and leans forward.

"I'm glad you've all gotten a glimpse of where this journey may take you. And, indeed, you'll all feel much better once you lose weight, physically and psychologically, but we are going to return again and again to my original premise: your weight is not your problem, it's merely a *symptom*. We'll be discussing exercise, nutrition, and strategies for handling different issues with your band that may emerge, but remember, the Lap-Band is going around your stomach, not your head. The most important goal of this group is to help you learn to address the habits and emotions that are driving you to food. If we don't eradicate the problem at its source, your attempts at losing weight or, later, maintaining your weight loss, will fail. Or other, even more undesirable addictions may emerge." Bitsy stops to evaluate her effect on the group. The expressions in the room are equally divided between *WTF is she babbling about?* and *Whatever—can we just go home now?*

Bitsy shakes her head and sighs. "People, dieting without dealing with your underlying issues is like playing Whac-a-Mole. Even if you hit the eating mole on the head, another mole will pop up somewhere else." I clamp down on my worst enemy before it shrieks *Whack this!* Bitsy looks around the circle like we're a bunch of morons.

"Okay, let's get back to learning about each other and the Lap-Band. Charlotte—Char, why don't you tell us a bit about yourself and your relationship with food?"

Char jumps to her feet, gives Sumo Girl a mock look of horror, and then raises her eyebrows at me. Another one of those fat-people conspiratorial gestures. I grin anyway.

"Hello, everybody! My name is Char Newman. I'm fifteen, I live in Westchester, and I'm a foodaholic."

"Hi, Char," we drone. Sumo Girl looks as if she wants to sink into the crappy linoleum floor.

"I've been in a serious relationship with food for about three years now," Char continues. "Some people start out slowly—they toy with their food, move it around on their plate, and then finally eat it. So not me. I'm hot and heavy from start to finish. Total scarf city."

"Even food you don't like?" says a dark-eyed girl in this very large, very orange I'M PHAT T-shirt. Char squints at her like she's a distant galaxy. Even petrified Sumo Girl laughs.

"There's no such thing," Char says, putting her hand on her abundant hip and raising one eyebrow this time. A couple of cheers from the peanut gallery, Jersey Boy's being the loudest. Sumo Girl rolls her eyes. Bitsy uncrosses her legs and leans toward Char.

"So you haven't always been overeating. Though girls often begin putting on weight when they hit puberty, it's not typically extreme. Can you tell us if anything specifically prompted this change in your eating behavior?" Bitsy Glass, Captain Freaking Buzz Kill. The room goes quiet again and Char glances down at Sumo Girl, who nods almost imperceptibly and then returns to studying the floor. Char glances around the room and then again at Sumo, who's now either wincing or has her eyes closed completely.

"Look, this is very personal, and I hope that East here doesn't mind me sharing," she says.

"Again," Bitsy says, "this place is our haven to talk things through and help each other. Please. Go on."

Char breathes deeply and goes grim. "Three years ago,

Mario's opened up less than four blocks from East and me. Pizza, calzones, and killer cannoli. But they also do a mean fried calamari and brilliant penne with vodka sauce. Not even going to mention their heavenly cream claws. We stopped in one afternoon, and Mamma Mia, that's all she wrote." Char stops talking and hangs her head. We're all just looking at her.

"So that's it?" Bitsy finally sputters. "Do you really believe you gained more than a hundred pounds because a restaurant opened in your neighborhood?"

"We're talking *four blocks*."

Bitsy's glaring at Char. Phat Girl starts choking on her gum, I'm about to die laughing, Jersey Boy is having an epileptic fit, the rest are bent over howling, and Bitsy is glowering. The only one barely reacting at all is Sumo Girl. Her face is red and her eyes are fixed on Char in disbelief.

Bitsy claps her hands and glances at the clipboard on her lap.

"Char, just sit down. Coco, your turn. Please introduce yourself, and tell us about your relationship with food and where it went wrong." Bitsy pretty much snaps this, so it's no shocker when Coco—red sweatshirt girl—jumps to her feet in terror.

"I don't know what to say. I've always been—"

"What's your name, girl?" Phat Girl heckles. Coco flushes.

"Oh, sorry. Coco Martinez, Flushing, New York. And I'm fourteen—closer to fifteen, actually. Um, I've always been heavy, and I can't really remember a time when I wasn't trying to diet. When I'm full, I have all the discipline and determination in the world, but no matter what diet I try, it falls apart the minute hunger hits."

Bitsy nods vigorously and *glides* over to the whiteboard on the wall just beyond the circle. "Let's talk about hunger." She draws a pathetic-looking stomach with a black marker. Then she takes a green marker and makes some *X*'s around the very top of the stomach.

"The green *X*'s—those are your stomach's largest concentration of nerve endings. They're the ones that send the message from your stomach to your brain that you're full and no longer need food. But what does it take to get us there? Around the room, starting with Bobby."

"Two pizzas and a six-pack of Red Bull," Jersey Boy—Bobby—says, doing nothing to change my opinion of the average jock IQ.

"The left three panels of the menu at Taco Bell," drawls a red-haired girl with a startling Southern accent.

"You go, girl!" says Phat Girl, waving her fist. A free-for-all breaks out.

"Two pints of Ben and Jerry's, any flavor!"

"Half a tray of my mother's lasagna!"

"Three triple Whoppers with bacon and cheese!"

"An entire dim sum cart."

"Hey—speaking of which," Char howls above the dither. "We know a great Asian fusion place called Chow Fun House just around the corner! Anyone in for a bite after group tonight?" The place goes wild. A heaping plate of sweet-and-sour chicken would be nice about now.

Bitsy reddens and raps her marker on the whiteboard.

"Char, I'd like to have a word with you after session. Everyone else—the time to start thinking about your food choices is now, *before* the surgery. The Lap-Band is not a magic wand and it's not a cure for obesity. It's a weight loss *tool* that must be used correctly to be effective. These presurgery weeks are not a go-ahead to binge—they're for developing the proper eating habits that are critical for your success with the band. If you can't commit to them now— *today*—you shouldn't go further." Bitsy breathes deeply and looks around the room. "So, there's room for thousands of calories before you get filled to the green *X*'s. Now, check this out." Bitsy encircles the top of the stomach with a heavy red band, leaving about an inch between that and her green *X*'s. "What if you only had to fill up to here before you set off the 'I'm full' signals to the brain?"

"That looks like about three pieces of pepperoni," Bobby says. I can't tell whether his terror is real or just for comic effect.

"How much space are we talking?" Coco asks, looking a little panic-stricken herself.

"About two ounces. At first, anyway," Bitsy says. "That's four tablespoons of food. And not heaping tablespoons either. Enough to fill an espresso cup."

The room goes silent and I'm wondering whether anyone's really going to that Asian place after group, and if I'll have time to join them before Carlo, Ronny's driver, picks me up.

Char is the only one who seems unconcerned about bird rations.

"Just think, guys! We'll so be able to get that *all's right with the world* feeling, as East here would say, in just a couple of bites." She's like Sumo Girl's voice box. East reddens and slinks in her chair.

But Bobby is right there with Char. "Yeah—like getting an excellent buzz on one shot—" Bobby turns red and coughs a couple of times. "Yeah—I get what you mean."

Bitsy narrows her eyes a bit, but nonetheless she seems relieved that the conversation is on track.

"Char is right, everyone. That's the most important thing the Lap-Band will do for you. It will prevent you from eating more than a few ounces of solid food, and signal your brain that your stomach is full. Emotional hunger, or 'head hunger,' as we call it—that's something different that we'll get to."

Bitsy puts down the markers and returns to her seat. She crosses her legs and leans in yet again.

"Here are some pitfalls: if you eat too much or too fast, your food will come back up. It won't be like vomiting—it's something called a 'productive burp.' Also, there are certain foods your Lap-Band won't like. For some people, it's fried foods or spicy foods; for others, red meat like steak, for example—requires about twenty chews if it is to stay down." Bitsy clears her throat and stands up again. "Remember to update your food diaries every time you put something in your mouth—not only what you're eating and when but also the events and thoughts that trigger your eating. Pay atten-tion to how your moods play into your food choices, folks."

Food choices my butt, I want to bellow. I don't get *any* choices about my life, not even about food. If I did, they'd stop feeding me this crap and send me straight into anesthesia.

LORD OF THE FRIES

Marcie (+2 lbs)

WTF? It took *weeks* for the stranded kids in *Lord of the Flies* to go from civilized schoolboys to bloodthirsty savages. Jen's only like six minutes late, and these Lord of the Fries lardies are already showing signs of wanting to run me off a cliff. If Lucia could liven up her "relationship with food" monologue everyone wouldn't keep checking their watches and glancing at me as if I'm getting telepathic updates about Jen's whereabouts and holding out on them. But Lucia is taking us through Twinkie by Twinkie, and with Bitsy all rabid about this group being our "haven," I'm not allowed to interrupt for permission to take out my phone and find out what's keeping Jen.

"Marcie?" Bitsy finally says when Lucia finishes her pathos-ridden "they called me fat in the lunchroom" story. "You're certain Jennifer is coming? We're only in session today to hear Jennifer share her Lap-Band experience with the group, and this has undoubtedly disrupted holiday weekend—"

"Of course she's coming," I say. Bitsy botched the scheduling, not me, but I manage not to mention this. "If you would just let me check my phone, I could find out if her train—"

"I'm so sorry I'm late," Jen says as she bursts through the door in all her size 2 glory. I just saw her a month and a half ago, and she's constantly sending me photos. Nevertheless, I don't quite recognize her. Even Bitsy looks like a cow in comparison. And there's something different about her—

Ohmigodohmigodohmigod—she got the breast implants after all!

The room goes so silent, you could hear a marshmallow drop. They're all stunned by how gorgeous she is. She looks like she had a lip job too—she's the spitting image of Angelina Jolie, only shorter and with black hair.

Bitsy rises and steps out of the circle to greet her. "I'm so sorry I'm late," Jen repeats, shaking Bitsy's hand. "A friend drove me down from Boston, and the holiday traffic was worse than we expected." I'm about to bark, "What's with the *friend*"—Jen's supposed to spend the weekend in Alpine with me—when Bitsy guides Jen to the edge of the circle.

"Group, please say hello to Jennifer. Jennifer, your pictures have caused quite a stir, and we're all eager to hear about your experience with the Lap-Band. Why don't you take the open seat next to Marcie so that we can begin?" Jen's greeting everyone as they fall over themselves and each other to get introduced. "*OMG, you're so tiny!*" "*OMG, you're amazing!*" and other sycophantic babbling winds down when Jen places her tiny tush on the seat next to mine. She elbows me with a grin and I elbow her back. Bitsy clears her throat.

"Jennifer, sitting before you is a group of teens who will

shortly embark on the same journey you've taken. What are the most important things they should know before they begin—experiences, for example, that you didn't expect?" She gestures to Jen that the floor is hers.

Jen surveys the circle with a smile and then folds her hands in her lap and leans forward—a motion, I realize, that is only for people who don't have seventy pounds of flab to balance on their laps.

"I see this more as a process than a journey," Jen begins, taking a beautiful whack at Bitsy's irritating "journey" metaphor, "and it's not as easy as you've probably been led to believe."

Bitsy clears her throat again and nods a little stiffly. "Excellent, Jennifer," she says. "Here at Park Avenue Bariatrics, that's the very point we try to get across—the Lap-Band isn't a fix, it's only a tool, and there's a lot of hard work and self-discipline involved. The band will solve the hunger aspect of your eating, but not the underlying reasons that you're self-medicating with food."

Jen smiles primly. "The 'solve the hunger' aspect is actually what I'm referring to." She pauses to enjoy the ensuing commotion.

"What the—" Phat Girl starts, but Bitsy raises her hand to shut Michelle down and gives the *hold off* signal to Geek Olive—neckless unibrow boy with the pimiento-red hair— who's raising his *index finger* in lieu of his arm. Talk about the sedentary lifestyle of today's teens.

"Please elaborate, Jennifer," Bitsy says, narrowing her eyes.

Jen grins like she doesn't mind the cool air. "If you go into the surgery thinking your eating will be restricted from day one, you'll be very disappointed. I know I was. But the fact of the matter is, until your band has been tightened enough to keep food from flowing straight through your pouch into your stomach, you're pretty much on your own with the diet—the band isn't going to help you feel full. It took over three months for me to get the band tight enough for meaningful restriction, and during that time, I actually gained two pounds—the pizzas and burgers still went down, they just took a little longer." Jen glances at me and suppresses a smile as all hell starts to break loose.

Bitsy raises her hands as if trying to fend off the questions being pelted at her. "People, please. Simmer down so that I can address Jennifer's *particular* experience."

"If you go online and read the Lap-Band message boards, you'll find that my experience was hardly rare or unique," Jen retorts loudly. As the murmuring rises in intensity, I lean over to whisper, "Jennifer raised an excellent point," and smell it—*liquor*—on her breath. WTF? Bitsy claps her hands for silence and I silently pull away.

"Everyone, Jennifer raised an excellent point. The first six weeks after surgery, your stomach will be healing. After that, you'll be scheduled for your first fill, and you'll be eligible for subsequent fills every three weeks thereafter. Some people can reach their 'sweet spot'—the level of band restriction that optimizes their weight loss—in their first fill, but it *can* take three, or even—"

"Whaaat?" Michelle bellows. "My stomach isn't going to be closed for business right after the surgery?"

"Hold on, Michelle. For many people, the band in itself and the initial swelling from the surgery provide some restriction before the first adjustment, or fill. Jennifer, you say you gained two pounds in the weeks after your sur—"

"Months," corrects Jen.

"But weren't you provided with any sort of eating plan following your surgery?" Bitsy says in a *so you didn't stick to your diet, did you?* voice.

"Of course," Jen says with icy politeness. "But if I had been able to stick to a diet, I wouldn't have needed surgery in the first place, would I?" A couple of kids giggle.

"Well, Jennifer, that's one of the reasons our teen patients attend group sessions—to become conscious of and responsible for their eating behaviors. So that they *are* able to stick to a diet," Bitsy volleys back. Faces turn back and forth watching the two skinny chicks go at each other.

"If group sessions are so effective, why not just slap a Weight Watchers sign on the door, and dump the surgeons altogether?" Jen returns sharply.

Bitsy lets out a sigh. "Jennifer, we're getting off track here. Let me just say that in *our* approach to weight loss, the Lap-Band is a tool used to address the physical hunger that accompanies dieting while we help our patients develop a healthier relationship with food. Can you describe the changes in your eating behaviors over the past eighteen months?"

"Of course," Jen says. "You're absolutely right about the Lap-Band limiting physical hunger, and it did finally work for me. I've learned to eat very slowly, take small bites, and chew my food thoroughly. And I never consume liquids while I'm eating—they'll come right back up if there's enough solid food already in the pouch, or they'll empty the pouch by washing the food down, and I'll end up eating more than I should."

"But what about your specific food choices?" Bitsy asks. "How have they changed?"

Jen pauses for a moment. "I go for softer foods now—lean ground turkey over steak, for example. And boiled chicken instead of barbecue or roasted. And if I find myself ravenous, I go for the foods that I know will fill me up quickly. One hundred-calorie ounce of cheese will eliminate my hunger in minutes, and keep me satisfied for several hours. Of course, I've completely eliminated all processed sugars—the band is useless in the face of junk food. Also, I stay away from starches, especially bread and pasta. Not only are they fattening, they can gum up the band and get stuck." Jen shrugs. "Did I miss anything?"

"What about your *relationship* with food?" Char bursts in, elongating the word *relationship* the way Bitsy does. Before Bitsy can jump on her for interrupting, Michelle chimes in.

"Yeah—how's *that* relationship working for you?"

Jen laughs and waves her tiny arm like she's casting something aside. "Oh, that relationship is long over. It's not gratifying anymore. I just eat because I need to—for energy and nutrition."

Bitsy nods. "So, would you agree that you now have a *healthy* relationship with food?"

"Of course. That's what I just said. Unless *healthy* and *ungratifying* are only synonymous in *my* thesaurus?" Jen and I look at each other and bust out laughing. Bitsy's smile tightens and I elbow Jen to stop.

"Jennifer," Bitsy says, "I have one more question before I turn the Q and A over to the group. The dramatic change in your eating must have been difficult to cope with in social situations, especially among your peers—most teens who get weight loss surgery prefer not to let others know about it.

Can you describe what that was like—were you self-conscious, and how did others react?"

Jen leans forward. "Dr. Glass, I'm not sure you've ever been told this, but I'm guessing you have never struggled with your weight. Because there are some unspoken rules among those of us who have fought the good fight—a sort of universal code embedded in the fat cell itself. Most fat people eat the same or less in social settings that involve nonfat people. Never more. By a show of hands, who's with me on this?" Bitsy shakes her head as the eleven of us raise our hands and wave them at her.

"Okay, put 'em down." Jen says. "One exception to the rule: your BFF isn't a porker, but she loves you just as you are, even when you're chowing big-time." Jen elbows me and continues. "Any other exceptions to the rule?" Hands start flying again and Jen points to Char.

"You're with your *porker* chub-buddy, say, and you're seated in the back of a restaurant—*not* the school cafeteria. As long as no one is within eyeshot of your table, you can eat normally. Or—more accurately—*abnormally*." Char takes a mini bow and we all applaud.

"Anything else?" Jen asks.

"My dad and my brother aren't big eaters, and I don't mind pigging out in front of them," drawls Jamie, this Southern girl.

"Okay, good. Family. Raise your hand next time. Anything else?" Coco, who's sitting on my left, flaps her jelly arm right in my face so Jen can see it. I brush it away.

"Okay, Coco," I say. "This'd better be good since you nearly gave me a bloody nose." Jen nods and Coco gives me the thumbs-up.

"For medical or medicinal purposes!" she shouts triumphantly—like she's a contestant on *Family Feud* and she's sure she's got the number-one answer. There's not a face in the room without *WTF?* written all over it, but Jen keeps it gracious.

"Interesting. Elaborate," she says.

Coco shakes her head like *we're* dense. "You know, if you're sick. Like when I had my tonsils taken out. I was in a hospital room with three regular-sized kids, but I was able to keep asking the nurse for more ice cream because my throat hurt so much." Naturally, everyone is dumbfounded, but this moron is looking right over me for confirmation from Jen, so it's taking every strand of decency in my DNA to keep from laughing, and the silence is killing me. *Please! Somebody say something.* . . .

"That's ridiculous," Tia, our Planet Pierce Observer, finally sneers—and Coco's hopeful smile evaporates.

"No, Coco—that's so totally valid," Char interjects. "C'mon, everybody. I bet there's not a person here who's never taken advantage of a sore throat to get extra cough drops. Or complained that a vaccination shot in the doctor's office hurt more than it did to get another lollipop or two."

"Once, when the urchin next door pummeled me especially badly, his mother baked me a chocolate cake?" Geek Olive offers meekly.

"And Char—remember when I was so upset you couldn't hang out for almost a week after your appendectomy that you bought me a huge bag of M&M'S?" East adds. Coco smiles gratefully at her.

Bitsy, who has quietly observed this interchange, claps loudly to get our attention. "Okay, gang. We've veered off into comfort eating—another topic for another day. We're talking about Jennifer's experience with food restriction. Jennifer, going back to your 'rule,' it's not as if you can eat even the *same* as thin people in a social situation. Fact is, you're not able to consume much at all, so even eating less than small eaters in a social setting creates a problem, which I was hoping you would honestly address for the group. In other words, if you're able to consume only a few bites of solid food at a meal, how can this not have caused issues in your social eating?"

Jen's smirk melts and she looks down at her fresh French manicure and slowly shakes her head as she shrugs.

"I've always been uncomfortable in social activities involving food—except now I'm involved in more social situations than I was before. I still order as much food as everyone else and I mostly push the food around on my plate. Still, it's a little uncomfortable and weird to not be able to even pick at your plate 'normally.' And until I lost half my body, everyone probably assumed I must be bingeing at home. Like most addicts, I've always tried to hide my addiction, so hiding the fact that I have a Lap-Band, well—I'm still a professional hider." Everyone's staring at Jen, riveted—even me. I don't think I've ever seen her look so vulnerable before. Bitsy's nodding her head slowly. Jen's still examining her nails when there's a rap on the door and someone unmistakably related to Geek Olive sticks a neckless head in.

"I'm sorry—it's past six and we need—"

"Oh! I'm so sorry!" Bitsy says, all flustered. "We're out of time, everyone. Let's thank Jennifer for sharing her Lap-Band experience with us, and remember—holiday or not, keep up with your food diaries."

Jen leans against my shoulder and whispers, "Saved by the beach ball."

"C'mon, let's blow this Popsicle stand before everyone starts asking for your autograph," I whisper back as everyone gets up. "Where's this *friend* of yours who drove you all the way from Boston?"

"Oh, that's Tom," Jen giggles in this suddenly alien, vomity, girly voice. "He just dropped me off and went back home." I stare at the tiny miniskirted girl with the breast implants and puffed-up lips who's now engulfed in a crowd of fawning fatties, and I've never felt more alone in my entire life—this isn't *my* Jen. It's a complete stranger.

The crowd evaporates toward the door and Jen emerges with her trademark *WTF* eye roll. "If that's Rich Ronny's limo I saw out front, we'd better hustle," a familiar voice says sharply. "That girl just invited me to her quince party. Get me out of here before someone asks me to marry them." And just like that, the world goes back to normal.

○ ○ ○ ○ ○ ○

Jen's telling me about her new fitness column in the *Fuller Review* and rifling through the minibar when Carlo turns right on Seventy-second Street instead of left.

"Shoot me now!" I moan, and slump down into my seat. Jen whips out her finger gun and fires a round off at my head. "Maybe he just took a wrong turn," I say, then undo my seat belt and hop across the limo and rap on Carlo's window— just as he pulls in front of Gran's apartment building. "Ugh!" I scream. Jen fakes terror and grabs a bottle of Dewar's and pretends to suck it down.

"Oh my God—remember that time your gran came with us to the Cape that weekend? The three of us were crammed in the backseat of your dad's Saab—her in the middle—and she kept telling me what a pretty face I had? Like for the whole ride?"

"Yeah," I mutter. "Granspeak for 'You're a fat slob, Jen.' "

"Not the subtlest person I ever met. Must be where you get it from." Jen laughs, and I lean over and whack her.

"Well, at least you won't be in the hot seat this time." I hop back to Jen's side of the limo and buckle up as Carlo opens the door for Gran—*and her luggage.* The whole weekend? Jen and I glance at each other as Gran daintily steps into the car and gently seats herself in the middle seat across from us.

"Oh my goodness, Jenny! Every time I see you, you get more and more beautiful," she rasps, and puts out her cheek for Jen to air-kiss. I'm thumbing through my idiot food diary as if it's my favorite novel.

"Hello, darling," Gran says to me expectantly, but I don't do air-kisses and her lipstick is the kind that stays on the victim's cheek, not on her artificially plumped lips. She quickly turns her attention back to Jen. "You must be fighting them off with a stick," she says, shaking her head admiringly. Jen freaking *blushes.*

"Well, I have to say, Mrs. Lipsky—there are a couple of guys . . ." Jen says a little too giddily—she's *inviting* conversation rather than our standard *whatever it takes to shut that woman down.*

"Jen and I were just talking about the new column she's been invited to write for our—her—school paper," I try, but it's more to myself than anyone. Jen is already gushing on about her new Boston–to–New York shuttle guy, and when she realizes I'm not listening, she gives her attention completely to Gran, and I throw myself back into my food diary for the duration.

○ ○ ○ ○ ○ ○

Jen shows up in my room at least fifteen minutes after we get home—long enough for me to curl up on my bed and pretend to be absorbed in a random book from the top of my library pile. "What's with you, girl? I have to say hello to your family, don't I?" She drops her bag on the floor and jumps onto the bed with me. "You know, you're going to be a lot happier once you lose weight, Marce."

"Really? Will I be getting all sorts of cosmetic surgery too? Because then I'll be extra *extra* happy, right? Just like you."

Jen elbows me and sighs. "I like feeling good about myself for a change."

"But Jen, if you feel the need for plastic surgery on top of being thin, how good about yourself can you really feel?"

"Okay, Marcie, I'll tell you what happened, and then we're going to drop it, because your attempt at dime-store psychology pretty much sucks. When I lost all the weight, I had lots of extra skin that had to be removed. So, while I was under anesthesia, I had a couple of other things done too. Anybody would." My mouth flies open. I turn over to lift the bottom of Jen's shirt to look for scars, but she slaps my hand and I turn away from her again.

"You know, Jen," I mutter, "kids typically don't need excess skin removed after major weight loss, because their skin is more elastic than adults' and it bounces back in time.

I guess you just couldn't wait. And that's why you didn't bother to tell me."

"You'll understand when you get here." Jen sighs. "It feels nice, not being angry at the world anymore. The world, like your grandmother, is nicer to *me*—fair or not fair. Everyone just treats me differently now, and so I treat them differently. You'll see. Soon enough, we'll *both* be giggling about boys—and deconstructing the universe as usual. Starting when we're roommates at Harvard and ending when, well, when we're way past your crazy grandmother's age." Jen leans her head against mine on my pillow and we lie like this until Abby calls us down to dinner.

II

FiLLiNG BOXES

Bobby (-0 lbs)

Syosset clears out for the summer. Kids do teen tours, work at sleepaway camps, and take classes on college campuses. I don't do stuff like this. My parents would let me and all. I just don't like the idea of living with other kids. I've never liked sleepovers, even at Zoo's, where we mostly hang out. Up until a few of us got our driver's license, I was the only one who didn't crash at his palace. But Dad was cool about picking me up late. Usually about the same time Zoo would buzz Oswaldo on his intercom and order more fettuccine Alfredo or O's signature *taquitos*. "*Rápido*, dude!" Zoo would yell. He's not a jerk, though. It's just the way he's grown up. Zoo's parents are like billionaires or something; his dad is some international financial whiz. So O is like their cook and he thinks we have this special fat-guy bond.

A couple of years ago, when I was waiting in the front hall for Dad to pick me up, the guys were watching *Ali G* reruns and O was bringing down this sick platter of dessert. He went back to the kitchen and handed me a wrapped paper plate to go.

"For you, my friend," he said. "Not as *bueno* as my *panqueques*, but you no here in the morning. *Yo comprendo*, my friend. I understand," he said.

"Understand *qué?*"

"The big man," he went on in his funny Spanglish, neck jiggling. "Our *secreto*. You no like it to fart in front of the other *niños*." My dad beeped and I nodded and rushed the hell out of there. Oswaldo, my fat compadre. He was right, though. *Is* right. I don't puff. Even when they all do. MT and Craig are insanely proud of their output, and we all laugh about it. I deny holding mine back, but I do. Because I wouldn't be like them. I wouldn't be Refrigerator-Man with my brand. Just a fat kid farting toxic fat-kid farts. Same reason I don't munch out mad in front of the guys. I'd never even eat a chip in front of a girl.

The guys took bets on whether MT or me would lose our V-cards. It's our summer assignment. Zoo says his money is on MT. As Craighead rightly said, if an ugly bastard like him could get with a girl, anyone could. He may have acne, but it's not the same as fat. Not many of my boys took me, the fat horse, to place first. MT went on a Fire and Ice Alaska-Hawaii teen tour. That's why they all said odds were in his favor—the only ass I'll be scoping this summer, they said, will be hairy butt cracks at the lumberyard. Still, I don't think it's just the lack-of-opportunity thing.

Anyway, MT wrote on my Facebook wall yesterday: *How's the wood, dude? 26 girls and 18 guys here and the babes are ripe. Get your blubbery butt on a plane. Operation Seminal Summer already has a target.* His message sent me diving into a gallon of Edy's cherry vanilla. "The only cherry you'll get," Zoo would say, and he's probably right. I'm lying in bed even though it's already after noon. Even though it's barely the second week of summer break, I have homework—this annoying piece of paper with all these boxes I have to fill in for the next six days.

"Preoperative homework" is what Betsy Glass calls it. I have to fill in squares. Write down what I eat for each meal and snack. The way the sheet is set up is stupid. Their expectation is that you'll have three meals, with two snacks in between. Six boxes. Like it's only six times you're eating. If whoever designed this had a clue, they'd put it in a database format where you could add spaces for breakfast, snack, snack, snack, lunch, snack, snack, dinner, and a string of snacks up until around midnight. It's not like the trial is for people who have gland problems—they're regular fat kids like me. All girls too, except for that one dweeby guy who wears shirts buttoned up to his neck. After the first group session at Chow Fun House (a sloppy greasefest Char suggested we *not* record in any of our food boxes), this girl Marcie said he reminds her of a big olive. Like his head is the pimiento peering out of his soft round body. If Char hadn't convinced me to join them, these seven fat girls—Ms. Lip Ring and Geek Olive didn't come—might have been talking about the friggin' moobies poking out of my jersey.

But Char's this mad funny blond chick, even if she's as big as a John Deere. She whispered that she and her friend ate a whole box of Cap'n Crunch on the train into the city. On the way to group! The surgery idea was hers, she said. She made her friend, East, sign up for it with her. I don't think she had to work it much—the chick clings to her like a barnacle and doesn't say a thing. That Char can talk, though! First, she tells me she's the type who will try *any-thing*. "I'm not just talking food either," she says, and flicks my arm. She said there was once this guy she partied with a lot, but now she's basically straight-edge. But in case I was thinking otherwise, she could most definitely Captain Morgan me under any table. Next, she's rambling about this bratty five-year-old girl she babysat for until the perv father, who finally gave up hitting on her, came up with some phony story about missing weed, so now she has like nothing to do all summer. This went down in the time it took the busload of girls to take a leak and her barnacle friend to make a call and scurry back to her side. But I can't for the life of me see any normal guy hitting on Char, not even with those mammoth boobs flying in every direction whenever she laughs. Which is like most of the time.

So at group, Betsy said I'm what you'd call a grazer—I'm always at the trough, even between regular feeding times. We'll all have to share more about our eating choices and behaviors next session with these sheets. So each time I eat anything I'm supposed to rate my degree of hunger on a scale of one to ten, then fill out *New Behavior Practiced* and *Reaction & Feelings*—the last two columns on the page. For *every bite.* This is not the kind of information I want people to know about me, not that I care what a herd of fat girls and one Geek Olive think. All of this stupid crap is killing my appetite anyway. And using these sheets is pathetic. Scary that doctors can still be in the dark ages when it comes to computer technology.

I go to MT's wall on Facebook before shutting my laptop and rolling over. I like my profile photo. In uniform, all padded up, I look more big than fat. Tough lineman. Not like some pussy keeping track of a leaf of lettuce.

My WOOD is good! Solid top-grade hardwood, Pencildick.

Just b/c girls are ripe over there doesn't mean you'll be picking any fruit. And dude, I'm mapping my options out here too. Gonna be filling in a lot of boxes, I write, knowing the guys would never think I'm talking about damn homework sheets.

Maybe a miracle will happen and a giant vacuum will come under these covers and suck off my boobs and fat butt. Maybe I'll fall back to sleep, into the dream I was having of fooling around with this girl Roxy. Yeah. That would be a dream assignment.

12

teenage waistland

East (-5 lbs); Char (-3 lbs)

Char notices my shirt immediately. "Whoa! Is this a non-Shroudity?"

"Whaaat?"

" 'Whaaat?' You insult me. You bought clothes without me." Char steps back to take me in.

"You're being ridiculous. It's nothing, from the Gap."

"Yeah? When'd'ya get it, then?"

"I don't know. A while ago?" I tell her. I bought it online yesterday and had it overnighted, but what does it matter when I bought the stupid shirt?

"It's not black. And you have flesh showing. Are you transforming before we're transforming?" Char shoves me. "Sistah, sistah, who are you?" She's cracking herself up.

I shrug. "It's just a shirt."

"*I* think someone is trying to be noticed by someone," she says all singsongy.

"You're wrong, Char. I'd tell you." I say this a little louder than I should.

"Okay. Relax. Thought I was just picking up on a vibe."

○ ○ ○ ○ ○ ○

We jam our way onto the uptown 4 train and grab the steel bar in the middle. At Fifty-ninth, it's clear that we're blocking people from getting out or pushing further into the train. Unlike Char, I'm supremely aware of who's watching us. She's two parts oblivious and eight parts doesn't give a crap, and is busy digging into her leather backpack for her iPod anyway.

Char's wearing a gauzy white peasant blouse, her black lace bra clearly showing through. *Again*. And she's tied the thin red string at the top of the blouse in a way that draws your eye to her ample cleavage. Now I'm sorry I bought this top. Why this boatneck? So Bobby can think of me as a tanker?

"This is ugly." I pull at my shirt.

"I like it. Stop adjusting!" She's swinging her wavy blond hair over her shoulder and stuffing her earbuds in. "Chill," she orders.

"Hey." I nudge Char. She unplugs one ear.

"Those boys are talking about that TV show, *The Biggest Loser*," I whisper. "That show is bigger than *Idol*."

She shrugs, sticking her earphones back in. A second later, she pulls them out again.

"They should so do a reality show about our Bandster group!" she exclaims. As if it's an actual possibility.

"Yeah, what are we going to call it—*Bigger Fatter Losers?*"

Char's scrolling through songs.

"*Teenage Waistland! W-A-I-S-T*-land!" she shrieks. I elbow her as people turn to look at us.

"Miss Clever, the clinical trial is supposed to be private.

We're not allowed to disseminate information about it." I guess Char is right. I'm always raining on her wacky parades.

"No matter!" Char says, undeterred. "We'll call our Bandster group Teenage Waistland!"

I mutter something about finding custom T-shirts to fit us all, but she's high on her idea and not listening. I just know she's going to announce this at group tonight, and everyone is going to be all over her even more.

At Eighty-sixth Street, we push our way out of the subway. Char's leading with her breasts. They seem to cut a path through the crowd like a machete in high grass. If I didn't love her, I swear I'd hate her. We have two blocks left to walk and we need to do it in a hurry. It's five of five, and group starts promptly at five p.m. "Walk faster," I say.

"Did you just see that guy? The Puerto Rican one. Cute. And him." She's throwing her head toward this muscle-bound European-looking guy.

"Char! He's probably like twenty and Turkish or something. You're crazy."

"No. Crazy, my friend, would be what we're doing after group tonight."

I turn to look back at Char. "We're going down to Fifty-third Street to buy a dildo," she announces. I stop dead in the middle of the sidewalk.

"We are not—"

"Yes, we so are. Marcie needs to get her slutty stepsister a graduation gift, and a dildo sounds like just what she needs." Char pulls on my arm and we're moving again.

"This was your idea, right?" I say. "No one normal thinks of this stuff. Remind me not to let you take me shopping for Julius's wedding gift."

Now Char comes to a halt. "Julius is getting married? When? Why didn't you tell me?"

"I thought I did. You probably forgot." I yank on Char's arm, but she stands firm. "Char? What's the big deal?"

"Hey," Bobby says from behind us. His voice is unmistakable. I'm in a panic now.

Char turns, and miraculously shifts to being all grins again. "Hey, Bobby—up for a little adventure after group tonight?" She *giggles* and gives him this playful shove. I'm ready to vomit blood on my dumb navy and white striped sailor shirt.

"What?" Bobby says.

"Hi," I blurt stupidly. *I'm an idiot.*

Bobby doesn't even notice. Char is chatting his ear off as I follow them into the building and onto the elevator. Betsy says, "Just in time," as I trail them into the room. Everyone is already there, and we take the three open seats left in the circle. Char grabs the middle one of course.

"Okay, everyone. Before we go through our meal sheets— wait, everyone has them—your recording of meals and snacks—right?" Betsy says looking around. Bobby's working his hand in his front pocket and pulls out a folded square. It looks like one of those paper fortune-tellers Char and I used to make. You pick a number, move the points, then pick another number, until you open a flap to reveal one of the fortunes you made up. *You will kiss Bobby,* I say to myself, and visualize it for a second. This is a ridiculous baby thing to be thinking. I'm embarrassed about my own mind sometimes.

"Hold on to them for a second," Betsy says. "I've got your surgery dates!" She's waving a sheath of paper like it's a victory flag.

Everyone claps, but not Char. No, she's *shimmying*! "Bring it," she shouts, and gets everyone into another round of clapping and laughing. I lean forward to glance at Bobby. He's laughing too, of course, but his eyes are, like, glued to Char's jiggling chest. I think Marcie's also catching this. She's got a smirk on her face. Marcie's okay, but I don't see why Char's getting so cozy with her. They exchanged phone numbers at Chow Fun House two weeks ago, after the first group session.

Char's really focused on everything changing. Lately, all her sentences begin with "After we get the bands . . ." I'm not sure if I *can* change. I'm not even comfortable not wearing black. It's like I'm falling further behind. When Char was blabbing away with Marcie and Lucia in the restaurant, I just sat there. Same thing with Bobby. I just sat there while they were giggling up a storm. It's like she's this champagne bottle and I'm a cork. She's the one transforming before we transform. I mean she's sociable enough in school, but here it's like a *Char Gone Wild* video.

"Most of your surgeries are scheduled for the third week of July," Betsy says, startling me out of my thoughts. "And—this is critical, folks—make sure you confirm your date and time with your parents and bring back this form signed." Betsy passes the surgery schedules to Coco, but before Coco can take hers and pass them on to Lucia, everyone is out of their seats grabbing for a copy. Char and I have our surgery on the same day. I'm in the morning, seven-thirty, and she's at three p.m. This is already backward: Char leads, I follow.

"Marcie and Bobby are two days before us," Char whispers.

"I can read," I say, and she makes a face at me.

Coco raises her hand and Betsy nods at her. "Is it possible to switch dates?" Coco says.

"Why? Is there a problem?"

"It's my birthday. My father's closing down his restaurant, Sunday, July twelfth, for the party."

Betsy looks at her sheet. "Oh, I see you're that first surgery the Friday before, Coco."

"Your dad is closing his restaurant for your birthday party?" Char interrupts. "Way cool." It sure beats closing his life for it, anyway.

"It's a big thing," Coco responds. "The fifteenth birthday, it's called a *quinceañera*. It's like a bat mitzvah or a sweet sixteen, but Mexicans do it at fifteen. I have family coming in from California and all over."

"So it's like a debutante ball?" Jamie asks. Marcie rolls her eyes at Char and Char grins back.

"Yeah, I guess." Coco shrugs. "Oh, and everyone here is invited."

"Anyone want to switch with Coco?" Betsy says, surveying the circle.

Bobby's hand shoots up, but Ms. Lip Ring—this is what Char and I named her last week—calls out, "I will. I don't do those kinds of parties."

"Bobby, you're one of the first as is, so let's let Tia switch with Coco," Betsy says. Bobby mumbles something about football practice, but Char leans into him to whisper. All I can make out is the word *waste.*

Bobby seems to like whatever Char said to him, because he's smiling and nodding. Then he leans into *her* and whispers something back. Char jumps out of her chair like she's just been lit on fire and shrieks, "Hey, everybody, we can all celebrate Coco's birthday at her party *and* have a final presurgery blowout commemorating the initiation of our group here as—are you ready?—Teenage Waistland! W-A-I-S-T-land!"

Dead silence. Could Char have bombed? I feel guilty for the little surge of glee I feel forming in my stomach. "Well, maybe we could call ourselves Blub Busters," I suddenly hear myself say in an almost-whisper. I'd like to think it was to try to save Char from the embarrassing silence, but I did come up with the name after Char's Teenage Waistland tirade on the train. There are a few murmurs in the room, but then I hear it—singing:

It's Alex—the one Marcie calls Geek Olive. And he's singing the Who's "Baba O'Riley"! And then Lucia. And Tia. Now Marcie. They're all singing it! By the time they get to "It's on-ly teen-age wasteland," the whole room is belting it out, Char and Bobby the loudest. I don't even know all the words to that stupid old song, but it doesn't matter— all everyone's howling now is "Teen-age Waist-land," over and over until the inevitable laughing and fist-bumping breaks out.

Betsy, totally red, claps her hands loudly. "Enough, Teenage Waistland. We've got important things to get to. Char, I need you to stay after group for a few minutes."

After the meeting breaks, Char emerges from the room looking a little solemn, but she lights up when she spots Bobby down the hall heading back from the watercooler. "Teenage Waistland, yeah," he says loudly, putting his fist in the air. She waves her fist back at him.

"Teen-age Waist-land," she chants again. "Right, East?" She elbows me.

"Teenage Waistland, for sure," I sputter, hoping this time to be more than the silent partner in this duet. Bobby joins Char, Marcie, and me as we head to the elevator.

"Are you guys still going to grab a bite?" he says, mostly to Char.

Marcie giggles.

"But of course," Char says. "Just as soon as we run a little errand for Marcie." Marcie clears her throat. "I mean, for Marcie's sister. And then we'll hit Chow Fun House. Hard."

I groan softly. She was serious about the stupid dildo thing.

Char puts her face in mine. "Lighten up. And stop adjusting your damn shirt. You *so* look fine." I'm about to ask her what Betsy said, but she skips ahead to walk with Bobby. Char's happier than maybe I've ever seen her and Bobby doesn't even know I'm alive. As Char glances back over her shoulder and motions for me to pick up my pace, I realize that I'm not a tagalong at all. I'm deadweight.

13

A GIFT FOR LISELLE

Marcie (-3 lbs)

We're tromping south on Lexington to Come Again Erotic Emporium. I'm in front, East is dragging a bit behind me, Char and Bobby are pulling up the rear. I'm marveling at the epic genius of Char Newman. Jen listened to me rip into Liselle and this ridiculously excessive graduation party Abby's throwing for her. For like an hour, we came up with hillarious schemes to embarrass Liselle and destroy her gala, but then in the end Jen said *seriously*, I should just get her a nice pair of earrings.

"Liselle's not nearly as bad as you say. Stop with this mighty vendetta of yours and chill out," Jen said. I growled that not only has she lost her feminist balls but she was also selling out to the forces of evil—she had borrowed a shirt from Liselle when she stayed over. There's no way I'm blowing my allowance on something *nice* for that witch—no way, no how. But Char—it took her, like, two seconds, right outside group last week, to assess the situation and come up with a graduation gift for Liselle that guarantees utter humiliation for her—and a one-way ticket back to Boston for me.

A dildo.

"Look, it's not *healthy* for Liselle to be humping every guy in a ten-mile radius. You'll be doing her and the world a favor by slowing the spread of STDs," Char explained while I stood gaping like an idiot. "It's the *charitable* thing to do."

It took about another two seconds for me to imagine a bikini-clad Liselle, presiding over her society of numnuts on the patio, opening gifts: First, Liselle's peeling back the tissue paper on her gift from June. It's a cute little beach hat, and she puts it on so the morons can coo over her for an hour. Then comes the David Yurman diamond bangle from Ronny and Abby, and she gasps—the ooohs and ahhhs reach fever pitch. Her attention still on her new diamond booty, she unwraps my gift and holds it up. The guys are hooting, the girls screaming, and the look on Liselle's face—once she realizes she's got a big plastic dick in her hand—is priceless.

I examined Char's face to see if she was screwing with me, but she didn't even blink. I threw my arms around her, told her she was very sick, and made her promise to go dildo shopping with me—and, of course, join the fun on Liselle's big day. Jen's coming too, but when I told her about Char's dildo plan, she was a total buzz kill. "Marce, stop! We hate all prejudice—against race, religion, whatever. But here you are imposing this whole 'slut' thing on Liselle merely because men find her attractive. It's not right, it's not even true, and it's not who you are." After we hung up, I ate almost a whole box of Double Stuff Oreos.

I turn around to ask Char what colors dildos usually come in, but she's busy gabbing with Bobby, so I wait for East to catch up to me.

"So, you and Char go dildo shopping often?"

East reddens, naturally. She's a little winded by the walk and wisps of her black hair are sticking to her face.

"Uh, no. This is our first time." She looks back toward Char, as if she's annoyed at being stuck with me. Oh. Like it's a big party for me.

I'm about to ask East some inane question about her family or something to break the ice, when Char shrieks, "This is it!" We cluster around a store window filled with whips, edible underwear, and various other items I can't begin to identify.

East starts laughing hysterically like she's having a nervous breakdown. "I'm not going in there!"

"Yes, you so are," Char says in a monotone. She slips her arm through East's and drags her to the window. Bobby steps back toward the curb and fumbles with his cell phone so it looks like he's not with us. The scene *is* a little freaky—three huge girls with their faces pressed up against a porn-store window like it's Godiva or something.

"This is an adult store, Char. Eighteen and over, it says," East whines.

"Like they're going to card us," I say. "They won't, will they?" I turn to Char.

"Don't be silly. Bobby has a fake ID anyway."

"Oh, right," East says. "You're going to send *him* in to buy a dildo?" Bobby's still holding his cell phone like it's his ticket out of here. Char walks over to him and whispers something in his ear. He starts laughing and puts his phone away.

"Okay, ladies. Let's go shopping," he says, and saunters over to the door. Char's right behind him and I'm behind her. East is still sulking by the window.

"Grab her," Char orders, and she follows Bobby in.

"C'mon, East. This'll be a scream. I promise—no one will get arrested," I say. But the door closes behind me.

Char and Bobby have already made their way past the racks of bright red satin lingerie to the counter. They're pointing at items behind the glass and laughing. "No clue. I'm going to have to look this up on the Internet," Char is saying.

"Over here, Char," I say. I'm standing before a dazzling array of flesh-colored penises twirling around in a large rectangular glass display case. Bobby is trying to be cool about it as Char guides him over, but his face is flushed and he mutters something about finding East and takes off.

"There goes our expert," Char says, and we giggle. A guy in tight black leather pants clears his throat.

"Ladies?"

"Oh, hello," Char says with a hint of an English accent. Like she's a freaking duchess or something. "We're looking for, um, one of those, sir." I'm dying to laugh out loud, but manage to make my choking sound like a coughing fit.

"Any particular size and color preference?" the man asks coolly, as if we're discussing bathroom tile.

Char and I look at each other.

"We're looking for the biggest bang for the buck," Char says, completely straight-faced. I turn away in peals of laughter. "Hey, how much do you want to spend, Marcie?"

I fumble for my wallet. "Thirty dollars?"

The man snorts. He opens the case and pulls out a large shiny penis and flicks the switch at the bottom. It starts to rumble, and it's all I can do not to start howling again.

"Basic version—no bells and whistles. Fifty bucks. Cheapest one here. Batteries not included."

Char pulls out a small slip of paper from her back pocket. She hands it to me. "It's a coupon. Ten dollars off any fifty-dollar purchase. I got it off the Internet."

"Done," I say, and hand the man the coupon and Abby's credit card—the one she gave me for emergencies. This *is* an emergency. If I don't get out of this store immediately, I'm going to pee in my pants.

14

chow and fun

Bobby (-3 lbs)

Last time at Chow Fun House, Freddie Kawasaki wanted to squeeze eight of us into a booth for six. Char had taken one look at where Freddie was heading, made a sharp left, and guided us straight to a table for twelve with a Reserved sign on it like *she* was the maître d'. Char and Freddie stared each other down for a few tense seconds, then Freddie took away the sign and brought back some tea.

This time, he takes one glance at Char swinging her curls and surveying the room and gives us a nice, roomy round table for six. She laughs and says, "Perfect, Freddie, thanks!" Dad would get a kick out of Char; he also firmly believes that a group that eats double its head count should call the shots in any restaurant.

Char plops down next to me, Marcie takes the seat next to her, and East, who was heading toward Marcie's chair, looks bummed to be on my other side. The girls go to the bathroom right after we place our orders. Guys don't make taking a whiz a group activity, but I guess the girls also want to blab on about this dildo thing in there.

The dildo thing. I'm thinking how to play it for MT. *Sex in the city, dude. Hanging with a group of babes I met in Manhattan. There's even a Charlotte, except she goes by Char and she's blond with a major rack. Exotic Asian chick too. Went shopping with these girls for some sex toys.* MT would cream over that. I'll close with, *Teen tour boy—I can't handle them ALL by myself—wish you were here.* And leave out the little fact that Char and her friend might outweigh our whole offensive line.

Truth is, though, these girls are fun. Especially Char. She was cool when I was acting like a loser at first in front of Come Again. She whispered, "C'mon, Bobby. Show us girls how it's done." And suddenly I wasn't a needledick anymore. Because of something a fat girl said to me. Which, I guess, makes me even more of a loser. If MT or the other guys get wind of me with them and this whole situation, I'll have to move out of state.

I'm watching the girls pile out of the bathroom and weave carefully, single file, through the tables toward me. East's hip bumps into a chair and she makes a great save before it crashes. She hangs her head so her hair covers her face, and I dump three more packets of sugar into my tea so she thinks I didn't notice. *Really* shy, that girl. We didn't say much to each other when I blew out of that store. Her back was to the window and her arms were crossed, and I went up to her and said something like "Char's looking for you." She got all uncomfortable and mumbled that Char knew exactly where to find her. So we just stood there staring at the pavement until East said we were blocking the view for window-shoppers, and we moved to the edge of the sidewalk. Then Char and Marcie came running out of the store together all giddy. East said, "Can we just go now?" and we headed over here.

Freddie Kawasaki is making his way across the room with a big steaming platter. I'm thinking we're all thinking the same thing: please be *our* order. Sure enough, he opens a folding stand and sets down his tray right behind East. Freddie delivers the soups and puts each appetizer in the center of the table, whipping off the metal covers like he's a magician making a rabbit appear, and announces, "Fried pork dumpling, shrimp spring roll, chicken teriyaki, double-order barbecue sparerib," and like three other apps. Then he says something to East in what I figure is Japanese, and she shrugs and gets all red. Char, Marcie, and I order even more dishes than last time, and once Freddie finishes broadcasting our feast to the entire restaurant, we look at the food and then each other. Marcie makes the first play.

"Next week, after we get the surgeries, we'll be licking postage stamps for a rush. Let's do it while we can," she says, and dumps a sparerib on her plate. "Who's got the duck sauce?"

After that, hands are flying all over the table and the appetizers are gone. Freddie's back in no time, chuckling, with another steaming tray, and I'm halfway done scarfing down my lo mein and some of Char's chicken *katsu* before I realize I've never eaten so much in front of any group of people but my family. And I'm having a blast doing it.

"Send over that tempura platter stat," I say to Marcie, and she passes me the dish. "Yeah, that's what I'm talking about."

15

COMING OF AGE

SUNDAY, JULY 12, 2009

East (–6 lbs); Char (–3.5 lbs)

The ceiling is covered in pink and white balloons with dangling pink and silver streamers. "Bat mitzvah, Mexican style," I mumble as I trail Char and Marcie through the doors of Coco Rosa. Marcie laughs and hits Char's arm.

"Told you she could be funny," Char says without turning around. Great. Char had to convince her I could be funny. *Big endorsement, Char.* I leave it. She's a little tense and I wonder what's up. There's a mariachi band blaring off to the side in the front entryway, and we stop at a little table strewn with tent cards to find the ones with our names and table numbers on them.

"Cool," Char says. "Check this out." She hands Marcie and me our cards, but there's no table number on the inside. Instead, it says *Teenage Waistland.*

"Great," I mutter. "It might as well say 'Fat Surgery Table.'" Char spins around and punches my arm.

"None of that Shroud stuff today. It's Coco's special day and she's so psyched we're all coming. Plus, as you may remember, we're also celebrating the initiation of Teenage Waistland. A big day all around."

I shrug, but Char has already turned back around to scan the rest of the cards. "It looks like Bobby's the only one to arrive so far." She takes off to find him, and Marcie and I quickly follow in the space she's opening in the crowd.

"With those boobs of hers, it's like Moses parting the Red Sea," Marcie whispers loudly, and I giggle.

Char, Marcie, and I have been together since yesterday morning, except for last night, when Marcie slept at Char's and I didn't because Mom doesn't like to be alone at night. Jen was supposed to spend the weekend too—a "best friends double date," but Marcie met us at Grand Central alone— something "important" came up, so Jen decided she'd "catch up with us" at the party tonight.

None of us had anything dressy enough to wear to Coco's *quinceañera*, so we went shopping—the Three Mooseketeers. I was the last to find anything I could stand, but by then I wasn't even embarrassed to try things on in front of Marcie. When Char was in the fitting room and Marcie and I were ragging on the plus-size selections, I explained our whole Shroud thing. She loved it. "The Shroud Shtick," she'd say whenever Char and I debated which acre of black fabric looked best on me.

There are maybe two hundred people here, and it seems like everyone speaks Spanish except for us. And Bobby, whom Char finally spots sitting at the bar. Bobby straightens up and waves when he sees her. He's wearing black chinos and a loose-fitting white linen shirt, and his hair is neatly combed. He looks seriously handsome.

"Drinks, señoritas?" he says with a big smile.

"Oh yes!" Char shrieks above the music. "Three sangrias." Bobby relays this to the bartender and reports back with bad news.

"Virgin sangrias," he says. "Coco's father left strict instructions that Teenage Waistland is *not* to get wasted. Something about valuing his liquor license."

The drinks arrive with floating orange slices and little cocktail toothpick umbrellas. Char grabs one and puts it between her teeth like it's a rose and she makes this tango move with one palm against her stomach, the other wiping a window in a circular motion. Bobby laughs at her as he passes the drinks around.

"Hold it," Char orders, and swings her large shoulder bag onto Bobby's lap. "Pull out the water bottle and spike them first," she says. "Marcie, East, and I will block everyone's view."

"Let's have yours later," Bobby says. He pulls a flask of tequila out of his pants pocket and pours some into each of our sangria glasses. Char laughs.

"Great minds think alike." She holds up her glass.

"No. Actually, the opposite," Marcie injects. She's about to explain why that is, but Char just rolls her eyes and goes on with her toast.

"To Teenage Waistland. May they get wasted after all." We clink glasses and drink to that. Marcie and Bobby throw theirs back like old pros. Char too. Even a little sip tastes bitter, and I put mine down on the bar to find my cell phone. Another check-in call to Mom. As our home phone rings, I wonder what's with Char sneaking liquor and why she didn't tell me earlier.

"Marcie, doesn't this *quinceañera* thing signal a sexual coming-of-age?" Char says.

"Liselle would be the expert there." Marcie's quick like Char.

"Ouch. *Tsss*." Char makes a sizzling sound when her finger touches Marcie's arm. I laugh and my eyes meet Bobby's for a split second before I quickly whisper into the answering machine.

"Get it? *Coming*-of-age?" Char asks Bobby, but answers for him first. "Ladies, this guy gets it." Bobby squirms a little, but he really seems to like Char being all over him.

Suddenly, though, Char's no longer my competition. Jen is making her way through the crowd toward us, and she's wearing this amazing black minidress that matches her hair and hugs her tiny waist. The stiletto heels on her shoes have to be at least five inches—if I even tried to wear anything like them, I'd puncture the floor. She's absolutely gorgeous.

"Jen!" Marcie screams, and then the two of them rush over to each other, hugging and jumping up and down and rambling on a mile a minute. I feel a pang of sympathy for Marcie. Jen can barely get her arms all the way around her, and wrapped around Jen, it's as if Marcie's an elephant gobbling up a peanut. Then, Marcie takes Jen's toned bare arm and drags her over. Bobby jumps up and *insists* that Jen take his stool. I glance at Char and then at Marcie to see if they have any reaction—Bobby didn't offer his seat when any of *us* arrived—but Marcie is still blabbering away with Jen while Char pours herself another shot of tequila.

"Great to see you all again," Jen says in a deep, throaty grown-up voice as she wiggles her little butt on Bobby's barstool to find the right position. "I love texting, but chatting in the flesh is much more fun." I didn't realize everyone has been texting with Jen!

"Totally," Char gushes.

"Yeah," Bobby says.

"Has anyone seen Coco?" Marcie asks while Bobby is ordering a second round of virgin sangrias. I'm the only one who hasn't said anything to him yet. I pick up my glass again and struggle to think of something clever before he turns from the bar to hand out the drinks. I might as well have had my vocal chords removed.

Lots of Coco's school friends are here and a bunch of people in their twenties. Coco must have one of those families with a zillion cousins. My family wouldn't need a restaurant to celebrate anything. Just a table for two, assuming Julius wouldn't be joining us.

Giving up on finding something unidiotic to say to Bobby and at this point, not even able to hear a word of the Char/Marcie/Jen gabfest over the music, I wander toward the dining area to find Coco. Tables set with white linens, hot pink napkins, and white and pink balloon centerpieces surround a large parquet dance floor. The DJ is on one side of the dance floor, and long buffet tables with empty silver hot plates are lined up along the other. Everyone's starting to sit, and people are already dancing. I wonder when they're going to start serving—I'm totally starving. I head back into the bar area as everyone pours out, and Coco and I spot each other at the same time.

"Wow. You look beautiful. Your dress is incredible," I tell her. It doesn't matter that she's huge and her bubble-gum pink dress looks a size too small—she's glowing. Her thick, wavy brown hair is tied loosely back with a pink bow that matches her dress, the napkins, the balloons, and her lip gloss, and she's got that big beautiful thing going on, just like Char.

"I'm so happy you came," Coco yells above the DJ bellowing the same thing over and over in Spanish. "He's asking whether everyone's ready to party," she translates.

Not quite. I take another sip of my not-so-virgin sangria. Coco's wearing an unusual antique garnet cross necklace, and I take it in my hand for a closer look.

"It's been in my father's family for ages," Coco gushes. "My dad gave it to me this morning."

"It's beautiful," I whisper. I feel tears welling up and look away.

"C'mon." Coco grabs my hand and takes me to the dance floor. "Once I get the waltz out of the way, I'll be able to hang with you guys. The father-daughter dance is an important *quince* tradition." Her dad is on the dance floor holding his arms out to her and everyone's forming a circle. I watch Coco and her father cling to each other as they swirl around to the music for a while, then suck down the last of my drink and return to the others.

Marcie and Bobby are still in the same spot, Bobby staring into his drink and Marcie glaring down the bar at Jen, who is laughing and doing shots with some tall, handsome older guy. Char, though, is nowhere to be seen. I turn around and head to the ladies' room.

Char's white pumps are under the last stall, but they're facing the wrong way—toward the toilet, as if she's puking. Which wouldn't be surprising. The Char I know never drinks. I knock on the door. "Char, are you sick?"

"No," she says. She unlatches the door and tries to pull me in, but it's tight and she has to cram up against the toilet to make room, nearly spilling the open Aquafina bottle in her hand. I see that her eyes are a little red.

"It's a good thing we're not lesbians, East. We're too large for the sex-in-a-public-bathroom thing," Char says once we manage to get the door shut.

"In a few months, we'll be able to squeeze into a locker if we want," I say.

Char sniffles. "Actually, there's a problem about that."

"A problem about being lesbians in a locker?" I laugh.

"No, East. A problem with my surgery. They're postponing it."

"Why? What's going on? And when did this happen?" I grab the water bottle with the tequila in it and take a swig. It tastes awful. I've hardly drunk anything, but I'm seriously queasy. Char gives me a weak smile.

"Take it easy, East. Not a huge deal, just an annoying paperwork issue. When you mentioned my appendectomy in group, it tipped Betsy off to the fact that I'd had an operation and she didn't have any of the hospital records on file."

"Char! I'm so sorry—it didn't occur to me that she might not know about it," I say. "The application asked if you were ever hospitalized—why didn't you say you were?"

Char stares into the toilet and shrugs. "It was stupid, I know. We never bothered including the appendectomy stuff in the application because we knew it would be a pain to get the hospital paperwork and it's completely irrelevant to this surgery anyway. Betsy's only making a big deal about it because I call out and make her stupid sessions fun." Char takes a long swig from her Aquafina bottle. I pull her arm to stop her and she yanks it away from me. Tequila spills all over her dress. She glares at me as she tries to wipe it off.

"Stop drinking and talk to me—you're going to get sick.

I still don't understand why it's a big enough deal to put your surgery on hold. Just have the hospital fax her the stupid paperwork," I say.

Char shakes her head. "My mom faxed the hospital permission to release medical info like last Monday, but when Betsy made me stay after group on Friday, she told me she never received it and said that if the file doesn't show up by tomorrow, they'll have to reschedule my surgery."

"Okay, so what makes you think they won't get the records by tomorrow? And even if it's like one day late, maybe it'll be okay?" I say, trying to control my panic. It's not like Char to get tripped up by something as stupid as paperwork, and I can't understand how faxing or e-mailing medical records from one county to the next can be such a big deal.

"Stop giving me the third degree, East. There's going to be a little delay in my surgery, okay?" Char barks. "As I said, no big deal, just paperwork."

"Char! I'm not doing this without you. Forget it. This was all your idea to begin with and I—"

"Stop it, Shroud. You're so doing it. Besides, it's better this way—I can take care of you when you get out of the hospital." Char seems back to her regular self now, all confident and ordering me around. I start feeling calmer.

"Are you sure?"

"Of course I'm sure. My mom will straighten those paper pushers right out," Char says. "Let's keep this between us, though. I don't want anyone else worrying about it."

"But won't they be able to tell you haven't had the surgery because you won't be losing as much weight?" I say.

"It'll probably only be a few days. And I'll be dieting

and exercising the whole time, so no one will know the difference."

"Okay," I agree. "I won't say anything."

"I know," Char says. "You're my girl. Now let's get the hell out of here. We have eating to do. Eating and dancing. And drinking." Char caps her water bottle and rams it back into her bag. She squishes herself against the toilet so that I can squeeze out around the door, and then she follows.

"There you guys are, thank God," Marcie says, barging into the ladies' room and leaning against the sink. "Jen's letting some smarmy jerk get her drunk—she brushed me away like a gnat when I tried to get her out of there! Uh, do you guys pee together too?"

"Yes," I say. "We're inseparable."

"Or lesbians?" Marcie suggests. Char and I look at each other and laugh.

"Not," we say together. It's the first time things feel normal between us since this Teenage Waistland thing began.

o o o o o o

The restaurant is alive with loud, rhythmic thumping as we go back to find Bobby and Jen. Bobby's sitting by himself and looks happy to see us. Jen is still whooping it up with one of Coco's guests. The guy puts his hand on her ass, and I'm thinking that maybe she's too drunk to realize how old this guy is—twenty-five, at least—and that we should just get her away from him and give her some cofee or something. Jen can't show up at Marcie's house wasted.

"Buffet table's open," Bobby says. Char is bouncing her

head and shimmying to the beat. More than back to normal. Back to Char Gone Wild.

"Char . . . ," I say. I want to ask her if we should do something about Jen, but Char is too busy horsing around with Bobby to respond.

"Not so fast with the buffet." She's grabbing his hand and then Marcie's and dragging them past the DJ, toward the dance floor. "You too, East! I don't have three hands." She finally yanks them onto the floor and shrieks, "Conga!" She places Bobby's hands on her hips and yells at me to grab Bobby's. While I'm shaking my head in violent protest, Marcie takes hold of Bobby and starts kicking out her legs, following Char's lead. Coco and her father grab on next, then some older ladies wearing pink straw sombreros. In about two seconds flat, there's twenty of them in the line, shaking, kicking, and shrieking, "Ba-ba, ba-ba, ba ba," to the beat. Char is the only one with free arms as the big pulsing snake winds around the dance floor, and she's waving them over her head, laughing like a hyena.

"C'mon, East," she screams as she tries to pull me in when the line comes around, but I wriggle out of her grasp. Her bag is banging against her leg and Bobby's holding her tight and cracking up. Coco's got her dad behind her and he's nuzzling her. I didn't even know Char knew how to conga.

I head over to the Teenage Waistland table. It's empty except for a few gifts and sweaters left on the chairs. I sit down, nibble on a tortilla chip, and try not to look at Coco and her father. And I especially can't look at Char and Bobby. His long arms are fully around her waist and her head is against his chest. A rush of anger flows over me, and I try to push it away by thinking about how bad Char must feel.

She's the one who made this whole Teenage Waistland thing happen, and now her surgery is on hold. But I just can't let go. As incomprehensible as the idea is, the only thing my mind can focus on is that if not for her, Bobby's arms might be around *me*.

16

the last supper

Marcie (−5 lbs)

There are few things in life more poignant than a heifer's final gorge on the eve of gastric surgery. Even the last meal of a death-row serial killer can't compare. See, the killer's last encounter with food is beside the point—he's got his impending demise to deal with. (Though chicken-fried steak smothered in mashed potatoes and gravy, with a side of slaw and chocolate pudding, certainly must ease the pain somewhat.) For the heifer, however, the appetite-dampening properties of being dead aren't going to kick in for many years; she faces decades of craving and longing before it'll all be over.

It's the night before my Lap-Band surgery, and Jen's gone. She spent last night puking in my bathroom after being a drunken slob at Coco's and then announced this morning that she was so hungover, all she wanted to do was go back home.

"But my surgery's tomorrow!" I shrieked at her. "You can't abandon me when I need you most. Eat something, or just go back to bed. You'll feel better soon."

"C'mon, Marce," she groaned. "I was here all last weekend—I spoke to your group because you wanted me to, I showed up at Coco's party because you wanted me to, and right now I just don't feel well and I want to go home to my own bed. Not such a big thing to ask."

"I went to Mexico with you," I grumbled.

"And got a great suntan. Big sacrifice," Jen snapped, and then held her hand to her head—her hair is freshly blown out and her makeup's perfect. "Please, Marce. I'd never leave you like this unless I was really sick."

"You don't look so sick," I said under my breath, and if Jen heard it, she chose to ignore it. I let her wrap her arms around me, and then she picked up her bag and headed down to meet Carlo in the driveway.

"I'll call you tonight, Marce—and I'll be there with you via text until the minute you go under," she yelled from the steps.

○ ○ ○ ○ ○ ○

Gran was the second-to-last person I wanted at the table tonight for my last supper before surgery, but when I complained about it this afternoon, Abby exploded. "She's your grandmother, and you're her only grandchild. I'm sorry she says things that hurt your feelings, but she only wants the best for you. Gran's sick, and when she's gone, you'll feel horrible about how you treated her. So I beg you—for me: act like a human being." Okay, maybe Gran *is* looking thinner and frailer than the last time I saw her, but I'm sure her big trap is still working just fine.

The table is heaping with some of my favorite foods—

macaroni and cheese (emphasis on cheese), barbecued chicken wings with four-alarm sauce, and steak fajitas. Well, *heaping* isn't exactly the word. The special dishes Abby made at my request are on small plates—single servings, a tasting, really. What *are* overflowing are the salad bowl and salmon and veggie stir-fry. I can't believe they're torturing me with paltry portions on the night before surgery.

I'm not even done polishing off my first fajita when Liselle starts in. "Ya know, Marcie," she says in her idiot East Coast Valley Girl accent, "June's mother got a Lap-Band last year, and she's gained, like, thirty pounds."

Gran is out of the gate before Abby or Ronny can respond, lest Liselle, God forbid, talk me out of anything. "Liselle, honey, your friend's mother is obviously eating things she shouldn't—"

"And the Lap-Band is a tool for weight loss, not an automatic cure," Abby cuts in, probably terrified that Gran will say something to set me off.

But Gran *never* lets anyone derail her train of thought. "Marcie is dedicated to losing her weight, and I know she'll do beautifully."

Dedicated? Hounded and harassed is more like it. The macaroni and cheese congeal in my mouth. I put my fork down. "Liselle, you're a brain-dead little bimbo. Which makes anyone who likes you, like June, a brain-dead bimbo. And, given how genetics work, it's highly likely that June's mother is also brain-dead. Therefore, I ask that you please keep your whole network of stupid out of my face."

Liselle cocks her head and puts on a little pout. *Poor angry fat girl.* I'm noticing that she's wearing the silvery blue eye stick that came in the Sephora makeup kit Abby got each of us, and it goes much better with her pale blue eyes than my crap brown ones. I'm tempted to wash it off her with my peach iced tea.

"Listen, Marcie," Liselle tries again in her fake sugary voice. "It's just so radical. I could help you with your diet and exercise, you know. Look at me, and I love to eat." I glance at Liselle's plate. A small lonely pile of overcooked vegetables. Yeah, a real gourmand. And that's when she *remembers* to eat.

I want to say—sweetly, of course—*Liselle, I know you don't like facts getting in your way, but nearly ninety percent of people who lose weight gain it all back—and more—within five years. And, surgery is the only clinically proven solution for long-term weight loss for people who get to be my size.* But my idiotic lip is quivering and I'm afraid my voice will break if I try to speak.

Abby smells another disaster and jumps in. "Sweetie, I'm sure Marcie appreciates your concern. But she's tried very hard to diet and she's convinced—we all are—that this surgery is the right answer."

"And she's going to do just beautifully, you'll see," Gran rasps again.

"She's going to have scars, you know," Liselle mutters before going back to moving food around on her plate. She knows how to hit the old lady where it hurts.

"Shucks! Now I won't be able to be like you and wear a thong bikini with my butt cheeks hanging out," I snarl. "So classy."

Gran shakes her head like she's bewildered about how a vile creature like me could descend from someone as delicate and refined as she, while Abby launches into her usual diatribe about my filthy mouth. She's halfway through the part about not raising a guttersnipe, whatever the hell that is, when I push away from the table and walk out.

○ ○ ○ ○ ○ ○

My dad's not picking up his cell and he's not in his office, so I dial his home number on a lark—he's hardly ever there. Tonight, someone is—a woman answers, and I slam down the phone and hit redial to make sure I dialed right. But the number's right. Dad's seeing someone and he didn't tell me. I speed-dial Jen to vent and maybe see what she knows, but her cell rings once and goes to voice mail. Out cold, probably, still sleeping off the booze. Some best friend! WTF?

I hop out of bed and pull out my stash from behind a huge bag of clothes in the back of my closet. It's not even seven p.m. yet—I have a good five hours before all food and drink must stop. Barbecue chips and an Almond Joy sound about right. And my favorite book, *Special Topics in Calamity Physics*. Blue van Meer is a smart and freaky sixteen-year-old who gets to travel around the country having adventures with her professor father after her mother is killed. Not that I'd ever want Abby dead. Just absent. That way I'd *have* to live with my dad. It'd be the two of us.

Book in hand, goodies in lap, propped up by a mountain of fluffy down pillows covered in cream Ralph Lauren linens, and sinking deliciously into my Tempur-Pedic queen-sized bed, I begin to calm down. Abby disapproved when she saw how Ronny's decorator outfitted my new bedroom when we moved in last year. White and cream everywhere, except for the part of the walls above the wainscoting, which are a cool mint green. "Marcie is going to get it filthy in no time," she wailed. Then she shook her finger in my face. "No food in bed—no chocolates, candies, nothing." Ronny just laughed.

My bedroom is the only aspect of my life that improved when we moved to Alpine. And I've been pretty good about keeping the duvet cover clean. There's only a small area of discoloration, from the time Jen came down two Thanksgivings ago—a few weeks before we went to Mexico for her surgery—and we ate pizza on the bed while watching *The Parent Trap* for the zillionth time. Yeah, on my thirty-six-inch flat screen that pulls out of the antiqued white armoire across from my bed. My father'd have a stroke if he knew. We didn't have any TVs in our old house, so I was an outcast as a young child, not knowing the Barney song. But while the other kids were still pooping themselves and laughing with glee at the moronic antics of a purple dinosaur, I was reading on my own by age four. Dad taught me how. He had teachers' hours and Abby was always working late. We didn't dissect the universe on long road trips, like the father and daughter in *Calamity Physics*, but we did go to lots of museums and libraries together. I'm back to the part where Blue van Meer starts hanging around with the Bluebloods, the cool, artsy clique at her new prep school. I glance at my clock radio. Nearly eight and Jen hasn't called me back. Neither has Dad, but at least he'll be there tomorrow. Dad wasn't all that hyped about this surgery—he asked me the same question about fifty times: Were Abby and especially Gran bullying me into it? "Of course," I told him, but I also told him that I wanted this too, especially after the writing-seminar chair episode. I'm not going to be gorgeous or anything, like Jen, when I'm thin, but my body won't get in the way of things like it does now.

Before I got huge, there was this kid at Fuller who sort of had a crush on me—Ralph Meyer. The superstar of geeks. He was tall, refugee-camp thin, and hideous besides, with razor-thin lips that could hardly cover his mossy braces. I instructed my friends to rescue me by faking a trauma if they ever caught him cornering me on campus. But Jen took it too far and made me look like an idiot. One Friday afternoon, Ralph was telling me about an open-mike poetry thing he was doing over the weekend, and Jen runs up to us fake weeping and shouting: "Marcie, Marcie, my father was running with the bulls in Pamplona and got trampled."

Ralph said, "Funny, weren't his legs just crushed in a freak train wreck in Botswana last week?" and walked off. I told Jen she didn't have to overdo it like that, but she huffed that her father *was* just in Pamplona and Botswana—he's some State Department bigwig who's always traveling. It was actually the bulls and the train wreck that I thought pushed the envelope, but there's no winning an argument with Jen, and that's one of the reasons I love her.

Still, I thought the whole thing was sort of funny until Ralph submitted a poem for the *Fuller Review*. It was called "Beauty Ain't My Truth," and it was about how two people who shared the same soul never found each other because they were wrapped in a skin that the other couldn't see through. It was such a beautiful sad poem that I texted Ralph to tell him I loved it and that we were going to run it, but he didn't reply. And when I'd see him around Fuller or in town, he'd look the other way. I couldn't get him out of my mind. Not that he was my soul mate or anything. But he was the most talented person at Fuller and even I couldn't get past his looks.

That's what the surgery is also about for me. I don't need to be beautiful, but I don't want to be a sideshow. When the other half of my soul comes searching for me, I don't want the blubber to stop him from recognizing me.

o o o o o o

WTF! My cell is almost vibrating itself off my night table. "What?" I groan into the phone. I can't make out the caller ID because I'm not wearing my glasses, but who else could it be so late at night?

"Marce—it's me, baby girl. How're ya? Just wanted to say I love you, girl, before your big day!" Jen is slurring through her sobs—and the sound of traffic in the background. New York City traffic!

"Jen, it's one in the morning. Where are you?" I bark.

"Marce, I need—" she blubbers.

"*You* need? My surgery's tomorrow!" I howl, cutting her off.

"Marce, please. Chuck kicked me out! I have no place—" Jen sobs louder.

"*Chuck?* That loser from Coco's party? You *are* still in New York!" I scream into the phone. Jen's betrayal is so mammoth, I can't even wait for a reply. I turn off my phone, throw it against the wall, and cry myself to sleep.

17

GOING UNDER

thursday, JULY 16, 2009

East (-7 lbs); Char (-4 lbs)

I'm in the downstairs bathroom so I don't wake anyone. It's three-thirty a.m. and we don't need to leave for the hospital for another two hours. I'm biting the inside of my mouth so I won't scream, *Forget it, I'm not going through with this.* I almost went there last night, but Char was so tense and overly sensitive about, like, everything, that I didn't want her coming down on me for being a big fat catastrophizing Shroud loser. Especially since she must be so upset about not having her surgery with me.

It started when we were in the family room, digging into the Mario's take-out bag in front of the TV—my "final pig-out," even though I just got a chicken Caesar salad without dressing. I got up to bring Mom's lasagna to her bedroom, and when I returned, Char had taken Julius's high school graduation picture off the wall.

"What are you doing with that?" I said. "My mom will kill you if you get tomato sauce on it."

"Don't get your panties in a twist, East," Char said. "It's

protected by glass. I was just thinking of how time passes, you know, and now Julius is getting married. . . ." Char banged the wall as she rehung the picture and left it cockeyed. We ate dinner in silence on the couch, not even bothering to turn on the TV. After we cleaned up, we went up to my room, and Char crawled straight into bed.

I asked her as casually as I could if everyone still thought she was having her surgery right after mine, but she flipped onto her side, putting her back to my face. "I don't see why your mom can't just pick the hospital records up herself. Then Betsy and Dr. Weinstein can lay off about this stupid appendectomy of yours and put you back on the surgery schedule. It's not right that I'm getting the surgery tomorrow and you're not," I said.

"I'm really tired, East, and you know how upsetting this situation is to me. I only told you because we're supposedly best friends—please don't throw it back in my face by bringing it up over and over again." *Supposedly?*

"I'm sorry," I said. "I just know how much you want this surgery, and this is like the dumbest reason on the planet to hold it up."

"Thanks. Can we just go to sleep now? You've got a big day ahead of you." Char pulled the blanket up around her shoulders and I shut off the light. I heard her tossing and turning for a few minutes; then she sat up and announced that the bed was uncomfortable, and could she sleep in Julius's room instead?

I switched the light back on. "Seriously? You used to always sleep in this bed, Char. Besides, the linens in Julius's room are probably all dusty. Why are you angry with me?"

Char rubbed her eyes. "I'm not angry at you. Honestly, though, I'd rather sleep by myself tonight."

I shrugged, and Char grabbed her pillow and blanket and left.

○ ○ ○ ○ ○ ○

All the forms and consents have been signed and I'm on deck. The nurses are really nice, and they've let Char sit with me while I wait for the anesthesiologist. More accurately, Char plowed her way through the doors that said Medical Staff Only and they were kind enough not to kick her out. I guess she felt uncomfortable sitting in the waiting room with my mom—a black velour mountain bent over a bag of wool, working her needles in a frenzy, as Char put it. I laugh nervously.

"She's fine—don't worry. But listen," Char says. She's all jumpy and speed-talking again like her normal self. "Big props for me on the blog idea." Char put up a blog for everyone to stay in touch while we're home recuperating, especially since it'll be over a week before Teenage Waistland meets again. "Oh, and Marcie says good luck to us." *Us*, the *supposed* best friends.

"When did you speak to Marcie?" I cut in. It's seven-thirty a.m. Certainly not this morning.

"Last night, when I couldn't sleep. It wasn't too late, so I called her. So listen to this," Char plows on. But I feel my blood start to boil. Char wanted to be alone last night and not with me so that she could chat it up with Marcie? I struggle not to react as Char continues.

"You know how Jen bailed on Marcie the day before her surgery because she was so hungover from Coco's party?"

"Yeah, you told me that already," I mutter, fighting tears. It's unbelievable how involved Char has become in every morsel of these people's lives.

"It turns out that Jen *didn't* go home early. She used Marcie's surgery as an excuse to hook up with a guy—the one she met at Coco's party. Ronny's chauffeur dropped her at Penn Station for her train back to Boston, but as soon as he pulled away, she got into a cab—"

"She just turned sixteen, right?" I cut in, completely nauseated. "That guy looked at least twenty-five. I can't believe Jen would do something that stupid—sober, anyway."

Char frowns and shakes her head. "Age means nothing when you're in love."

"Love? Right." I laugh. "Obviously it was a booty call. Why else would a guy with an apartment want anything to do with a sixteen-year-old? Isn't that statutory rape or something?"

Char stands up briskly like she's ready to take off. "That's *so* not the point, East! Jen called Marcie from the street, *drunk*! At one a.m., the night before her surgery! Marcie hung up on her, so Jen spent the night at Marcie's grandmother's apartment."

"Can we please forget Marcie and Jen for now, Char? I'm about to have *surgery*! And I'm scared." Char sits down again and her expression softens.

"Chill, girl. You'll be completely knocked out. You won't even know what's happening."

"They put you out when you had your appendectomy, right? Did it hurt? Do you remember any of it?" I ask.

"*Yes, no,* and *no*! And I'm sure it'll be the same with this." She's snappy all over again.

"I'm still freaking about that video," I offer, trying to find a neutral subject.

Yesterday, Char and I watched a Lap-Band surgery video she found online. It started with three surgeons in scrubs and masks standing around a fat inert body. They're holding long metal rods that have barbecuelike tongs with teeth at the end, and they're smiling for the camera. The next scene is inside the body—they pumped air and shoved a flashlight into the abdominal cavity so you could see the goings-on. One of the tongs pointed at all the organs for the camera. *See, here's the liver. Fatty! And there, if we just lift up the stomach for a moment, is the spleen.* We watched in horror as two pairs of tongs guided the Lap-Band around the stomach while a third was moving globs of fat out of the way. One wrong move and a vital internal organ could get punctured. Just as they finished sewing the band around the stomach, Crystal popped in to ask us if we wanted some sandwiches. Char shut the browser.

"We didn't get a chance to see them close the incisions," I say. Four of them, each supposedly about an inch long, across the upper stomach. And then a bigger one closer to the belly button for installation of the port.

"So you could be catastrophizing it and wondering if you'll bleed to death?" Char says, finally smiling again. "Or is pooping on the table while you're unconscious your Shroudtastrophe of the moment?"

"Don't be silly. I got over those scenarios minutes ago. Now I'm working on never waking up from the anesthesia."

● ● ● ● ● ●

All I can remember is the anesthesiologist injecting something into my IV and saying I'd begin to feel sleepy.

"You're done," Char says, hovering over me in the re-covery room, where she's probably not supposed to be either. "It went perfectly. No pooping whatsoever. Or none that Dr. Weinstein mentioned to your mom when he came out of surgery."

I'm still drowsy, and in excruciating pain.

"Where is she?" I croak.

"She went home."

"She left me?" My stomach is killing me and I start to cry.

"It's okay, honey," Char says, and takes my hand. "When Dr. Weinstein said you'd be in the recovery area for another hour or two before being taken to your room, she was so re-lieved and exhausted from the stress that I suggested she go home. If there's an open bed in your room, Dr. Weinstein said I could stay with you overnight."

A nurse comes in and asks me to rank my pain on a scale of one to ten. I tell her "a million," and she promptly pumps a cylinder of morphine into the port on the hand Char isn't squeezing. And as a warm, happy feeling floods everything else away, I squeeze Char's hand even tighter. Char. My one and only "we."

18

HOTSTUFF

Bobby (-10 lbs)

This is the third time Roughshod, a low-ranked seventh grader from some farm in the Midwest probably, has sacked me on a crucial play, and I'm pissed. Madden Xbox links you up with other players over the Internet, but all you know about them is their screen names and whatever crap they make up about themselves—it's not like they're next to you on the couch. So I'm thinking that the real Roughshod is out, like, milking cows and his older brother is using the screen name. Every other time I've gone up against this jerk-off, I've sliced through his defense, stifled his offense, and dominated the scoring. Today, he's eating my lunch.

At least someone is.

I'm pounding vanilla, chocolate fudge, cookies and cream, and banana protein shakes. Dad and I stashed a case of each behind his spare tires in the garage. Third day after surgery means I'm still on liquids. So when I'm not drinking, I'm peeing. And burping.

The postoperative instructions say that I can have stuff

like broth, juice, milk, gelatin, or ice pops, but yesterday Dad said, "That's the girl version, buddy. We need to get you some protein shakes. They'll keep your muscles from wasting. And, help your incisions heal faster." When Mom left the house to pick up some of the foods on the post-op diet sheets, Dad marched me over to the list. "See, buddy, *yogurt*. Yogurt's for girls. Protein shakes are for men." And then he went to the Bodybuilding Warehouse and picked up four cases of them before Mom returned.

We've all been sort of irritable since I got home. The air-conditioning died while I was in surgery, so we've got fans running, but they're just pushing hot air around, and with this heat wave going on, fat chance the repairman will show up anytime soon. Dad's had Sam, his general manager, run the store over the past few days so he and Mom can be home with me. I appreciate it, but I'm fine, really, and don't need them both all over me. Especially Dad. He tells Mom we're in the basement so much because we're working on a lifting program for as soon as I'm up to it, but that's where he's having me suck down the contraband. I keep thinking the more protein shakes I drink, the faster I'll heal. But my abs still feel like they're on the bottom of a ten-man pileup, and all I really want is to chill out *alone*.

I escape to the pool with my laptop to catch some rays. The sun is strong, but it feels good. Nice tan wouldn't hurt this pale whale. I've lost seven pounds already, and I'm not even hungry. Not very, anyway. The water looks seriously refreshing, and I'm dying to jump in. I could probably wrap myself in a Hefty bag to keep the bandages dry, but just the idea that I've got five stitched-up holes in my blubbery stomach that go clear through to my insides is enough to keep me out. Not that staying dry will make me any less screwed. Preseason practice starts in exactly one month, almost two weeks before I'm allowed to do any strenuous physical activity.

MT is ranting on my wall about this girl Alicia who's ready to give it up to him, like, any minute. They're going camping on some active volcano on the Big Island tomorrow, and he's got these plans to sneak out and meet her up on the mountain after lights-out. *Gonna be erupting soon, sucker. Lava will be spilling into an ocean in no time at all hahahaha.* Count on MT to get his V-card snatched in style—on a freaking volcano. I'm on MT's wall with no creative ideas for a V-card counterattack when an IM from Char flashes on my screen.

Check it out, she writes, and gives me a link to follow. I catch myself almost hoping she's posted post-op photos of herself lying around in some low-cut satiny nightgown. She and East got done yesterday, and they're obviously home now. No photos, though. It's the Teenage Waistland blog Char's been saying she was going to put up.

I'd rather see your stitches, I IM back. For some reason, in the hot sun, I feel like seeing Char's skin. And even crazier, I don't feel gay telling her so. Online, anyway. But Char doesn't reply, so I check out her blog. There's already a little action on it.

Teenage Waistland—Friday, July 17, 2009—2:30 p.m.
Gang! Charmer here. Lay off those Percocets (you too, Tila Tequila) and gather round. I've created this space for us to hang out together while everyone's recovering.

This is a public website and anyone can comment, so here's some screen names for us to hide behind.

Fuzzball replies Friday, July 17, 2009—2:40 p.m.

Excuse me, *Charmer*, but what's with Fuzzball? Are you saying I've got fuzzy hair?

Charmer replies Friday, July 17, 2009—2:41 p.m.

Fuzzball's a compliment! It says you're warm and soft and cuddly!

Fuzzball replies Friday, July 17, 2009—2:42 p.m.

Screw that. Change my name to Marcelous. As in MARVELOUS.

Charmer replies Friday, July 17, 2009—2:44 p.m.

You got it, marvelous Marcelous.

Hotstuff replies Friday, July 17, 2009—2:47 p.m.

Hey—what up? No kidding with the *Hotstuff*. AC has been busted for 3 days now and it's so hot here, paint's blistering off the walls.

Charmer replies Friday, July 17, 2009—2:48 p.m.

Interpret your screen name any way you like, Hotstuff. ;-)

Hotstuff, huh? I lean back in my lawn chair and stretch my arms over my head, until the sharp pain in my abs comes back. *Very close to an intensely hot V-olcano myself, Loser. Am right on your tail.* Yeah. With a girl who could win a Guinness Record for the biggest tail.

Marcelous replies Friday, July 17, 2009—2:51 p.m.

Is anyone else burping like every minute?

I'm like the freaking Goodyear Blimp here.
Even Scrotum-breath (my screen name for
Liselle Rescott, Alpine, NJ) feels sorry
for me.

Charmer replies Friday, July 17, 2009—2:53 p.m.

L is going to KILL YOU! Since I'm the moderator, I can edit that out of your post.
About the burping, no worries. It won't
last. They pumped air into your abdominal
cavity to make room for the camera and the
surgical instruments. Shroud and I watched
an actual surgery on YouTube before ours.
Check it out.

Hotstuff replies Friday, July 17, 2009—3:10 p.m.

Man, that's nasty. 'Specially all those
wads of fat they have to plow through to
get to the stomach. Nice to know that this
flab is more than skin deep. Gonna run and
puke now. Later.

I'm about to get up and take another piss and my nine-
teenth protein shake of the day when Char IMs me back
about my stitches comment.

I'll show you mine if you show me yours.

And suddenly the idea of seeing her skin reminds me of
hiding mine at Zoo's pool party, and I slam my laptop shut.

19

HAPPY GRADUATION, LISELLE

Marcie (−7.5 lbs)

In seven hours Liselle's friends will begin to arrive, and I've yet to figure out how to wrap a dildo for maximum impact. The rolls of wrapping paper in the back pantry have birthday designs or flowery granny prints, and I'm going for sophisticated and elegant. Something to throw Liselle completely off the scent.

I'm hoping that Char and I can walk to the card store in Closter to buy paper, but it's a couple of miles away and Char's surgery was only three days ago, so she might not feel up to it. I'm grateful she's able to come at all—I wouldn't have the balls to pull this off alone, and I'm finished with Jen.

I hear voices downstairs and shove the dildo box back under my bed. I'm not moving very fast, but I'm halfway down the front staircase when Abby bellows that my guest has arrived.

"This place is unbelievable," Char whispers as I lumber down the last few steps. "You didn't tell me you lived in a palace."

I snort. It makes me uncomfortable when people go gaga over Ronny's money. Char throws her arms around me. "How are you feeling?"

"Ouch," I laugh, pulling away. Our stomachs bopped against each other when we hugged, but Char's taller and hers rides higher than mine, so I'm the only one in pain.

o o o o o o

We're heading down Closter Dock Road to the card store, and Char's raving about the McMansions—these fabulously huge homes crammed on top of each other. If I had money, I'd want lots and lots of land so I'd never see my neighbors. But Char likes crowds—she's what Abby calls a people person. I used to be more like that. Now, I guess, I'm what they call a *GTF out of my face* person.

"You sure you're okay to walk?" I ask. "My stomach's still bothering me when I jiggle it, and my surgery was almost a week ago."

Char nods but slows down anyway. "So—you and Jen patch things up yet?" she says.

"What are you on, Char?" I snort.

Char sighs. "That's crazy, Marcie. You're best friends. You haven't even tried to call her?"

I stop short. "I should call *her*? Not only does she leave me when I need her most—the night before my surgery—but then she literally goes and sleeps with the enemy!"

Char narrows her eyes at me and shakes her head. "C'mon, Marcie. Was your grandmother supposed to leave Jen on the street all night? You're lucky Jen even knew where your grandmother lives—if she spent the night at the train station, God knows what could have happened to her."

"Jen blew me off for a *guy*! I can't believe you're taking her side on this, Char!" I'm ready to blow off the damn dildo plan and turn back around, but Char gently puts her hand on my arm.

"Of course I'm not taking her side—Jen totally screwed up. But I—"

"But nothing! She still had the chance to show up at the hospital for my surgery. Again, no less than I did for her, but instead my grandmother put her in a taxi to the train station and came to the hospital by herself."

"Yeah, but . . ." My *there's no freaking excuse for her behavior* expression nukes the topic and shuts Char up. She jerks her head in the direction we were headed and we just resume walking. "So, what about your dad? Have you spoken to him?" she finally says.

"Nah, not since he left the hospital," I say, removing all anger from my tone. I pick up my pace a little to keep up.

"But why are you pissed at him about his new woman? Shouldn't he move on—I mean, your mom has been remarried for what, over a year now?"

"It's not about moving on. He's got to make a new life for himself, I know. But he's raised me on words and ideas like they're the most important things in the world, and now he's fallen for a certified piece of meat with a third-grade vocabulary. Plus, how the hell could he think that my surgery day was a good time to introduce us?"

"He probably figured you'd be in la-la land from the painkillers, maybe a little less *zealous* with all them words?" Char quips.

"Don't make me laugh! It hurts!" I hit her arm. "Zealous! Good word, though."

"C'mon, she can't be *that* bad," Char says. I elbow her arm so she sees I'm serious.

"You know what my dad does now? He says something and then like two seconds later, he repeats the same thought—*using smaller words*. The two-step dumb-down. When we were alone together—Jill was downstairs with Abby—he even did it with me. I had to remind him he wasn't talking to a moron."

Char covers her mouth with her hand. "Ruff! Ruff! How'd he take that?"

"Not too well. He shook his head like I disappointed him and said, 'Jill is kind and a joy to be around. I taught you to think, Marcie, not judge.'" My eyes tear up. "Sorry, I'm being so emotional, Char. It must be the food deprivation." She rubs my shoulder for a second.

"You know, Marce, there's something to be said for kindness. People can be cruel—especially to fat people."

I nod. "I know. People treat me a lot differently since I packed on all this weight. They talk *about* me more than they talk *to* me."

Char hesitates. "Not to sound like Betsy Bitch Glass, but how long have you been ob—overweight?"

"Wow—*bitch* is harsh for you, Char." I laugh. "What gives? I mean, I know she's kept you after group, like, every time, but, as someone who does her share of running off at the mouth, isn't being forced to stay after class par for the course?" Char smiles and does Bitsy's sweeping *the floor is yours* motion. "I guess I've been seriously packing it on for maybe two and a half years? Pretty much since Abby landed this high-power job and started brawling with my father. But that was nothing compared to the weight I've put on since we moved here," I say. "Put it this way: compared to PSJ—presurgery Jen—I was a *babe*. With a lot of friends. Hard to believe, I know."

Char flicks me away like I'm a gnat. "You'll be a babe again before you know it. And now you have some great new friends!" As a rule, I hate positive people—happiness equals stupidity in my book. But this dumb little comment makes me feel better.

"How 'bout you?" I say. "What's your true fat-girl story? It's not really that Mario's thing—which was so freaking funny!"

Char stops in front of a Georgian-style brick monstrosity. Her eyes are red and her expression so un-Charlike that I immediately regret being so glib.

"I guess I starting gaining all my weight about three years ago too, but it's really horrible. And so complicated. I wish I could tell you everything—really, Marcie, I do. But there are other people involved and I can't." Char turns away to hide her face and her shoulders are shaking. I don't know what to do, like whether I should put my arm around her or just give her space. When Jen would try to comfort me about the crap going down at my house, it made it harder to hold in. So I just say, "Char?" in a soft voice.

Char puts her hand up. "Don't," she sniffles. "I'm fine. I—I just can't go there right now, okay?"

"Sure," I say. I'm dying to press for info, but I manage to just stand quietly and watch her. She's wearing a turquoise top over white capris, and it strikes me that Char is three times Liselle's size, but maybe even prettier. Char's "Don't

Stop Believin'" ringtone suddenly starts blaring. She pulls her phone out of her pocket, sighs loudly, and sends the caller to voice mail. Then she turns back toward me and wipes her eyes with her sleeve. "Damn, Marcie. If I wanted to be depressed, I'd go hang with the Shroudmeister."

She hooks her arm in mine and we start walking again. My stomach is bouncing and hurting like hell, but we're women on a mission and can't be undone by our little melodramas.

○ ○ ○ ○ ○ ○

I'm eyeing the huge platters of food wrapped in colorful cellophane spread out all over the kitchen countertops when Liselle prances in fresh from the salon. Her blond hair has been highlighted almost all the way to platinum. And her makeup looks professionally done—the smudged charcoal eyeliner is perfect on her. She looks glamorous and way older.

"Marcie, you're so right about your sister. She's gorgeous," Char says loudly. She waves at Liselle. "Hi, I'm Char. Congrats!" Benedict freaking Charnold! Most people hold off at least two seconds before dropping to their knees to kiss Liselle's feet, but Char just set a record.

"Aren't you sweet! Pleasure to meet you," Liselle coos, all sugary. Then she turns to me and says, in the same voice, "Where's Mom?"

"*Abby* is—I don't know. You freaking find her," I mutter, hardly audible. I don't want to be a jerk in front of Char, but Liselle's "Mom" act makes me ballistic. I used to think she just called Abby "Mom" to freak me out, but she's "Moming" *my* mother to death even when she's on speaker with Abby and doesn't know I'm right there listening.

Liselle snatches a carrot stick from under the cellophane, waves it at Char, and walks out. "Mom?" I hear her call as she moves through the house. Mounds of sheer decadence surround us—marzipan cookies, éclairs, cream-filled pastries, etc.—and Liselle goes straight for the *veggies*. The veggies and my mother. WTF.

"Marcie," Char chides, "you're not getting with the program. You don't want Liselle to think you're out to get her tonight, right? Play nice and let the dildo do the talking." It's so hard to be pissed at Char. She's so funny it literally hurts.

"Abby got us some fresh chicken broth from the deli. I guess that's about all we can have," I say. Char also can't take her eyes off the platters.

"Just heartbreaking," she sighs.

o o o o o o

Char and I are totally not hanging out at Liselle's party, but we are sort of stalking it. This thing is a monster, and impossible to avoid. It's spread out on the patio, the covered porch overlooking the patio, and the living room with its wall of French doors opening out onto the porch. There are a few jokers in the pool—males, of course. But this ain't no pool party—everyone is so coiffed to the hilt, I'm half expecting Paris Hilton to show up.

When Abby isn't schmoozing with the guests or hammering the caterers, she's hanging out behind Liselle like her fucking handmaiden, smoothing her top or holding her drink whenever Liselle goes to hug another fan. It strikes me that

Abby could pass for Liselle's real mother. They're both blond, fine-featured, and a hundred percent fat free. And very pretty, even if in a high-maintenance way. Ronny is walking around patting everyone on the back and laughing at every stupid thing. He's dark like me and has a paunch (smaller than mine). I wonder how many people think I belong to him.

Liselle's gifts are in a huge haphazard pile on the dining-room table, but Char and I managed to situate the dildo—spectacularly wrapped in heavy high-gloss cream-colored paper, with a pale green taffeta bow—right on top, like the happy couple on a wedding cake. But the hours are ticking by, Char and I are so tired we're ready to pass out, and the un-wrapping ceremony has yet to take place. Finally, when Liselle brushes past me in the hallway on the way to the bathroom, I call her name. She turns around and smiles.

"Marcie, baby. Char, baby. How goes it?" She's drunk, real shocker. Kids obviously snuck in the booze, but I have the fleeting impulse to call the police and report Abby for serving alcohol to minors—an even faster ticket back to Boston than the dildo. The thing is, with Jill in the picture and Jen out of it, Boston looks different.

"Great part—" Char tries to gush, but I cut her off at the pass.

"We were just wondering when you're going to open your gifts," I say as sweetly as my DNA will allow.

Liselle smiles dreamily. "Sometime tomorrow, probably." But she must catch my *kill me now, God* expression, because she straightens up and adds, "What kind of party do you think this is?"

20

least

East (-9 lbs); Char (-7 lbs)

"Did you order the Cream of Wheat?" I call over the TV. It's eleven a.m. and I'm lying in bed. I check my phone again—Char still hasn't texted. She, my *supposed* best friend, probably stayed up late with Marcie.

"Mom? Did you place the order?" I yell again. She said she was going to do it online last night, but I probably should have done it myself. Though I don't see why I should be the one to order all the groceries when I'm mostly on water, broth, juice, and skim milk for another three days. Blended yogurt and hot cereal are the only foodlike things I can eat.

"East, we have the instant Quaker Oats. Do you want me to make some for you?" Not at all. Why should you be taking care of me? I'm just your only daughter who just had surgery. What happened to being with me "every step of the way"? Even the steps to the recovery room were too difficult for you—and you were already in the hospital! And the only steps I've seen you take since I got home from the hospital are the ones leading back into your bedroom. You were so engrossed in your precious TV that when Char helped me to the front door, we had to ring *four times* before you answered, even though I called from the car to say I'd be home in five minutes.

"No, Mom. I'll get it. You want some?" I say, my voice flatter than even her spiritless tone. I slip into my bathrobe and kill my stomach bending for my slippers. "*Owww!*" I scream.

The TV clicks off. "You okay? What happened?" Mom comes in, the stupid remote with CH and VOL worn off the buttons still in her hand.

"Stomach's a little sore, that's all."

"C'mon downstairs with me. I'll make the cereal," she says.

"Not too much. I'll probably only be able to eat a couple of mouthfuls."

"That's all?" Mom says. Yes. Most mothers would know. But that was part of the post-op instructions and . . . What is the point?

"Yes, a few mouthfuls eaten very slowly," I tell her.

"Why don't you come down and order what you want while I make the oatmeal?" she calls over the clatter of cabinets opening and closing.

I want Cream of Wheat. If Char wasn't at Marcie's, I could have asked her to bring some over, and yogurt or something. Of course, she also could have asked if I needed anything. But no. When she called yesterday morning, it was to say she was off to Marcie's for Liselle's party.

"Whatever," I said.

"C'mon, East. Marcie needs support."

"What about me?"

"I'll be home tomorrow. I'll come over and support you all you want."

"No, I mean about going to Marcie's."

"Shroudness, you're not back to that again? Besides, you said you feel like crap."

I said nothing.

"Look, you won't be missing a thing. I'll text you the scoop on Liselle's little surprise as it goes down. It'll be just like you're there," Char said.

I've had enough with this stupid dildo already, but I didn't want to fight. So I don't tell Char how she could always come back from Marcie's tonight and sleep over *here*. In my room this time. Or that she should have tried to include me in her plans whether I wanted to go or not. And I definitely don't touch the fact that I've been wondering, with all the flirting she's doing, if she's purposely not noticing my crush on Bobby. Char knows me better than that—I know she's always catching me staring at him. . . . At them.

"Whatever. I'll hold my breath for the transcript."

"Love ya, Shroud."

"Yeah, yeah. Okay," I said again, and we hung up.

○ ○ ○ ○ ○ ○

It's now almost seven p.m., and I send Char another text—the eighth one, counting the four yesterday afternoon and three last night. Starting with *Tell Marcie hi from me* and *How's the party?* and ending now with *Char, where ARE you?* Nothing back. Complete radio silence. *Just like I was there.* I decide to call Char's house—maybe there's a problem with her cell. Crystal answers.

"Hi, Crystal, it's me. Is Char home yet? I can't reach her."

"East! How are you feeling, honey? Still a trouper?"

"I'm good—a little sore, that's all," I say.

"Haven't spoken with Char since I dropped her at Marcie's. I'm sure she'll reach me when she's ready to come home." She chuckles. I don't. "Maybe there's no cell service at Marcie's—her house is practically its own state," Crystal says brightly.

"So I hear." It's as if Crystal's trying to make me feel better for being abandoned by her daughter. A thought strikes me: "So, how soon do you think Char will be able to get her surgery? I mean, the hospital records finally got there, right?" I say, hoping to sound totally casual. Crystal hesitates—I hear her other line beeping.

"I'm not sure," Crystal finally says, "but hon, I've got to take this call. Char'll talk to you about it."

Actually, Char *won't*. Every time I bring it up, she either rips into me or freezes me out.

It occurs to me that there may be signs of Char on that Teenage Waistland blog, so I log in.

And lo and behold. She and Marcie have been whooping it up all day!

Teenage Waistland—Monday, July 20, 2009—
1:20 p.m.
News flash, gang. Operation Dildo a bust.
But more exciting anyway is Marcelous:
she's lost nine pounds, probably more not
counting her humongous nightgown. A big
round of applause, pls!
Marcelous replies Monday, July 20, 2009—1:22 p.m.

Charmer is no slacker either. She's lost
seven!

Hotstuff replies Monday, July 20, 2009—1:25 p.m.

With or without the nightgown, Charmer?

Charmer replies Monday, July 20, 2009—1:26 p.m.

Mine's more of a negligee, Hotstuff. All
satin and lace.

Marcelous replies Monday, July 20, 2009—1:30 p.m.

Bull. Charmer's got on a big ratty flannel
thing. And it's got wasabi sauce all over
it. She's the worst influence—Charmer had
us sneak downstairs last night to pit our
Lap-Bands against the leftovers from
Scrotum-Breath's graduation party. This
band thing's a farce in the beginning, just
like Jen said—the band didn't stand a
chance.

Charmer replies Monday, July 20, 2009—1:31 p.m.

It was so not like that!

Hotstuff replies Monday, July 20, 2009—1:31 p.m.

If you want to see something grosser than
wasabi stains, you should see my pussed-up
stomach. Probably popped a couple of
stitches trying to lift.

Charmer replies Monday, July 20, 2009—1:31 p.m.

You're a bigger idiot than Marcelous. We're
not supposed to be lifting *anything* yet,
let alone weights!

I've probably read the first few entries a dozen times
now, and I can't decide what's most upsetting: Marcie and

Char horsing around in their nightgowns all day—Char's obviously in no hurry to come home—or the lingerie flirty *Hotstuff* chat with Bobby? And the *"we're* not supposed to be lifting anything." I scroll back through the previous posts and get a sicker feeling in the pit of my stomach. A pain that has nothing to do with my operation: Char is clearly leading everyone to believe she's already gotten banded. Sure, she's being clever by not saying anything outright. But there's absolutely no doubt about it. Char is lying·to Teenage Waistland.

It's after eight now, and I'm so angry I could bust my stitches. Char's cell still rings, but she's not picking up. I check my out-box status again: every text I wrote definitely got sent! I go back to the blog and scroll through the entries. I just can't believe it.

Teenage Waistland—Monday, July 20, 2009—6:40 p.m.
Anybody there? Marcelous is showering.
Hotstuff replies Monday, July 20, 2009—6:45 p.m.
I'm on, Charmer. Messed up my stomach more today. I'm screwed for football. Our first preseason game is in exactly five weeks and practice starts sometime the week before that—if I don't show, I'm benched for the season. But if I do, the first head butt in my gut is going to lay me up for a year.
Charmer replies Monday, July 20, 2009—6:50 p.m.
Ouch! Don't you studs wear like serious padding?
Hotstuff replies Monday, July 20 2009—6:51 p.m.

Yeah. On our shoulders and legs. No stomach
gear. Basically, I'm screwed. My dad's
going to kill me.

Hotstuff replies Monday, July 20, 2009—6:58 p.m.
Still there?

Charmer replies Monday, July 20, 2009—7:00 p.m.
But of course! What are you doing tomorrow?

Hotstuff replies Monday, July 20, 2009—7:01 p.m.
Same as today. Nada. Why?

Charmer replies Monday, July 20, 2009—7:02 p.m.
Need to do some research. Think I have a
plan for us. Will call you in 20.

Char has plans for Bobby? I bet he wouldn't be so into her
crazy plots and plans if he knew she was lying about her
surgery—he seems like someone who may care about honesty. And to top it all off, she's passing out *advice: We* should
do this, *we* should do that.

If Ms. Know-It-All won't speak to me on the phone,
maybe she'll answer on the blog. I make up a username she
won't recognize and log in.

Meltdown replies Monday, July 20, 2009—8:34 p.m.
Great blog! Was researching Lap-Band surgery and just came across it. I'm having
the surgery next week in Boston. (Not a
teen anymore, thank god.) Am nervous and
hoped you'd answer questions since you just
did it. What do your incisions feel like
after surgery? Can you actually feel the
band and the tubing and the port under your

skin? And how many days before you're up
and around? Thanks!

Marcelous replies Monday, July 20, 2009—8:40 p.m.

Charmer's the moderator here, but I just
had the surgery too. Can I help?

Meltdown replies Monday, July 20, 2009—8:45 p.m.

Nothing personal, but she seems to be the
most knowledgeable person on the blog, so
I'd like to hear her take on it.

Charmer replies Monday, July 20, 2009—9:00 p.m.

Hi, Meltdown! Congratulations on your impending surgery! The incisions are sore, of
course. But they don't hurt too much. And
the extent to which one can feel the band
under their skin probably depends on how
much blubber's on top. ☺

Meltdown replies Monday, July 20, 2009—9:02 p.m.

How long did your surgery take?

Charmer replies Monday, July 20, 2009—9:05 p.m.

They usually take somewhere between 45 minutes and an hour and a half, depending on
how hard it is to reach the right spot.

Meltdown replies Monday, July 20, 2009—9:08 p.m.

My doc already told me that. But how long
exactly did your surgery take?

And then *Char-latan* disappears. Again.

21

AN UNEXPECTED PLAY

Bobby (–12 lbs)

I spot Char half a block away. Alone. She's smiling and waving to me in this pink flowy shirt thing that looks see-through from here and her curls are flying everywhere. I'm outside Starbucks on the corner of Seventy-ninth and Park waiting to hear this great idea of hers—something to do with my stomach and practice starting in a few weeks.

"Marcie bagged out," she says, standing on her tippy toes to kiss me on the cheek. I'm busy checking out her blue toenails and flip-flops, and like an idiot, I bump her forehead.

"Sorry."

"No worries, Bobby. We're not allowed to have Frappuccinos or anything, but how 'bout a water?"

"Yeah. Sure. I got that," I say, grabbing the door.

"A real gentleman, aren't you?"

"No doubt."

She laughs.

"So, what's your big idea?" I ask.

"You don't like surprises, do you?"

"Not if the surprise is going to another dildo store," I say.

"Are you sure? They sell other things too." Char laughs, and I feel my face burn. And something else. Char hits my arm. "Seriously—my *brainstorm* is a chest protector. I read about it online. People use it to protect their chests after open heart surgery but we can use it as a shield for your stomach. Genius, right?"

"I don't know. You really think it'll work?" I say as we get up to the cashier with our waters.

"Of course, Bobby—that's what makes it a brainstorm." Char laughs and I pay for both bottles. We're heading out of Starbucks single file through the lunch crowd piling in, and I see a familiar yellow football jersey up ahead—Massapequa. Massapequa juts his chin at me and I nod back. Professional courtesy. I'm about to turn to Char and tell her that this is one of the guys we're going to crush at our preseason opener, but I spot the hot little blonde he's with and beeline to the door, holding it for an old guy, who then has to hold it for Char. She catches up to me on the sidewalk and we start walking.

"So, Bobby," Char says, "what comes after the chest protector? A suit of armor?"

"I thought you were sure about the chest protector thing."

"No, silly. I mean, once you start losing weight. I saw that huge football player in Starbucks, and it occurred to me that someone would need to be pretty huge himself to get him out of the way," Char says. I flex my bicep and hold it out to her, and she squeezes it. "Very impressive," she laughs. "But seriously? You just finished telling me how being a line-man is so important to you and your dad, and how you absolutely need this year's best-player plaque for the Konopka trophy hall in your house and all that other legacy stuff. Why in the world did you get this surgery if all this is so life and death for you? Oh, look—we're here!"

It's this surgical pharmacy near the bariatric center we've passed a bunch of times before. The place is crammed with boxes of neck braces, bedpans, and humidifiers. There are these weird handicap potty-seat things too, and the place smells like cleaning fluid in a sweaty locker room. And the few customers shuffling around in here are so old, they're like three-quarters dead.

"Follow me," Char says. I'm having trouble pushing my way behind her. The aisles are narrow and the shelves are spilling over with sick-people stuff.

"Check out these wheelchairs," I call to Char, and send a big one rolling right at her.

"Are you crazy?" She crosses her eyes as she jumps out of the way.

"Not any more than you," I say.

"I'll give you that," she says, ducking around the next aisle while I put the wheelchair back.

"Bobby, ready for your sponge bath?" I hear, and it's Char wearing a shower cap and holding a long stick with a loofah on the end.

"Gimme that," I say, and grab it. She grabs another and now we're fencing in the aisle and cracking up.

"Excuse me! Can I help you?" It's another old guy, but this one is wearing a pharmacy smock.

Char puts the loofah stick back in the bin and says, "Yes, in fact, you can help us. We need a chest wall protector." Dad would never believe how well this girl can take complete control of a situation *with a plaid shower cap on her head*.

"Down to the end of the last aisle in the back," Old Man Pharmacist says, all cranky.

Char grabs my hand. "Let's go," she says, winging the cap like a Frisbee back into the bin the minute he turns around.

Char finds the chest protectors first. "You see?" she says, waving a box at me. "It's a hard shell with a thin cushion underneath. All we have to do to make it a stomach protector is turn it sideways and reengineer the straps. Take off your shirt real quick so we can see which of these models would work best."

"Not here, are you kidding?"

"C'mon. No one's looking."

"Yeah, but . . . Someone might come."

"Here." She pulls me to the corner by this door that says Employees Only and peeks in. "Your dressing room, sir," she says. "Boogeyman's gone."

"But—" I say. Char puts her finger in front of her lips and motions me to enter, and I do. She grabs a roll of paper towels from a shelf and jams it so the door stays open and we have a little light. We're like in this really tight space between the door and a shelving unit, and every time we move, we hear something—plastic or cellophane maybe—crunching underfoot. There's no air in here and it's boiling hot.

Char pulls the first chest pad out of the box and says, "*Now* take your shirt off." I'm panicking about her seeing my fat stomach. And moobies. There's not even enough room. We're six inches from each other, and if I lift my arm I'll asphyxiate her with my sweaty pit. I just stand there frozen. "C'mon. It's no big deal. It's only me here," Char says softly. She begins lifting my jersey and I don't stop her. When she gets it up around my neck, I just pull the damn thing over my head and stand there, naked from the waist up, trying not to act like a self-conscious pussy.

"Here—hold the pad over your stomach while I try to work the straps around your waist," Char says, straining to thread the strap around my back and pull it through with her other hand—her face like two centimeters from my right moob and only a few more than that from my sweaty armpit.

"Let's just forget this," I mutter, leaning away from her and reaching for my jersey on the shelf behind her at the same time.

"What?" she says. "Why 'forget this'? I don't really understand what you want, Bobby." She drops the arm holding the chest protector and looks up at me with her big blue eyes. "Do you, Bobby? Do you understand what you want?" She's so close I can feel her breath. And there's no place for me to look away. My whole field of vision is her face, so full of concern. And those eyes.

"I don't know what I want. All I know is what I *don't* want," I hear myself say. My chest is heaving and I feel a strange rush of emotion—like something big or important is happening whether I want it to or not.

"Tell me," she whispers. And that's all I need.

"Char, I don't want to be a fat lineman anymore. And I don't want to run a hardware store. I don't want to have the same life as my dad and my grandfather. I don't want the Konopka legacy, I want to make my own life." I can hardly breathe; I can't believe I'm saying this stuff, let alone telling it to another person. But it's like, just as long as I keep looking into her eyes, nothing bad can happen. The concern on Char's face melts away into a huge smile.

"Of course you want to make your own life, Bobby," she says softly. "It's okay. It's your right. How else could you ever be happy?"

My chest starts heaving even harder as relief floods my body, and I can't understand it. How can something this simple be a revelation? I'm huddled in a cramped airless stockroom that's got to be at least a hundred degrees, and I've never felt so free in my life. Char's arms go back around me as she tries again to work the straps, her body pressing up against the pad on my stomach. Her lips brush against my chest, and something else feels simple and obvious too.

"Char?" I whisper. "Forget the straps."

"Wait, I'm almost there," she says. I feel the latch click behind me, but I put my arms around her to keep her from pulling away, and when she lifts her face to look at me, I lower mine and kiss her. Char steps back, but only to wrap her arms around my neck and pull me in closer. And then we're kissing and hugging and laughing—I don't know how long—when the stockroom door flies open and Old Man Pharmacist starts going berserk.

We're still laughing when we come crashing out of the pharmacy, me with my jersey on backward, holding the bag with the chest protector Char talked the pharmacist into selling me before he kicked us out, and Char with her hair all wild and messed up. I grab Char's hand with my free one and pull her into a small alley, and we kiss again, this time a long slow one.

"Drop the bag," Char giggles when we come up for air. "The corner of the box is digging into my neck. Why'd you even buy it?" I drop the bag on the ground against the cement building wall and cross my eyes at her.

"Duh, football practice, Char. Are you the same person I spent an hour with on the phone last night talking about it?"

Char sticks her tongue out at me. "Of course, Dr. Jekyll. But where's that bummed-out Hyde fellow from the closet who doesn't want to be a lineman anymore?" She laughs and whacks me on the arm, but that old sinking feeling in my gut comes back—she sees it in my face and gets quiet.

"Yeah, you're right," I say. "It's complicated, though. What am I supposed to do? Crush my dad's dreams? Tell him that it's not just the weight I want to drop but everything that comes with it—playing lineman at a Division One university, taking over Grandpa's stupid lumber store one day, and then passing all of it on to my own fat kids? It's not like I have some really great alternative life planned out that I could tell him about. It'll be like saying that any loser life is better than—"

"You mean, you've never expressed *any* of this to him before?" Char says.

I shake my head slowly and stare at the pavement. "You're the first person I've said any of this to, but I think my mom sort of knows it. I mean, she knows I'm not the happiest guy in the world. But whenever she makes a suggestion about something new I might try, my dad cuts her off and accuses her of trying to 'pussify' me. Like, when I wanted to take a computer programming course instead of some intramural sport for one of my electives." Char puts her hand on my arm, and words start flying out even faster. "My dad's the greatest—I mean, he's always done everything with me. Much more than most fathers. But he's never asked me what I like or what I want—he just takes it for granted that I'm *him*."

"He sounds like a great dad, Bobby. But if you've never told him any of this, how is he supposed to know?"

"Char, imagine spending your life programming a character in a video game—you know, coding in the actions he can perform and the ways he can respond to events. But then *your* character—the one you created—decides he doesn't like his environment or any of the things he's supposed to do in it. Don't you see how that would be? Don't you see why I can't tell him?" Now Char's got that smile on her face again and she's shaking her head. "Okay, wise one. What?" I say.

"Why tell your father anything right now? You don't have life-altering choices to make this minute. Spend some time trying new things on to see how they feel. Like, losing weight may mean that you won't be such a great lineman anymore, but it doesn't mean you have to give up football. Last night you said that you'd love to get into running if not for the fact that it'll burn up too much muscle. So what? Go for it. Football teams need great runners—" I grab Char and kiss her again, hard. I get it now why East can barely take a breath without this girl. I'm even ready to be Char's barnacle. . . .

"You're the first girl I ever really kissed—a kiss that means something," I whisper into her ear while I'm kissing her neck. "You're like this crazy truth serum that's making me say—making me *realize*—all these pussy things."

Char pulls me closer. "Bobby, you're my first real kiss too," she whispers back. "I can't remember anything feeling this real." And then we go back at it.

22

HOT & SOUR

tuesday, July 21, 2009

East (-13 lbs); Char (-9 lbs)

"I don't know why you like this place. So crowded and noisy."

"The hot-and-sour, duh." Char rolls her eyes. "You said you were fine with it."

"Whatever. We're here."

"You're going to stay like this?"

"Did you honestly expect me to be all cheerful? How would you feel if you were me?"

Char finally called today around four o'clock with another one of her brilliant plans—she'd catch the 5:19 from Grand Central (I didn't even know she was in the city!) and I'd take the 5:42 from Chappaqua and we'd meet in White Plains. "We'll do our usual. P.F. Chang's for dinner, cruise the mall after," she said.

"I don't think so," I said. "I'm still only allowed to have liquids mostly."

"Shroud, please. I *have* to tell you something. For your ears only!"

"Go with Marcie. Tell *her* your big secret," I said. She told me to hold for a sec, and then I heard Bobby talking in the background. "What—you're with Bobby?"

"East, I should have called. You're right to be mad and I'm really, really sorry. But you have to give me a chance to explain. Bobby's like right here and I can't talk now," she whispered more urgently. "Just meet me in White Plains at six."

"You think I like checking my phone every minute for two days straight to see if you care whether I'm alive or not?" I said. Though looking to see if Char called probably trumps having nothing to look for at all.

"I'm sorry. Completely sorry. I need you. *Please.*"

"All right," I finally said. Because I wanted to know about Bobby. Because the TV is driving me nuts. Because I've been picking my nose inside that house for four days straight and I couldn't stand it for another second. And . . . Char needs me.

· · · · · ·

Char puts a Hale and Hearty bag on the floor at my feet. "Pea soup for you. It'd better be good. My arm's killing me from carrying it," Char says.

"I appreciate it, but—"

"I don't blame you for being mad. But I'm raging starving. Can we order some food first and then you can yell at me?" she says.

"Aren't *we* dieting and trying to lose weight so no one knows we *didn't* get banded?"

"*We* need to eat! And I thought *we* hated people who use *we* when they mean *you*." I don't say anything. "So, can you believe that story?" Char had texted me from the train about these four wasted college guys who asked her to sign their bare asses for their fraternity pledge. She did it. Initialed every one.

"Crazy," I say, monotone. I want to hear what she was doing alone in the city with Bobby. "Why didn't *Marcie* go with you?"

"She was supposed to—we were going to show Bobby this chest protector thing he can use to cover his incisions for football practice. But at the last minute, she didn't feel up to it."

"Why couldn't you just give him the store address? What—you're his personal shopper now?" I mutter.

"How could I be? I'm yours, aren't I?"

My napkin is mashed into a tight ball by the time the waitress comes. She takes Char's order, which includes an extra hot-and-sour soup for me. Then Char lets out this deep breath. "This really big thing happened, but I'm also screwed because—promise you won't tell a soul?"

"Fine! What already?"

Our soups get put in front of us. Mine's steaming up into my face and I'm about to burst into tears. And it's not because Char has a Diet Coke and I can never have carbonated drinks again, or that the soup smells so incredibly delicious—and too spicy for me to even taste. I have a very bad feeling.

"You hooked up with Bobby, didn't you?" I blurt. Char's leaning forward and watching me. "That's it, right? Right?" And then I put my spoon in the soup. All these yummy little pieces swirling around—I'm not supposed to eat bits of anything yet!

"Sort of. Yeah. We kissed. But that's the second part." Char pauses, still studying my face.

"Details," I say calmly. "Very cool. Very great." I must be emphasizing *very* way too much, because Char's still dissecting my every micro expression.

"Really? You're fine? I mean, if you weren't, then I wouldn't—"

"Enough, Char." I cut her off. "I'm happy for you."

"You sure?"

"Absolutely."

"Then why are you shredding your napkin?"

"No reason other than that I'm a freak," I say, straining to get one clear spoonful of soup without pork or vegetable in it. Char laughs, I don't.

"Don't be mad at me, East. Sunday night I couldn't find my phone and then I didn't plug it in to charge it the full way and—"

"You could have called from Marcie's phone."

"I'm an idiot. I'm sorry. Please don't be mad. You're like— you *are* my best friend. I have no one to even tell all this to." She pushes her empty bowl away. "Damn, I'm so hungry."

"I ate two spoonfuls of yogurt before you called and got full. Not really ever hungry anymore," I say. It's mean, and it's not even true, but there it is. "Go ahead and tell."

Char starts nibbling bits of fried noodle from the bowl in the center of the table. "We're in the back of that surgical supply store and Bobby needs to measure the thing against his stomach, so we sneak into this stockroom and it's dark and tiny, so we're piled up against each other. And I don't know. We were talking and that's when he put his arms around me and kissed me."

"A long one?" I'm queasy watching Char as she licks and sucks on this one fried noodle. *Just shove it in your mouth already.*

"Long—with tongue. I mean, it felt really long, but I guess it couldn't have been *that* long. Maybe three minutes?"

"And?" I'm digging my nails into the flesh behind my knees under the table.

"It was really nice, East. He stared into my eyes. And then—it was so funny—the owner of the pharmacy opens the door right in the middle, and the poor old guy almost has a heart attack, and while he chases us out, the whole time I'm saying, 'But sir, we need to buy this first.' Then, like two seconds after, we're back on the street, Bobby pulls me into this alley, and he like just won't stop kissing me. And then—and swear you won't tell anyone—"

"Stop, Char! Who would I tell? Marcie?"

"No, I told Marcie. I mean, just a little, on the train. But not anyone else in group. So, Bobby told me I was his first real kiss—and that I'm like this truth serum for him, and East—I think he might really like me." Char's watching me like she expects me to jump up and award her some kind of medal. I'd rather have Bobby give her some of that truth serum.

"So, then what? Did you make plans?" I end up saying.

"Yeah, sort of. When we were waiting at Grand Central he said we should maybe chill together after next Friday's session. And then after we kissed on the platform for a few minutes, he mumbled something about me coming to watch him play football in a few weeks—his preseason opener. But I'm not sure—"

"He walked you to the train?"

"Yeah, when Bobby was paying for the stomach shield, that's when I called you and—"

"Wait. Bobby knew you were calling me?"

"I guess. I told him I had to head back because I had to get you soup and then he said, 'I'll go with you. You shouldn't be carrying anything.' How nice is that?"

"Really nice. So, he has no idea that—"

"That's the other reason I need to talk to you, East." Char pauses. "I really screwed up. Bobby thinks I had the surgery. Marcie too. Everyone who read the blog."

I play dumb. "What do you mean? You *told* them you had the surgery?" Char is no longer sucking each fried noodle. She's drenching them in duck sauce and plunking them in her mouth, one after the other.

"Of course not. I'm not that bad! But they assumed I had it, and I just let them." Then Char puts her head in her hands—a gesture of desperation I've never seen from her. "Oh, East. What am I saying? I *am* that bad. I pretended like my stomach hurt and stuff like that. I lied to them. I did." Char looks so miserable that I'm truly feeling sorry for her. And glad that she's finally coming clean with me.

"Char," I say softly. "What's really going on? I know *something* is. Otherwise, you wouldn't lie about having had the surgery." Char puts her head in her hands again.

She looks up at me helplessly and whispers, "Swear you'll never breathe a word of any of this. I don't want anyone else thinking something's wrong with me that isn't."

I shake my head. "I would never tell."

Char dabs at her eyes with a napkin and then leans forward. "Okay, look. The issue with my hospital records—"

"Don't even tell me the hospital still didn't send the records?"

"East, yes, they did, but that's not it. After the appendectomy, do you remember how I couldn't hang out with you for like *days?*"

I nod. I'm afraid if I utter another syllable, Char will stop talking.

"Well, I was back at the hospital having my stomach pumped."

I'm gaping now—silently. Char wipes her nose with her napkin.

"Look, I was in a lot of pain from the a—operation, my parents were fighting, so I didn't say anything, I just went into their bathroom cabinet and took some Percocet. I mean, the doctor said I could take something for pain. Anyway, I took a few and soon I got really drowsy and began having trouble breathing. When my parents heard me hit the floor, they came running, saw the bottle, panicked, and called an ambulance. The point is, I was in a lot of pain and I was just being careless, but Betsy and Dr. Weinstein are making a federal case out of nothing. They keep bringing my parents in, telling them I might have been *trying* to hurt myself and all this other crap. So, until everyone's comfortable that I'm not a nutcase, they're going to hold off on my surgery."

This was only three years ago, and Char's been my best friend forever—I don't know how I didn't know about this! I'm just sitting there with my mouth open, shaking my head. "Char, what's 'a few' pills? You had to have taken enough for them to get this idea in their heads," I finally say.

Char smiles sheepishly for a second. "Yeah, well, I don't remember exactly. Maybe four or five. Not a lot, but, yeah, obviously enough to get them all bent out of shape. I was just in a lot of pain, but they won't let it go, and now next week

I have yet another meeting with my parents and a new doctor they want to evaluate me."

"Oh, Char! You didn't need to keep this from me! I know you'd never do something to hurt yourself. Never in a million years! What do your parents think? They believe you, right?"

Char leans forward again. "Well, that's just it, East. I mean, they do. But whenever they try to make Betsy understand that I would never hurt myself—then or now—Betsy gives them her psychobabble about how quote resistant unquote I am to *admitting* to emotional issues, let alone willing to deal with them. And then she spooks them further with her rap about how when people who don't address their emotional reasons for eating get weight loss surgery, they can end up seeking substitutions, like alcohol and drugs. So then, they come running back to me and make me swear that I'll never even take so much as a Tylenol, and I have to convince them all over again. The whole thing is a stupid circus, but Betsy thinks it's important that I continue with group for the time being, which hopefully means she's coming around."

I feel a surge of relief. "So what's the big problem, Char? All you have to do is become serious about addressing your 'emotional issues' instead of disrupting all the time, and you'll get your surgery. If Betsy wasn't still open to letting you have it, she'd have kicked you out of group already."

Char looks up at me, reaches her hand out for another noodle, and then abruptly pushes the bowl away. "Yeah, you're right, East. I'll just give Betsy what she's looking for, keep starving myself, and then, once I have the surgery, no one will ever know that I lied. But you swear you won't tell anyone about any of this, no matter what happens?"

"I promise: I'll never tell a living soul about any of this," I say solemnly.

A cell phone starts buzzing, and I don't even bother going for mine. "It's Bobby," Char says, miraculously all lit up again. She's showing me his text: *You made your train right?* "Yeah with East now," she says out loud while typing. *Say hi,* she shows me.

"One more sec, East. Let me just tell him I'll call when I get home."

"No doubt you'll call *him* when you say you will." But I'm smiling as I say this. My best friend's got enough on her plate.

23

INVASION OF THE BODY SNATCHERS

tuesday, July 28, 2009

Marcie (-11 lbs)

Teenage Waistland is a freaking mausoleum this session, the first group meeting since we've all had our surgeries. I mean, yeah, there was high-fiving when we all first got into the room, and everyone spewing stuff like, "Oh, but how do *you* feel?" and, "Wow, I can see a big difference in you already," to each other. But after we took our seats and Bitsy had us *clap for ourselves* like we just climbed Mount freaking Everest, all the life pretty much got sucked out of the room. And it takes me only like two seconds to figure out why: Char's gone mute.

Seriously. She's sitting there between Bobby and East as usual, but it's like the invasion of the body snatchers! And instead of snarling and watching Char's every move, East has gone freaking *Buddha* on us—she's all happy and calm, like she's at peace and one with the universe. And Char. Well, Char's sitting here beaming as usual, maybe even more so, but it's like she's had a lip zipper installed and that's *all* she's doing—beaming! I mean, she's beaming at me, and beaming at Bitsy, and beaming at the other kids depending on who's talking, and beaming at East, and beaming at Bobby. . . . Especially at Bobby. And the two of them are constantly like leaning into each other and smiling into each others' eyes and touching each other's hands and all of this frankly vomit-y crap. Yeah, they're cute together and I'm happy for Char, and I haven't even minded analyzing "the Kiss" one hundred times. But what about me? This whole lovey-dovey serenity thing is B-O-R-I-N-G, and, I swear, if there was loaded artillery within reach, my brains would be splattered all over the wall.

Everyone is getting up and droning on about how their surgeries went—*Oh, and two seconds later I was out like a light*—and how the nurses were so nice, and how changing the bandages was gross, blah blah blah. I expect the tiniest bit of action when the "sharing" gets to Char, but she stays seated and waves *demurely*—like she's passing on a tray of hors d'oeuvres being offered to her at some elegant cocktail party. In a tiny sweet voice she says, "Oh, nothing to add— let's move on to East." And Bitsy, who doesn't normally sanction hesitation in the sharing department, clears her throat and says, "Okay, East, your turn. Tell us about your surgery experience."

Each second here feels like an hour, and I'm just dying for this torture to end so that we can head out to Chow Fun House. The gag is, none of us can get more than two bites down before we're full. So I can't wait to snap the photo of Freddie Kawasaki's face when the four of us—or however many kids join us tonight—waddle in like freaking mall Santa Clauses, and order *one* dumpling appetizer. To share.

Abby's been on my case to visit Gran in the hospital after group tonight since the hospital is literally two blocks away. I'm not sure exactly what's even wrong with the woman. She's only like seventy, which I think seems early for all that lovely organ-failure crap that happens when people get really old. But my only theory on the situation, based on the paucity of available facts, and, admittedly, my own piss-poor level of interest, is that Gran's fifty-five years of bulimia are finally catching up to her.

Abby says that Gran keeps asking for me (and asking if I've called Jen yet!) and that the least I can do is visit for a few lousy minutes. *Gran's mind is going,* Abby pleads. *You shouldn't hold anything she says against her.* But Gran's never been interested in my high grades or all the creative writing awards I've won, or anything like that. It's just always about my appearance. Oh, and my mouth—how men don't like women who have minds and speak them or women who curse like truck drivers. Which, I believe, is yet another one of her unfair stereotypes, since I highly doubt Gran's ever *met* a truck driver, let alone gotten into an obscenity-riddled conversation with one. Mind or no mind, Gran is still an expert at making me feel like crap, and there's no way I'm missing our after-group soiree just to get harassed, especially now that my own blood has taken Jen's side!

Chow Fun House won't take long anyway. The dumpling will be quick to eat, and Freddie will probably kick us out pretty quickly: the last thing he needs is a bunch of raucous fatties hogging a table when they're no longer ordering half the menu. *Then* I'll get over to the hospital—just in time for visiting hours to end. Abby's my ride back to Jersey tonight, and she'll be furious with me, of course, bitching the whole way about my heartlessness. But traffic is usually light on the George Washington Bridge that time of night, and a twenty-minute barrage in exchange for another great evening with Teenage Waistland sounds like an excellent trade to me.

● ● ● ● ● ●

Here's the scene. Group has finally ended and we're in the elevator: Char and Bobby are sucking face and mauling each other, and East and I are rolling our eyes and sticking a finger into our mouths like we're about to hurl chunks. And then on the street: Char and Bobby are sucking face and mauling each other, and East and I are rolling our eyes and blowing our brains out with imaginary guns. And then outside the entrance to Chow Fun House: Char and Bobby are sucking face and mauling each other, and East and I are rolling our eyes and pretending to throw ourselves in front of moving traffic. Finally I screech, *"Get a freaking room!"* and Char hits me and laughs and Bobby blushes and East gives me a high five, and we go into the restaurant.

But the joke's on us. Freddie is nowhere to be seen, and another fellow leads us to the table—a table big enough to comfortably seat us without Char getting to pull any theatrics. Then, after this new waiter says something to East in Japanese (presumably—it could be Swahili, for all I know) and she reddens and ignores him, he takes our order of one fried shrimp dumpling appetizer without even twitching. But the irony of this failed gag turns out to be hilarious too, so we're shaking our heads, laughing so hard that our eyes tear, and thumping the table with our fists. That is, until a booming voice—sickeningly familiar—fills the restaurant.

"Marcie! Get over here right now!" I spin around. It's Abby storming toward us, and I've never seen her this crazed before. She digs her fingernails into my arm and yanks me out of my seat so hard the chair falls onto the floor.

"Your grandmother is dead."

o o o o o o

It's like all hell has broken loose *everywhere* in the city tonight. Ambulance sirens blaring, crosstown traffic crawling an inch per minute, and Abby's face glistening with tears as she sits frozen behind the wheel.

"Mom?" I try. "Maybe we should pull into a garage and have Ronny come get us? Or I can drive. I mean, not legally or anything, but Carlo's been letting me practice. I'm not bad, although I'm not quite sure I could pass a road test if parallel parking a fifty-foot stretch limo is involved." She remains stone-faced, not even a hint of a smile at my attempt to cheer her up. At the intersection of Seventy-second Street and West End Avenue, an ancient bag lady wearing ten layers of clothing in this miserable summer heat crosses in front of us pushing a shopping cart. Abby finally turns to me, her face hard and tight.

"You know what your grandmother's very last words were, Marcie? I've been debating in my mind whether I should tell you, but at this moment, all I can think is how much you deserve to know." I shrug, but only to myself—no point in getting Abby freaked out with me. Abby takes an angry swipe at her eyes, leaving a black streak of mascara—it looks like war paint—across her face. "I'm at her bedside and I'm holding her hand. Her breathing is so shallow that I'm grateful for each tiny exhale. And here's my mother, so delirious she doesn't even recognize me. Instead, she thinks I'm *you*! 'Marcie, my beautiful baby. I'm so very happy you're finally here. . . .' That's it—the last moment with my mother that I'll ever have. And it was all about *you*, the selfish granddaughter she yearned for in her final breath. The one who wouldn't give her one lousy inch! The one who wouldn't give her the tiniest bit of time, love, or warmth. Even if you couldn't find it in your heart to do it for a dying old woman, what about me, *your* mother?"

I can't for the life of me decipher the reaction Abby's looking for. It's not like my feelings about Gran were a mystery to her. "I'm sorry, Mom," I say. "It should have been your moment. But it's not my fault that Gran—"

"What? I don't know where you came from," Abby cries. "It's not about 'my moment' or fault! It's about acceptance!"

"I know it's about acceptance!" I cry back. "She didn't accept me! I wasn't good enough!"

"My mother was a good woman," Abby practically spits. "For all her flaws and all the 'beauty baggage' you hate so much, she loved you the best way she knew how! She never said, 'Oh, Marcie and I aren't on the same page, so I'll just write her out of my life!' the way you did to her. All she wanted was a little love from you, a little respect. But every time you opened your mouth—almost from the time you were a toddler—you made her feel small, like she was a pathetic moron living a silly shallow life. Who are you to judge anybody? You didn't grow up in *her* generation, you didn't think for one second to put yourself in *her* shoes—you simply chose *not* to understand her. And then you shut her out. Why couldn't you just love her the way she was? Because it's Marcie's way or the highway, that's why. Right?" We're finally *on* the highway now. I just clench my teeth and stare out the window.

24

KONOPKA & SON

tuesday, july 28, 2009

Bobby (-15 lbs)

I'm scanning codes into the computer, part of testing this
new software program I convinced Dad to try at the store—
they've been tracking inventory (or not tracking it) the same
way since my great-grandfather's days—when I spot yet another exposed rear end as a contractor crouches in an aisle
examining pipe fittings. I almost laugh out loud. *Okay, Pencildick, you're dead wrong about hairy butt cracks being the only
ass I'll be scoping this summer*, I mentally type on MT's wall for
like one second. But then I think about the size of Char's and
all the abuse the guys would give me if they came face to face
with it—especially MT. It's not that I'm a prize, but meeting
her would make the guys think I'm even more of a loser with
girls, or desperate. Or both. Thank God Char hasn't brought
up the opening game to me—I want so much for her to see
that I'm not this totally insecure pansy. I want her to see the
"local hero" part too. But the guys . . .

While I'm working on this computerization project—
Dad gave in and spent big bucks on the hardware and software

for it despite knowing dick about technology—I have to try hard to push Char—this whole dilemma—out of my mind. It's fine that she's totally there when I'm running, because the thought of her and me together, both seriously buff and all over each other in front of everyone, is part of my motivation to keep going. I'm up to almost eight miles a day, dragging myself out at six a.m. every morning, rain or shine, so that I make it to the store by nine. I'm so into the running, how tight and agile and just *good* it makes me feel. And my weight is like falling off—fifteen pounds already!

The other part of the motivation is harder to think about. Even though my incisions probably won't be an issue for me with brilliant Char's stomach shield, I'm nowhere near as ready for the upcoming season as I usually am this time of year. The whole thing gives me the same horrible friggin' feeling as the thought of the guys finding out about my summer. The pussyband and the *not* hot babes. And my hypothetical V-card, which I should laminate since I'll probably have it forever. *Refrigerator.* Just saying the word in my head makes me want to put on my running shoes and bolt. From this store, from this town. From my life.

I shake it off, scan the last inventory code into the system, and am finally set to test it when hairy-butt-crack pipe-fittings guy strides up to the counter. Without even looking up, I motion to the right and say, "Paul is on the cash register this morning, sir. He can help you."

"Little Bobby Konopka! You've gotten so much taller—and leaner—since last season!" I lift my head and give the guy my full attention now. He's no contractor. It's Mr. Dawson, as in Dawson Depot—Konopka & Son's biggest competitor next to Home Depot, which thankfully, according to Dad, doesn't carry most of the higher-end wood products that we do. Dawson Depot has expanded, with two other stores in neighboring towns, while Konopka & Son Lumber is as it's always been, just this one location.

"Good to see you, Mr. Dawson," I say as enthusiastically as I can fake, and put out my hand. Dawson Depot is also our team's biggest sponsor and Mr. Dawson comes out to most of the games.

He pumps my hand. "So when's the big preseason opener, my man?"

"Saturday, August twenty-ninth," I say, nodding, with my idiot smile plastered on. I have no idea what he's doing here.

"Practice must be starting pretty soon," he says, squeezing my bicep. "I guess you'll be hitting the iron hard until then— they've still got you on the first string, yeah? You look great, kid, really, but not quite as big as the Refrigerator we all know and love." He chuckles.

I half nod and half shrug. "I've gotten into running lately."

Dawson raises his eyebrows. "I got word there'll be a few Division One college scouts at the opener, but you didn't hear that from me."

"Mr. Daw—" I start, but change my mind halfway through his name.

"Go on, kid? I don't have any pull with the scouts, if that's where you're going."

I shake my head.

"Well, just a hypothetical question. What would happen if, say, Notre Dame signed a big lineman, but then the guy got, like, mono his senior year and lost a ton of weight. I mean, I know he couldn't play that position, but do you think they'd look at him for, say, running back? I mean, if he was super lean and fast?"

Dawson looks at me weird and then, as if to change the subject, he peers around the counter and checks out the computer screen. "You guys are finally coming into this century— good for you! We've been using that system for, I don't know, eight years now?"

"Well, *this* is the RFID version—released just two weeks ago," I say, all smug. "It doesn't just track inventory in the store—it can track any product through the entire supply chain. When a customer asks when we expect an item in, we just punch in the code and we're able to tell them that it's on a truck sitting at a light two blocks away."

Dawson cocks his head and nods thoughtfully. "Impressive, kid. Very impressive. You're quite an asset to your old man. I hope he doesn't have you hauling boxes in the stockroom. Would be a waste of your talent." Dawson shifts to his other leg and pivots to survey the store. "Where is the big guy, anyway? We've got a lunch appointment." He checks his watch and grins. "Oops. Guess I'm a little early. I like your expansion into plumbing supplies, by the way. Not enough room for a big selection, I see, but the bestselling items are all here."

I'm kind of turning *impressive, kid* and *asset to your old man* over in my head, so it takes about a minute for the rest to hit me. They have a cordial relationship, being football stars on rival teams back in the day and all, but what's Dad doing having lunch with this guy?

"Uh, Mr. Dawson. The running back thing was totally hypothetical, so—" I stop when the front-door bells chime, and Dad's flying in toward us, hand outstretched.

"Good to see you, Harry! Pumping my kid for trade secrets, I see?" They laugh and shake hands and then turn and head for the door. "Be back in about an hour," Dad says with a wave.

Mr. Dawson turns back toward me and winks, like he got my meaning and won't mention anything to Dad. Then he puts his hand on Dad's shoulder. "He's no kid anymore, Rob. A man now. With a good head on his shoulders," I overhear him saying as they leave. And then I get that same high happy feeling like when I'm running.

in the basement

East (-17 lbs); Char (-13 lbs)

I'm back at the basement door, this time standing behind Char and clenching a paper lunch bag in my hand; as it shakes, it sounds like kites flapping in the wind. Like the last family vacation we ever took, when the four of us were running on a white Bermuda beach flying kites.

"I'm not sure this is such a great idea," I say to Char.

"Are you kidding? It's brilliant. Breathe into the bag through your mouth and you won't gag." *I'm not talking about the moldy smell.* But Char's full speed ahead with digging out old pictures from when we were thin so we can finally be on Facebook. She says she wants Bobby to get a "taste" of what he can look forward to, but I'm thinking she also fears that, even if she can keep up with her crazy starvation diet and all the miles she's putting on Crystal's treadmill, she won't lose as much weight as the rest of us. And, though I don't say this to Char, it wouldn't be so terrible for Bobby—or anyone in Teenage Waistland—to know that I used to be something to look at too.

My father was heavily into photography and always taking pictures. And Char's in practically all of them—we were always together. When she said her parents can't even find baby pictures of her, and I told her ours were all boxed up somewhere in my basement, instead of saying, "Okay, just forget it," like I hoped, Char said, "Excellent. They're all in one place—much easier to find!"

"Ready?" she asks as she flings the door open.

I'm looking at the wooden stairs in front of me—I shove my face deeper into the bag. My dad's life finished in this stinky unfinished basement—I don't see how I can get even as far as the first step. "Why don't we wait until Tuesday when Elsa is here and I can have her dust off the boxes and bring them up? I'll just bring the pictures to your house and we can pick through and scan them in then," I say, pulling on Char's sleeve. She yanks it free.

"No. C'mon!" And we're in tandem on yet another exploration, Char in the lead, dragging yours truly behind her. "Over here," she calls when she reaches the bottom of the staircase and spots the boxes marked PHOTO and VIDEO in my mother's handwriting. I'm proud of myself for not even looking to the right as I make my way over to where Char is.

"Stepladder, Shroud. We so need one," she orders, before spotting it behind her.

"You know she removed like that whole wall of pictures after? And almost every other photo we had displayed around the house?" I say, but Char's busy wiping off cobwebs and sending clouds of dust in my direction. "This is my first time down here," I mumble, more to myself than Char. But this time, she freezes, clamps her cobwebby hand over her mouth, and gets right down off the stepladder.

"Shroud! Oh my God. East!" she cries out as I struggle to contain my tears. She stammers, "You—you're doing this for me when—and here I—" And then she stops talking and throws her arms around me. I want to pull away and tell her I'm fine, but I just stand with my face against her neck and sob uncontrollably.

"Shhh. Shhh. It's okay."

I want to say I'm sorry for being such a basket case, but I'm shaking too hard to form any words.

"Shhh. This is good. Let it out," Char murmurs, gently rocking me side to side.

"I'm—I'm okay," I finally sputter, and pull away. Char offers me her sleeve to blow my nose, and I sob-laugh and use the neck of my T-shirt.

"You go upstairs," Char says once I'm calm again. "I'll bring the boxes to your room and we'll open them there. You shouldn't be lifting stuff anyway."

○ ○ ○ ○ ○ ○

I move one of the dusty cartons over to my desk and peel the tape off fast, like a Band-Aid, but it doesn't lessen the pain: my parents' wedding album is on top. There's a maroon chamois cloth covering it, but I recognize the brown leather peeking out immediately—it used to sit on the family-room coffee table.

Beneath the album is a file folder filled with loose photos. There's my mom in a hospital bed with a newborn baby. I think it's me, but there's no date on the back. Her hair is pulled in a tight ponytail, all pretty and shiny, and her eyes are shimmering. She's *happy*. Then there are some of

Julius and my old-fashioned wooden rocking horse. He's standing on it like it's a surfboard. Next are pictures of me, around two years old, on the horse. I'm in a yellow and kelly green plaid jumper and my arms are wrapped tightly around the horse's neck like I'm on some terrifying bucking-bronco ride. I put the folder aside—I'll come back to those early ones later. I dust off the album below it—an older one covered in rice paper—and place it in my lap. The first photo is yellow and faded and when I realize what it is—a huge extended Japanese family—tears start flooding my eyes.

"All done," Char suddenly says. I hadn't heard her come back with the final box. She sits next to me and examines the photo over my shoulder.

"I saw some of these people once," I say, staring into the picture. "The day my dad died."

"Is the little boy standing next to that woman in the flowered dress your dad?" Char whispers. "That *must* be your grandmother—you look exactly like her."

I nod slowly. "It could be. She looks like she could be the younger version of the lady Dad took me to meet," I say, studying the woman with the cold eyes holding my dad's wrist.

"I never knew you met anyone on your dad's side of the family. Actually, you told me you didn't—that time that lawyer called the house and spoke to you about your grandmother's inheritance because your mom wouldn't get on the phone," Char says, still peering over my shoulder.

"Yeah," I say, remembering. "I couldn't say I met them in front of her—my mom would have been furious about Dad taking me to see his family. His parents were children in a Japanese internment camp in California during the Second

World War, and they never forgave America. They refused to accept my mother, without ever even meeting her."

"So messed up," Char whispers.

"Anyway, Dad had read about his father's death in the paper, and we drove to the house where he grew up in Queens, just the two of us. I remember how thrilled I was to be on a secret mission alone with him—Mom thought we'd gone out for a pre-birthday father-daughter dinner—and Dad was excited too. He was sure that with his father gone, his mother would soften, especially when she saw me. Then, he said, he'd fix things between everyone."

"And?" Char whispers even more softly. Now it's like she's the one afraid that I'll clam up.

"Well, he was all chatty about his childhood on the drive, but when we pulled up to the house, he became really quiet. After we sat in the car for what felt like a long time, he slapped my leg and said, 'Okay. Ready?' Then he came around to my side and opened my door with this big smile. 'It's time for you to charm your Japanese family, Annie.'"

"Oh, East," Char murmurs, and rubs my back.

"All these Japanese people were inside milling around, and when they started noticing us standing in the doorway, everything got quiet. This old lady with a cane, my grandma, made her way over to us slowly. She didn't even look at Dad—just me. I mean, she couldn't take her eyes off me. She knelt down and took my hands in hers and whispered something. But I had no idea what she said, or how to respond, so I just looked up at Dad. She stood up suddenly—as soon as she realized I didn't speak Japanese, I guess—and shook her finger in Dad's face, screaming things I couldn't understand. But Dad understood them—he looked like he had been punched. And then he grabbed my hand and led me away."

Char flips the album closed and tosses it back in the box. "These people are not even worth looking at!" she says.

"Well, at least my grandmother came to regret it—she died shortly after my father," I say, "and we'd be on food stamps if not for her. Now I have a college trust fund, and her money paid for the surgery, of course."

"Your mom must have been wondering why your grandmother suddenly had a change of heart and left your family all her money," Char says. "Why didn't you just tell her about your visit?" I shake my head, and Char sighs and rips open the next box. "Awww," we both squeal. The picture used to hang in the center of the family room wall. It's an eight-by-ten of Char and me, our faces near a sprinkler head with streaks of water spraying out. In the next photo, we're going to dance class. I'm in a yellow leotard and purple tutu and she's got a purple leotard and yellow tutu—Char's idea to trade tutus, of course. And then, us in the fifth-grade play dressed up as trees. "Oh my God!" Char screams, waving an old Halloween picture. Julius is the Tin Man, Char is Dorothy, and I'm Toto.

"Put that one here—I miss Julius. I'm hanging that in my room!" I shriek. We go through the entire box like this, carefully pulling each stack of photos out like treasure, laughing at all these forgotten pieces of our lives together.

"On to the next box, Shroud," Char orders. "We're not even past age ten yet and I need at least one good skinny pic with me older. Help me," she says, yanking on the tape.

There's a yellow padded envelope on top and I grab it and pull out a picture mounted in a paper frame I remember making. It's of me on Dad's lap, his arms wrapped tightly around me. "This was like the week before he died," I say, staring at it. "He'd given Julius a Polaroid camera for his birthday—you know, the old kind that develops photos instantly. I think this was the very first picture he took with it—me and Dad." I study the photo up close, trying to decipher my father's expression with me in his arms. "You know, my father didn't say one word the whole way home. When we got back, I said, 'I'm sorry, Daddy.' We were walking to the door and he stopped and stroked my head, and then knelt down in front of me and said in a very soft voice, 'It's not your fault, Annie.' But I'll never forget how tired and old he suddenly looked. I remember throwing my arms around his neck, but he didn't hug me back. He just stood up and said we'd better go in now. And he killed himself later that same night, Char! Maybe if she had liked me—"

"Oh my God, East! Stop! It's completely crazy for you to even think you had anything to do with what your father did. He knelt down and looked you straight in the eye when he told you it wasn't your fault. That's because what he was telling you was important and he wanted you to remember it. And you did!" Char puts her hand on my shoulder and rubs my neck. "I bet your mother thinks it was her fault too," she says softly. "She must always wonder about the things that were on your dad's mind before it happened."

I shake my head.

"Does Julius know?" Char says.

"No, I never told Julius any of it either," I say, still shaking my head. "Julius was in such terrible shape, I couldn't."

"Nothing?" Char's incredulous. "You've been sitting on this for three years without a word to anyone—even me? East, how could you not tell your mother?" Char's just looking at me while I shake my head. I don't even know how to answer. Then Char's eyes widen and she clamps her hand over her mouth. "Oh, East, my poor crazy freak of a friend—*do not* tell me you didn't tell your mother about what happened with your grandmother because you were afraid that *she'd* blame you for what your father did?"

I gently shake free from Char's massage. "We'll never get through all of this stuff at this rate." Then I dump the rest of the photos in the envelope onto my carpet. The pictures from that vacation in Bermuda are strewn in with Julius's Polaroids and other more recent photos, and Char and I are giggling about the queer bathing suit Mom has me wearing.

"Oh God—check this one out." Char picks up a photo and screams. "My mom is laughing and trying to get out of the water while her bikini bottom is being pulled down by the undertow. Hysterical!"

But I'm staring at the photo that's underneath it.

It's a blurry Polaroid of Julius in his underwear laughing, with his arm around some topless blond girl. But it's not blurry enough for me not to be deadly certain that it's not just any topless girl. It's *Char!*

Suddenly, it's like I don't recognize anything around me—the walls of my room, my bedspread, the girl next to me. Everything is completely alien, like I'm seeing it for the first time. It's not until I start heaving that Char notices something's wrong. She spots the photo and dives for it, but I yank it away and scramble to my feet.

"What the fuck? What the *fuck*!" I'm roaring and screeching. "You *fucking* slut! Get the fuck out of here!"

"East, wait, wait, you don't understand." Char's crying and pleading as she comes toward me, as if she has a shot in hell of calming me down. I hurl myself at her and shove her out of my room. And then I'm shoving her down the hall and as she's flying down the stairs I'm behind her screaming, "Go! Go!" and stumbling after her trying to keep my hands down and to control myself. I swear I could push her down the rest of these stairs headfirst.

"Go! Faster!" I'm screeching. She skids across the foyer and I push her once more, and as she's just heading through the screen door, I slam the heavy wood door as hard as I can behind her, barely missing her back. "East," she screams from outside, and I scream, "Fuck you!" through the door and race into the kitchen. I fling the pantry door open and I'm in there knocking over ramen noodles and boxes of rice and oatmeal. C'mon, where's your stash, Mom? I know you have one. Where the hell are the Oreos? Where's that fucking bag of sour apple rings? I need them now. "Where is it?" I'm screaming and pushing every-thing around, when a bottle of salad dressing falls and oil and vinegar go all over the place. All over my new run-ning sneakers. Ruined. I come out of the pantry and slam my back against the door struggling to catch my breath. I close my eyes and try to focus on my breathing to calm down.

"East!" Mom's yelling from her bedroom. "What's going on? Are you okay?" *Am I okay?* I pull my greasy sneakers off and throw them against the fridge and charge up the stairs in a bigger rage than the one I was in on the way down. I stomp toward her room and punch open the door so hard it bounces off the wall and hits my shoulder as I tear in.

"Something happened with Char and Julius!" I'm screaming. "Is that why you sent him away? I need to know what you know about Char and Julius, and I want to know it *now*!"

charred and feathered

Bobby (–17 lbs)

"You're fine, Bobby. We're just getting started now," Betsy says as I come tearing into the room. Everyone's watching and waiting for me as I head for the empty seat next to Char with her bag on it, but Geek Olive's on her other side, so I sort of stop dead in my tracks thinking she's saving that seat for East. Except there's East on the far side of the circle next to Marcie, and all the rest of the seats are taken.

"Here, Bobby." Char laughs as she picks up her purse. I'm such a douche. If there's only one open seat in the circle, obviously it's mine. But at least I'm not late. *And* my pits don't stink.

"Thanks," I say, settling into it.

"Hi," Char whispers.

"Hi," I press my shoulder against hers but she doesn't respond. "Your twin looks mad you didn't save her a seat," I whisper back. Char's too busy trying to catch East's eye to respond, but then she leans over and whispers, "It's not like we're conjoined." I'm still lost in thoughts of Char and me *conjoining* when I feel her breath hit my neck again.

"I don't feel so hot, Bobby."

"Really? What's wr—"

"Uh, hello?" Betsy calls out frowning at us, and I catch the kissy face Marcie gives Char. East, though, still seems mad as hell—like she's fuming and trying to look in any direction but ours.

"Sorry," we both say to Betsy at the exact same time, but Char doesn't laugh. She straightens up and shifts and now our arms aren't touching.

"We're up to you, Lucia," Betsy says softly.

"One and a half pounds," Lucia mumbles miserably. "Just under."

"Lucia, that is on the low side, but it's moving in the right direction," Betsy says. "Do you want to stay after group and go through your meal sheets to see if we can spot the problem?" Lucia shrugs and nods, then changes her mind and shakes her head. "Okay, just be sure to stay extra vigilant next week. Who's next? Coco?"

"Seven," Coco says, and Jamie high-fives her.

Tia is next, then Geek, Char, then me.

"Five," Tia grumbles, but the edges of her mouth go up.

"Ten and five-eighths, with a possible point-five-pound deviation related to variation in instrumentation." Geek's mumbo jumbo kills me.

"What the hell?" Marcie mutters, cracking everyone up.

"Yeah, our scales aren't consistent either," Char agrees. "I solve that problem by selecting the reading I like best—which is eleven!"

I'm looking around the circle waiting for the laughing to end because I want full attention when I announce my number, and I notice East biting her lip and staring at the floor like it's a roach she'd like to crush.

"Okay, people, don't be jealous," I finally get to say. "I've been running. A lot. I've lost about sixteen pounds." I don't add that I have Char to thank. But when the applause starts, I smile at her, and she doesn't react.

Now Michelle's up. "Nada," she whines. "Nothin'! I swear—I started out with one jar of baby food, got through three, and then ate two bowls of chili. And that was just lunch. So, I'm not losing *and* I'm starving."

Betsy stands up. "Michelle, how are you doing on your meal sheets? I'll bet you anything I won't see the chili on it. Am I right?"

Michelle nods. "Busted."

"People—these sheets aren't for my well-being, they're for yours. Writing in them faithfully will help you observe the connections between your emotions and your eating be—"

"I—I need to go to the ladies' room," Char croaks, her voice really weak, like she's trying to catch her breath.

"Sure—are you okay?" Betsy asks. "You do look a little pale."

Char nods, but she is pale and all sweaty, actually. "I'm okay, I'm okay," she says as she reaches under her seat for her bag and rises all shakylike to her feet. I stand up and take her arm to help steady her, but she pulls it away, saying, "Really, Bobby, I'm fine." She's two steps out of the circle—behind the back of my chair—when her legs buckle and she totally crumples to the floor!

East springs to her feet as if she was on a seesaw with Char and Marcie screams. But then everyone's yelling and I'm over her face saying, "Char? Char?" but she's not moving. Betsy pushes me away and crouches next to Char and feels for a pulse.

"Someone call nine-one-one!" she orders.

Marcie's wailing. "Is she breathing?"

"Calm down, everyone. Please."

"Nine-one-one in transit. On the way," Geek yells.

"She's breathing but her pulse is rapid. Everyone back up and give her air," Betsy barks. "Bobby, Marcie, I need you to move back. Please, everyone!"

"Where's Dr. Weinstein?" Marcie shouts. "We *are* at a freaking doctors' office."

"He's in surgery, Marcie. And it's okay—Char's regaining consciousness." Betsy's cradling Char's head in her arm and speaking softly to her when two paramedics burst in with a stretcher. They make me, Marcie, and even Betsy clear out, and then they're hovering over Char, checking her breathing and pulse and stuff.

"Let them do their work," Betsy says loudly. "Everyone back to their seats!" That's when I notice that East hasn't been anywhere near Char, and she's already back in her seat. The rest of the girls are crying and whimpering and touching each other's backs and hands, but East is completely still— like maybe she's in shock.

Char turns onto her side so the paramedics can slip the stretcher under her, and then, in a weak voice, she says, "Bobby? Are—" but one of the paramedics gestures for me to keep back while he puts an oxygen mask over her face before she can finish. Lucia completely freaks out all over again.

"What's happening to her? Why can't she breathe?"

"Oh my God! It's our bands!" Coco yells, putting her hands on her stomach.

"What kind of side effect is this? Is it going to happen to

all of us?" Tia jumps on the what's-wrong-with-the-band bandwagon, screaming. All the girls are going nuts.

"It's not a side effect of anything but Char starving herself," East says calmly, but loudly enough that everyone hears.

"What are you talking about?" Coco says to East. Except for the sound of the paramedics strapping Char in and closing their medic cases, the room goes dead silent.

"Group—we'll pick this up next week," Betsy breaks in. "Don't worry—Char'll be fine. I'm going to ride to the hospital with her." She briskly follows the stretcher and the EMS guys as they head to the door, and I take off with them. If they don't let me in the ambulance, I'll run the two blocks to the hospital and probably even beat them there.

"Char never had the surgery." East's words ricochet through the room and pelt me in the gut. Betsy juts her face in East's direction as she walks out. I jerk to a halt and spin back around to face the circle.

Everyone's stunned and sort of in shock and *What the hell?* Marcie's ranting, "Are you hallucinating? Char's surgery was right after yours, East. She was at my house a few days after!"

East still hasn't moved from her chair, but her voice is shrill. "What don't you understand? She *never had the surgery*! She's been starving herself so you would all think she had it. But she didn't."

"On the blog—" Coco starts, but East snaps, "She was lying. *Lying!*" The girls go back to shrieking the same stuff— "Oh my God!" "Can you believe it?"—over and over.

"So what's wrong with her? I mean, if it's not a complication from surgery," I cut in.

"She simply fainted, of course. From dehydration or low blood sugar. Or some combination of both," Geek responds.

"If she was starving herself as East indicates, and let's say her blood sugar level—"

"Save it, Alex!" Marcie shouts. "I need to make sure I got this straight. Char fainted because she's starving herself because she wanted to dupe us all into thinking she had the surgery?" Geek Olive looks up at the ceiling like he's doing the calculations, but East just closes her eyes and nods like she's exhausted with the whole thing. Marcie goes mute and stands gaping at East. Then she puts her hand over her mouth and staggers out of the room.

"Why?" Geek Olive asks simply during the brief break in the hysteria. But then it all starts up again.

"Yeah, why! Why didn't she have the surgery?" Coco and a few of the other girls peck at East like a bunch of lunatic chickens.

East crinkles her face in disgust and finally stands up. "What does it matter why?" she yells back at them. "Something in her records. Who cares why?" And then she takes off, slamming the door behind her.

"No," Geek Olive says as the room quiets down after East's dramatic exit. "I'm not asking why Char didn't have the surgery. I'm asking why she'd lie about it." But by the time the girls break out into another frenzy, I'm already out the door.

27

ménage à trois

Marcie (-13 lbs)

Carlo and I are camped in hellish rush-hour traffic on the West Side Highway, sucking in a toxic brew of carbon dioxide, hot humid air laced with its own potpourri of local pollutants, and New Jersey's usual wretched stink wafting in from across the river. We've got the windows wide open, Cuban music blasting on the satellite radio, and Carlo chain-smoking his filterless Camels. I could hang in the back of the limo, where it's quiet and cool, but I don't feel like being alone.

Carlo's rapping his fingers anxiously on the side of the car. He glances into the rearview mirror and cranes his neck to check his blind spot. "Maybe we should get off at Ninety-ninth Street and take Riverside to the bridge. Mrs. Rescott wants you home as soon as possible. It's the last night for sitting and shivering, I think she said."

I snort. "It's called 'sitting shivah,' Carlo, and it's how Jews mourn their dead. For a whole week, people come to the house and sit around stuffing their faces, sucking down the Manischewitz and telling stories about the person who died. So for God's sake, forget Riverside! Shivah ends at sundown, which is not for well over an hour, so there's no rush. Let's just relax and enjoy the fresh air."

Carlo sighs and wipes the sweat from his forehead with his shirtsleeve, then shakes his head when he notices the grimy residue he left on his white cuff.

"Forgive me, Miss Marcie, but there's nothing fresh about this air. And we're moving about twenty feet per minute. Really, I think there's been an accident and we should try another route."

"Marcie, just Marcie," I say for the zillionth time. "And please, Carlo, I need this ride to last as long as possible. It's the first time Abby's let me out of the house since my grandmother died—a whole week ago now! I even had to beg her to go to group. Which turned out to be a freaking disaster." I mutter the last part under my breath, but Carlo catches it and shakes his head.

"Not a nice word for such a nice young lady," he says, all fatherly-like.

I turn to study Carlo. Despite his clean shave and carefully combed hair—and that ridiculous chauffeur getup they make him wear—he has a rough and gritty look about him.

"Tell me, Carlo. Have you ever driven a truck?"

o o o o o o

It's nearly dark by the time Carlo punches in his code to open the driveway gates, and thankfully, everything looks quiet now—no more cars parked in the driveway, and the main downstairs lights are out. Carlo called the house to let them know about the big traffic jam at the bridge, so I'm not going to catch any crap from Abby, who would otherwise conclude that I blew off Gran's shivah to go out after group. She's totally rabid with me these days, as if what turned out to be a fifteen-minute outing with Teenage Waistland last week was the moral freaking equivalent of slipping into Gran's hospital room and pulling the plug. Add to that the lingering hostility from the Ronny-Liselle sector surrounding the dildo gag, and it's no exaggeration to say I'm entering enemy territory.

This place is so large my footsteps on the marble floor freaking *echo*, even though I'm treading as quietly as possible so as not to rouse the natives. I head straight for the kitchen. I can't explain it. It's like I have a kind of SAD—seasonal affective disorder. Sunlight or special full-spectrum lamps solve the problem for others; for me, refrigerator lighting. Ridiculous how soothing it is.

Tonight, though, I'm going further than merely basking in the glow of Abby's new Sub-Zero; if there ever was a time for a ménage à trois with Ben & Jerry, it's now. They're all I have. My mother hates me, my best friend since fifth grade had her frontal lobe removed when her Lap-Band went in and is now officially brain-dead, and the only person I've made a real connection with since I left Boston just turned out to be a lying sociopath. I spend a few moments deciding between Cookie Dough and Butter Pecan, but then a fresh rush of self-pity hits, and I grab both pints. I'm crying so hard, I can't see a thing—every freaking utensil I grab from the silverware drawer turns out to be a fork.

"There's a clean spoon over here, Marcie," a sickeningly

familiar voice behind me says. I put down the ice cream so that I can shove my glasses onto my forehead and wipe my eyes with my sleeve before I turn around. Liselle's standing by one of the dishwashers in a black tank top and size 0 Seven jeans, and she's dangling a tablespoon.

I grab the pints in one hand, walk over, and swipe for her spoon with my other hand. But Liselle pulls it away and holds it over my head.

"Marcie. Stop. You really don't want to do this, do you?" she says. I brush a tear from my face and nod. "C'mon. You're doing so well. How much now?"

"Thirteen pounds," I mumble miserably. A drop in the freaking ocean.

Liselle rummages in her handbag and pulls out a pack of cigarettes. "A much-lower-calorie addiction," she says. I snort, but it's a bad move—a ball of snot shoots out of my nose onto my lip. She sighs and hands me a napkin. "Come sit on the porch with me? We should talk." I stand numbly for a second, then return to the freezer and toss the Butter Pecan back. When I turn around again, Liselle's already gone. I grab the spoon she left on the counter and make it halfway to the staircase before turning back and trudging through the living room, out to the porch. This is how desperate I am to talk to someone.

Liselle's sitting on a wicker chair and she motions me to sit on the one next to her. I do so wordlessly. The first spoonful of ice cream hits my system, and I'm already calmer. Liselle lights her cigarette and inhales deeply.

"Don't say anything about this, okay?" she says, waving her cigarette. She flicks her ashes over the porch railing. I detect another smell—something different than cigarettes and perfume—and I realize she's been drinking. This explains her being nice to me.

"You shouldn't drink and drive," I mutter.

"What's the matter with you, Marcie? I haven't left the house in a week. While you've been holed up in your bedroom, I've been stuck down here chatting and making nice with all *your* family friends and relatives. Besides, I wouldn't ever drink and drive, and you know it—that was a nasty thing to say."

Crap. My worst enemy again. Liselle's mother was killed in a horrible car wreck—the drunken idiot who slammed into her was a retired policeman who walked away with a small bruise and a suspended sentence. I nod miserably. "I wasn't thinking. Sorry."

"That's okay, Marcie. There's something personal I want to tell you without you throwing it back in my face later." *Man, you are drunk,* my worst enemy wants to shout, but I give Liselle the nod/shrug combo and shovel another spoonful of ice cream into my mouth.

"My mother was six months pregnant when she died—with a girl. She had sorta been hoping for a boy to even things out, but I was ecstatic—I was dying for a baby sister! Even though she was never born, I always felt her loss too. Twelve years later, Abby enters our lives. She's lovely and warm, but the best part for me is that she comes with a daughter—you." A small tear winds its way down Liselle's face and I stupidly offer her the napkin I wiped the snot off my face with. She accepts it anyway.

"Finally, the little sister I could share things with, teach things to. Except it doesn't quite work out that way. My new sister turns out to be this snippy, angry, dildo-toting ballbuster who hates me from the moment she lays eyes on me."

"That would be me," I mumble, and hold up my spoon. "Sorry. About the dildo part."

Liselle laughs and shakes her head as she pulls out another cigarette. "The dildo part is the least of it, Marcie. And maybe if it were in a different size and color . . ."

I almost shoot my wad of ice cream across the porch. "*Nooo*—if you let me off so easily, I'll feel even worse about the whole thing," I laugh.

"*Nooo,*" Liselle says, shaking her head again and not laughing. "There's too much you feel bad about already. I'm trying to take this in the opposite direction."

I nod slowly and plow down another scoop of ice cream. "I get it. The beautiful princess takes pity on the poor little fat girl."

Liselle sighs. "Stop that, Marcie. I don't feel sorry for you. *You* do. The fact is, I envy you in a lot of ways."

I snort right into the ice cream container and examine the chocolate chips to make sure that's what they really are. "Name one, Liselle."

"Okay, you're really funny."

I wave it away with my spoon. "You've got potential in that department."

"All right," Liselle says. "You're a lot smarter than I am."

I nod—there's no getting around that. "Yeah, but so what? Being smart isn't important to you. And when you're beautiful, you get everything you want without having to be smart."

Liselle starts puffing furiously on her cigarette. "That's my point. When you're beautiful, you don't have to develop any skills or talents to get noticed or define yourself, so you only turn out to be what everyone expects you to be. Isn't that why anyone does *anything* in life? To be special? To be loved?"

"*That's* dumb, Liselle," I say. "People do things because they find them interesting, not so somebody will love them. Do you think Jen's poetry rants about men being nothing more than sperm donors is a personals ad in disguise?"

"Jen's exactly what I'm talking about!" Liselle exclaims, like suddenly her stupid notion is going to click and I'll see the light.

"Yeah, what about her?" I say.

"I searched for Jen online, Marcie—just today. There's not one poetry clip of hers left on YouTube—but I found at least twenty where she's jumping around in her little tights demonstrating some new exercise routine."

"I know she hadn't done any poetry rants in a while, but I didn't realize she took them down," I say slowly. "They were mad funny and got zillions of hits."

"Did you know she took down her Lap-Band blog too? In fact, I can't find one smart Jen anything on the Web—if you only knew her by her Internet footprint, you'd never know she was smart. Or ever fat. She's still out there trying to attract attention, Marcie. The difference is, now she has a more marketable product to sell," Liselle says. "I could add that she's switched her target market from angry feminists to, um, sperm donors, but then I'd sound too much like my dad and I'd have to kill myself." She laughs.

I am so furious at Jen all over again, I'm about to explode. "You're right! That stupid superficial witch. When she was fat and I wasn't, I didn't care one bit. I didn't care that I was like her only real friend—I always brought her wherever I went even though she wasn't invited. Someone even once told me that hanging with Jen made me look like I was 'as weird' as her, but I never even thought about how being with Jen affected how others saw me. But after I go to Mexico with her for her surgery, I have mine in *New York*, and she cuts out on me for some loser she just met. All that time, she never really cared about me—I was just the only one available. And when she got thin, she stopped needing me anymore! You know, she never even called or texted me. Not once after my surgery."

Liselle tosses her cigarette butt into the shrubs. "You amaze me, Marcie. How could you make this all about you? You left your best friend drunk and crying out for help in the middle of a strange city—you're damn lucky she remembered how to find your grandmother's apartment building or she could have been hurt! Jen needed you then, Marcie. She *needs* you now, more than ever! Don't you see how unhappy she is—how desperate? Where the hell are her parents? A sixteen-year-old girl is allowed to get breast implants and a lip job? Did you know she stole a bottle of my dad's twelve-year-old scotch when she was here July fourth weekend? Do you even know she's drinking?"

My Ben & Jerry's has melted on top, and I take a swig straight from the container.

"Okay, Marcie. Let's forget about how you've abandoned poor, sad, love-hungry Jen for the moment and talk about someone else you've taken great pleasure in hurting."

I make a Bitsylike sweeping motion giving Liselle the floor. "My life runneth over with morons. Who's up next?"

"Your gran," Liselle says gingerly, like she's afraid—with good reason—that she's going to set me off again.

"Oh, you also think I've done her wrong? She was on my back all the time telling me I wasn't good enough. What am

I supposed to understand about her that makes *that* okay?" I nearly shout.

Liselle motions me to keep my voice down and lights up another death stick. "Your grandmother was like from ancient times when the only thing women were supposed to do was get married," she says. "But she loved you a lot."

I shake my head vigorously. "Sure, she'd *say* how much she loved me. And then, in like the same breath, she'd catalog everything that was wrong with me. If I wasn't good enough for someone who loved me, what chance did I have with the outside world? That's why I couldn't—*wouldn't*—deal with her anymore. And I won't be a phony and sit down here acting like I gave a crap about her dying when I couldn't stand her alive. I don't understand why I can't get anybody to understand this."

Liselle takes a last inhale of her cigarette, leans forward, and snuffs it out in my ice cream. There was still a good five-hundred calories left. "What the fu—" I start, but Liselle puts her finger in front of her mouth and moves her chair closer.

"Marcie, I heard the saddest story in my life tonight at the shivah while you were at group. It was about your grandmother and I think you need to hear it. Especially now, with what's going on with Jen. But listen—don't say a word of this to anyone. Your aunt Lucy was sloshed when she told me, but afterward she was terrified that Abby would find out that I knew."

"Fine, I won't rat out the old lady, but nothing you tell me can change how I feel about my grandmother."

Liselle smiles. "Let's make a bet. If this story doesn't change your mind, I'll be your slave all summer and drive you wherever you want to go. But if it does, then you're going to clean up your act and take your crabby self-absorbed head out of your butt."

"Not an enticement, Liselle. You drive like a maniac. And I'll get my license soon anyway."

"Yeah, but I have a cool car," Liselle says.

"None of your nitwit friends will be in it with me, right?" I say. Liselle lights yet another cigarette. If Marlboros were ice cream, Liselle would be twice my size.

"Okay, Marcie. We have a deal. Until you decide you like my friends, they will not be in the car when I drive you around. Which I won't have to do, because you're going to lose the bet."

"Fine, but I don't see what you get out of this either way," I say.

Liselle smiles again. "That's okay—I do." Then she takes another puff and inhales deeply. "You know how your grandmother talked about her boyfriend, Michael? You know—how wonderful and successful he was. How he kept her in fresh flowers? Her whole 'he was the love of my life' rap?"

I nod. "They were together for over ten years or something—ever since my grandfather died. What about him?"

"Well, did you know that when your gran first got sick, she told Michael that she didn't want him to watch her waste away, that she wanted him to leave now so that he would 'always remember her as beautiful'?" Liselle's doing the air quotes thing. I let out my loudest snort ever.

"No, I didn't know that. What a drama queen!"

"Marcie," Liselle says softly. "He did it. He went away. Just like that. No more visits, no more telephone calls, no more flowers. He just disappeared. He didn't even show up to her funeral."

"He did it?" I am absofreakinglutely incredulous. "When Gran said, 'I want you to remember me as beautiful,' that was his cue to say, 'Darling, you'll always be beautiful to me, no matter what you look like.' "

"Of course!" Liselle says. "That's my point! Can you imagine how awful that was for her? Can you even begin to imagine how abandoned and alone and unloved she felt? It took your grandmother her entire lifetime to discover that beauty doesn't guarantee happiness, and that it doesn't guarantee finding love. Not one that lasts, anyway."

I hadn't realized Michael wasn't in her life anymore. She must have been heartbroken! And as heartbroken as she must have been about him, it was me she wanted to talk to at the very end. . . .

A lump begins to form in my throat, but then Liselle sniffles and I pull in closer and see that her eyes are wet. "Liselle, are you crying? You didn't do anything to Gran— you were really sweet to her." Liselle waves me away with her cigarette like she's fine, but then she starts crying even harder. "Liselle?"

"After I heard that story, Marcie, I felt so sad, and I needed to talk to you." She wipes her eyes with my snotty napkin.

"You needed to talk to me? That's why you came downstairs? You didn't take me out here because you knew I needed to talk to someone?"

Liselle shakes her head, sobbing harder. "It was about me. And then, when I saw you crying, it became a little about you too. But mostly, actually, it was about us."

I shake my head. "I have no idea what—"

Liselle interrupts with a combo laugh/sniffle. "Marcie, I envy you because you know who you are. I'm practically done with high school and I still have no clue who I am or what I'm good at. I was a complete spaz at cheerleading—I was only captain of the team because everyone voted for me. And that leaves me alone like your grandmother when I get old, because if people like me only for my looks, then what happens when I'm a shriveled-up hag?"

"Or if you get hit by a bus?" I add, probably not too helpfully. Liselle laugh/sniffles again.

"When I was up in my room crying, I thought if you knew I felt like this, maybe you wouldn't hate me anymore. And I didn't want to go off to college in September without taking one more stab at that little-sister fixation of mine."

Liselle wipes her nose again and looks up at me so sweetly—with such hopefulness in her eyes—that something in me cracks, and I erupt into sobs.

"See?" Liselle laugh/sniffles. "Gran's story changed how you feel. Time for Marcie to take her head out of her butt."

I take off my glasses and wipe my eyes on my sleeve. "Sorry, Liselle. You're driving me around all summer, even once I get my license. Gran didn't make me cry really. You did."

"Oh no!" Liselle shrieks.

"Don't worry," I laugh. "I'll consider removing my head from my butt anyway. Or at the very least, I'll make up with Jen—if she can ever forgive me for being such a horrible selfish person, that is." Liselle nods and wipes her nose again on my skeevy snotrag.

"Uh, Big Sistah?" I say. "Now that I've listened to you

whine about your problems, something major happened with Char at group tonight, and before I do something head-up-my-butt selfish again, I need to talk. Would that be okay?" Liselle smiles and nods. And then she bursts right back into tears.

28

the unforgiven

Marcie (-14 lbs)

Marcie Mandlebaum here, riding back into town with my faithful steed Carlo. My mission is to right a terrible wrong, and I'm packing a weapon far more powerful than a pistol— *information*. As soon as I can shoot some into East—and good aim will be critical because she, like Jen, hasn't returned one of my texts or phone messages all week—she'll *have* to forgive Char. Just like Jen will have to forgive me. And then, together, we'll set things straight with Teenage Waistland so that Char can return and get her surgery.

"Miss Marcie," Carlo says, "I hope you brought your shovel. That girl is in some deep you-know-what." Deep I-know-exactly-what. I'm still reworking my pitch for East when Carlo pulls up in front of Park Avenue Bariatrics.

"Same bat time, same bat-channel," I tell him as I open the limo door.

"Miss Marcie, you must wait for me to come around," he says, reaching the passenger side in time to close the door behind me. *Don't bet on it, Carlo. Miss Marcie's last name isn't Rescott.*

I get to the room about fifteen minutes early, but East is already there, along with Michelle, Lucia, and Alex. East's huddled in her seat away from the others, and I head straight for the chair beside her. Mobilizing East to see Char's side is going to be a nightmare—she looks *dour*.

"Looking good, East," I say as I plop down and stow my cell phone and my bag under my seat like I'm on a freaking airplane. "I bet you've lost more weight than anyone." She forces a smile. "Speaking to Char yet?" I say in a more hushed tone. Given my nonstop conversations with Char, though, I already know the answer.

East lowers her eyes. "No. And I'm not going to."

"Ever?"

East shakes her head.

"Never *ever*?" I say, eyes wide. East shakes her head more violently. "Wow, that's a crazy long time." For a split second, I think I have her, but East quickly purses her lips and fixes her eyes on the floor. "East," I say, "this is serious and we need to talk." I stand and gently take her arm. "Let's go out into the hallway."

East shifts her shoulder forward as if to escape my grasp, but I hiss, *"Please,"* and when we spot Bobby coming into the room, she reluctantly follows me out. We walk down the corridor in silence and turn down another hallway so we'll be out of view from the rest of the group as they arrive. When we stop, I move in to comfortable talking distance, but East backs away like a cornered animal, tears brimming.

"East," I say softly. "I know how awful this thing must be for you and I don't want to upset you further, but talking out what happened with Char will make things better." East looks me in the eye without bothering to hide her crying.

"Marcie, I've already talked it out. With my mother. And Char can go to hell! She goes after what she wants regardless of how it affects anyone else. After my father died, Char practically moved in with us, to comfort *me*, I thought. But she was really there to *screw my bob*—*my brother*. She was there to screw Julius!"

"You're shouting, East," I say. She's actually frothing, but I don't say that nor do I comment on the Bobby slip. The only one who *isn't* aware of East's crush on Bobby is probably Bobby himself, but if I even hint that East's anger toward Char might also have something to do with Bobby, she'll really flip out.

"Sorry, Marcie, but the truth is the truth. Char gets pregnant, but *Julius* has to leave town because *her* mother threatens mine with criminal charges. That doesn't make what Julius did right—my mom and I know that. But Char's not innocent either. She knew what she was getting into. She *wanted* him—*she* went after *him*! Julius was having enough trouble staying above water—we all were. Because of Char, I didn't just lose my father, I lost my brother too! And even my mother— If Julius had been around, maybe my mother wouldn't have shut herself up in her room. So you tell me," East hisses the last part, "how can *anything* make this better?" Tears are streaming down her face, and she crosses her arms tightly.

"I agree. It's horrible, and nothing can make *that* story better," I say softly, marveling at the sheer volume of East's verbiage. "*But*, that's the story from your perspective, East. Char has her own story, and it's only fair that you hear it before you end your friendship."

East laughs bitterly. "Char always has a story—she has

millions of them. I've watched her spin her webs of lies since we were toddlers. So I'd advise you to take Char's 'story' with a whole tablespoon of salt," she spits out—literally. There's a tiny bit of spit on my glasses. "Sorry," East mutters, and hands me a tissue from her pocket.

"Granted, Char has a knack for schmoo," I allow, "but can you remember even one time that Char lied with the intent to hurt someone?"

East frowns, a look not dissimilar to Liselle's *if you're so smart, why are you such an idiot?* expression. "No one lies to hurt other people, Marcie. They lie to protect themselves."

"Or to protect people they care about," I say. "Like you."

East puts on a tight smile and shakes her head. "Is that what Char told you? That she lied to protect me? Or was she honest about her lies? They're always just about her getting what she wants."

I shake my head. "East, I'm not here to justify Char's actions. I just want to tell you her story. Both your stories share the exact same facts, so Char's lying has nothing to do with this, okay?" East turns her face from me and crosses her arms again, but she doesn't move her body. I calculate that I've got maybe a minute before she storms off, so I decide to go with the abbreviated version.

"So, yes, Char did practically move in after your father died to comfort you, East. But she was a twelve-year-old girl who fell under the influence of an eighteen-year-old *adult* she had known and *trusted* all of her life. He gave her drugs and alcohol and then had, er, unprotected sex with her and got her preg—"

"So Julius is a pedophile and a rapist?" East rages. "Is *that* Char's story?"

I put my hand up to fend her off. "Wait—that came out wrong, East. Let me tell you a completely different story. About people you don't even know. Okay?" East slowly eases back against the wall.

"Once upon a time, there were two little girls named Mary and Elizabeth. They've been best friends since they were babies because their mothers were best friends since high school. Mary has a big brother named John—and Elizabeth has a huge crush on him. Nothing unreasonable about that—Elizabeth and Mary grew up together, so Elizabeth has also spent a lot of time around John."

"Group starts in three minutes." East is looking at the floor now and tapping her foot.

"So we've got two best friends, one with a crush on the other's brother," I continue, my words racing to meet the deadline. "On the day Mary turns twelve, there's a terrible tragedy in her family, and the world is turned upside down—for everybody, including her brother, who starts spending a lot of time in his room drinking beer and getting high. One night when Elizabeth gets up to go to the bathroom, she notices the light on in John's room. His door is slightly open. She pokes her head in to see if he's okay and they end up talking. She thinks she's being good company, and to be nice, he tells her she can try his weed. No pressure at all. To be nice back. Of course she accepts—he's treating her like someone his own age, not like the stupid-little-sister treatment she gets from her older sisters. The next time Elizabeth sleeps over, she gets up in the middle of the night and visits John again, and again, they smoke together. It's fun, but remember—even though Elizabeth developed early and looks way older than she is, she still has no experience as far as anything—drugs, boys, nothing!" I pause to take a breath. East is still with me—she's even looking at me now and her foot tapping has stopped.

"So John and Elizabeth are in his room, high. They kiss, and she's over the moon. He tells her it's a mistake, but the next time she visits, they take it further, and soon they're getting wasted and fooling around a little more every time Elizabeth spends the night. And even though John keeps saying, 'No more, never again,' it happens—again and again. And he's really so nice to her, never pushing. Elizabeth thinks John is in love with her like she's in love with him.

"One day soon after, though, John stops talking to Elizabeth. Stops cold. Won't even look at her. Elizabeth is heartbroken. In her mind, John has stopped talking to her because she's too young to go all the way. Obviously John stopped because he sobered up and realized that not only what he was doing with Elizabeth was wrong—it was *illegal*. He was eighteen and Elizabeth only twelve. That's *statutory* rape." I pause and quickly try to assess if my emphasis on *statutory* let *rape* slide in without ruffling East up too much. She's still watching me intently, so I move on.

"Elizabeth is devastated and tries to visit John during her next sleepover with Mary, but his door is locked, and he doesn't open it when she knocks. One night a few sleepovers later, though, his door isn't locked, and Elizabeth enters and says she wants to be with him. She takes off her nightgown, and drunk, with Elizabeth standing there naked, John gives in.

"Fast-forward six weeks after this all began, and Elizabeth realizes she's missed her period and she's peeing all the time. She goes online and suspects she's pregnant. So when Mary and Elizabeth go shopping with Elizabeth's mom, Elizabeth shoplifts a pregnancy test. And, lo and behold, she is pregnant. But before she has a chance to figure out what to do, her mom finds the positive pregnancy test wrapped in newspaper in the garbage in Elizabeth's bedroom and goes *ballistic*—she's got two daughters in college, but her *baby* is pregnant!"

East is crying, but her fist is pressed up against her mouth so that she doesn't sob out loud. I move in closer and gently push the hair out of her eyes, and she doesn't even flinch. It's happening. I am getting to her.

"So Elizabeth's mom whisks her away for an abortion. And as soon as they get back home her mom confronts Mary and John's mom. She demands that John be kept away from Elizabeth or she'll report him to the police—John would go to jail, not college. And by then, he has already been accepted into, er, Columbia University. Mary's mom, sick with grief and with concern over little Mary and, of course, John's sudden drinking, responds with 'So keep your slutty daughter out of my house, then!' and hangs up on her now former best friend.

"At this point, Elizabeth's mom has no choice. She forbids Elizabeth to set foot in Mary's house again or have anything to do with her entire family. Elizabeth goes insane and it takes her mother hours to calm her down and get her to rest. Later, when Elizabeth's mom hears a thud from upstairs and runs up to check on her daughter, she spots a bottle of painkillers. Unable to rouse Elizabeth she calls an ambulance just in—"

East starts shaking her head violently and making like she's about to take off. "Enough, Marcie, enough! I can't be late for group."

"Please, East," I plead. "Group can wait a couple of minutes. I'll hurry up and finish."

East relents, shrugging like I'm free to knock myself out if I feel like it. I hightail it to the finish line.

"While Elizabeth's in with the doctors having her stomach pumped, her mom completely loses it and calls Mary's mother, screaming that Elizabeth just attempted to kill herself.

"But a few days after Elizabeth and her parents get home from the hospital, her mom and Mary's mom meet at the corner to talk things out. Everyone's calmer now and the moms both agree that Mary and Elizabeth really need each other—now more than ever, and that to forbid them from being together would be too damaging to them both. Mary's mom promises Elizabeth's that John will finish the last half of his senior year at a boarding school hundreds of miles away and that she'll ensure he never sees Elizabeth again." I take a deep breath and close in for the kill. "You see how tragic this situation was for Char too, don't you, East? How everyone just wanted to protect you?"

But East's suddenly holding her hands over her ears and my mind races to remember other points I had planned to make. She cuts me off before I can formulate something else.

"Stop!" she cries. "I get the stuff that happened three years ago. But what about all the lies Char's fed me just in the past week? How about all the lies to everyone? Explain that!" East abruptly takes off down the hall and I dash off after her and grab her arm.

"Char wanted to tell you everything! The real story! From day one! The mothers made a pact to never tell you any of this, and they forced Char to swear to it—it was what *your* mother wanted. She said you had already been through too much. Don't you see, East? In order to protect *you*, she sent Julius away. It was almost like a choice—between you and your brother. And she chose you!"

East's eyes are brimming again, but she yanks herself free and breaks into a run. I take off again after her, but we both freeze as we round the corner. Abby is talking to Bitsy in the hallway in front of Teenage Waistland. They both spot us at the same time and watch as we approach. Mom's eyes are red.

"What? What?" I screech, breaking into a run again. My voice is shaking in panic, my mind racing with all the possible reasons why she'd be here. It's not Dad—we spoke just a couple of hours ago. And then, a vision of Jen standing alone in the middle of the city in the middle of the night crying for help pops into my head, and in the pit of my stomach, I just know. . . . Even before Mom wraps me tightly in her arms and murmurs, "Oh baby, thank God I got to you first."

29

LOST NOW, LOVED FOREVER

SUNDAY, AUGUST 9, 2009

East (-19 lbs); Char (-9 lbs)

Jen's plot is on a quiet hillside overlooking a mist-filled valley. There are only a few gravestones nearby. Inscribed on one is JANE REDDING, 1915–2005, and then below that, LOST NOW, LOVED FOREVER. The stone next to it reads SAMUEL REDDING, 1919–2003, CHERISHED HUSBAND, FATHER, SON, GRAND-FATHER.

My dad isn't buried near anyone we know. No trees or hillsides or valleys, just long rows of graves stacked tightly together as far as you can see. That's about all I can remember of his final resting place—Mom never went to visit him and I was always too afraid to ask her to take me. I can barely even remember the funeral. Except how I traveled to the cemetery in the backseat of Crystal's car with my head on Char's lap the whole way. The hearse wouldn't start in the funeral parlor parking lot, and my mom and Julius were inside waiting for someone to find jumper cables. I didn't want to be by myself in the family limo parked behind my father's coffin, so I got into Char's parents' car and stayed.

Char and I are standing under her big black umbrella at the second burial we've ever been to. The sheets of rain that pounded Abby's Land Rover throughout our four-hour drive have stopped, but there's a cold, light drizzle and water is running off the metal points of the umbrella onto my shoes—I'm fixating on the droplets that are wobbling around like liquid mercury balls on top of the black patent leather. Char's wearing sandals, and there are globs of cut grass sticking to her heels and unpolished toes. We're both struggling to keep our balance as our heels sink into the soft muddy ground.

People huddle closer around the graveside as Jen's coffin is lowered into the ground. In this cold dense fog, it's hard to make out Jen's family and Marcie and her family in the swarm of raincoats. But it's easy to hear them, even above the sixty or so people crying out from under their umbrellas, and the rabbi's prayer that other mourners softly join. Jen's mom is screaming, "My baby, oh my poor baby," over and over again, and Marcie's bent over heaving as if she's throwing up. Abby and Liselle are clutching her, one on each side, and Marcie's dad is holding her up from behind.

"Marcie looks terrible. So horrible." Char sniffles.

"I know," I say. I can't stop sobbing. The balled-up used tissues I'm clutching are so soggy they're falling apart, and I can't find any more in my pockets.

"Here," Char offers, ripping the last one in her pack in half. Suddenly the collective crying grows even louder. Jen's dad throws a shovelful of soil into the grave and hands the spade to Jen's mom, who just stands holding it limply until Jen's dad puts his arm around her like he's teaching her to golf and guides the shovel into the dirt and then the dirt onto the coffin. Next, other relatives do the same, and then Marcie and her family. One by one, people silently step forward, slice into the mound of dirt next to the grave, and empty it. The sound of rocks and pebbles hitting wood fades as the grave gets filled. Char and I approach to take our turns with the shovel and Marcie, her face swollen and devastated, smiles weakly at us and mouths, *Thank you*. Then Char and I step carefully as we make our way back.

"That was so frightening," I whisper. "Not just seeing the coffin get put in the ground like that, but filling the grave ourselves."

"It's a Jewish custom," Char says in a hushed tone. "Liselle warned me that we might find it upsetting—that it's *supposed* to be. The wisdom behind it, she said, is that when the mourners fill the grave themselves, it forces them to confront the reality of their loss head-on. It's more painful at the moment, but it starts the acceptance, which starts the healing."

I shrug. I confronted my father's body dangling at the end of rope, but the only healing I've experienced took place in my incisions.

The burial is over and people are making their way down the hill to their cars when Char touches my arm. "What I did after your dad died was terrible, East," she says. "I never meant to hurt you. Never. I hate myself. I was stu—"

"Please, Char. Not here."

"Yes here!" she says, and stops walking. "*We* need to bury this! It was such a terrible tragedy, and I made it worse! I'm so sor—"

"Please! When you called to ask if I wanted to come along to Jen's funeral to comfort Marcie, I told you that I didn't want to talk about any of this. And then I told you the same thing in the car on the way up here. Now I'm saying it again. It's done. I understand and I forgive you. Okay? Can we just let it lie?" I turn to head down the hill, but Char grabs my arm.

"It's so not done, East! I know Marcie spoke to you, but how can you and I ever get past this if *we* don't talk it out? I'm not trying to blame—"

I snatch my arm out of Char's grip. "Blame who? Julius? Fine. Here's what you get to blame Julius for, Char. You can blame him for bad judgment. It was the worst period of his life, he was drunk or high practically all the time, and he should have known better. If he wasn't drunk, I'm sure he would have used better judgment. So stop apologizing." Something moving on the hill behind Char catches my eye—it's Marcie crouching by Jen's grave. She's all alone—everyone else is grouped in clusters on the hill or heading for the parking lot. Char turns and watches her with me.

"At least we still have each other," Char murmurs, but I act like I don't hear. I'm about to suggest we go up to be with Marcie when we spot Liselle making her way toward us.

"Are you girls okay?" she asks. We nod and Liselle nods back as she continues up the hill toward Marcie. "Oh—we're going to stop briefly at Jen's family's house for a shivah call, and then it'll just be the four of us driving back—Marcie's spending the week with her dad." She smiles tightly and walks on.

"I'm glad that Marcie has Liselle now," I say softly. Char's eyes suddenly brim with tears, making them bluer and shinier than ever. The odd thing is, I just don't recognize them. "I'm going back down," I throw in.

"Shroud. P-please," Char stammers. "Please just talk to me." I don't turn around. Suddenly, Char crashes into me from behind and grabs at my arm for support, but not before her knees have hit the ground. She starts crying.

"C'mon, Char, get up. You're not hurt," I say. I yank on her arm to help pull her up but she refuses to budge.

"You don't forgive me! You have to!" she whimpers. I start to head back down the hill and leave her in the wet grass, but my anger resurfaces and I turn around again.

"I needed Julius. And my mom too. And he needed us. Because of you, we didn't have each other when we needed each other most. But yeah, Char. I even forgive you for that," I say through gritted teeth. "But here's the thing. When you were explaining why Jewish people fill the graves themselves, I was wondering why I was never able to accept my father's loss. And just this moment, as I left you alone in the mud, I realized that all this misery and weight gain and all the stuff you call awfulizing wasn't really about my father at all. It was about what *you* did to me."

Char's arms are hanging limply at her side and she's looking at me in complete bewilderment.

"You know what I'm talking about, Char. It was *you* who let me go on believing that my mother kicked Julius out because she wasn't up to dealing with his problems. Do you know how long I've lived in fear that if I did something wrong, if I had a problem, if I needed anything from her, if I wasn't the best little girl ever, she'd send me away too? As you said, I do what I'm told, no questions asked. *But that's why!* Do you know how much my mother's suffered alone for three whole years *needing me*, while I was in the next room choking on my own anger—my hatred for her for abandoning Julius? My fear of my mother, and my hatred for her was all because of you. And because of that hatred, I wouldn't even try to help her—talk to her about how she was feeling, convince her to get help, nothing. And here *you* were *supposedly* my best friend."

"East! You have to know that *we* kept this secret from you to save you from more pain—not make it worse. They made me swear to not tell you."

I laugh loudly in Char's face. "Suddenly Char Newman plays by the rules? You'll say anything to anyone to get what you want—to Bobby and Julius, to Teenage Waistland, to me, to everyone—you don't care what crazy lies you have to tell. But the one thing that might have helped me accept my father's death and saved me from drowning in all this fear and anger was the truth about why my brother got sent away, and that's the one thing you wouldn't tell me. Now get up and wipe yourself off. You're a mess and Abby and Liselle are waiting for us." This time when I head down the hill, I don't turn back.

o o o o o o

My eyes are closed and I'm huddled in the backseat of Abby's Land Rover shivering from the dampness. The engine is running and the heater is on, but I don't feel like I'll ever get warm. Abby and Liselle are with Marcie and her dad a few cars down, and Char, for all I care, is still on her knees in the rain. But I hear a door open and feel the weight on the leather seat as Char climbs in next to me. She slams the door loudly. I shrivel further into my corner and tighten my eyes.

"Okay," she says. "I should've told you the truth regardless of any stupid promise. I saw you suffering and I knew you so needed to know. But, y'know, East? Our moms were best friends from high school—at least twice as long as we've been, and this thing completely destroyed their friendship. I was terrified that it would wreck ours too. For a while, I kept thinking you would ask me why they stopped talking, but mostly I just worried. I didn't want to lose you—and I used their pact, to never talk of what happened to anyone, as my excuse not to tell you. So yes, that was selfish of me, I so understand that. *But* I wasn't *completely* selfish and you weren't the only victim." I feel Char watching me scrunch my eyes to keep myself from looking at her, and I'm starting to feel idiotic acting like I'm back in kindergarten, so I just open them.

"Okay, Char. I'm listening. Tell me who else got tangled in the spiderweb besides my brother and mother. And Bobby—you hurt him too, you know."

"Listen to yourself, East! I wouldn't have believed you were even capable of being so hard if I didn't actually see your lips move. And why are you bringing Bobby up? He's got nothing to do with Julius. Or us!"

I just stare at her coldly, and she stares back at me the same way for a couple of minutes until I drop my eyes. "All right, Char," I say. "You're right—I shouldn't have brought Bobby into this. Tell me how you weren't completely selfish and who else is on the injured-party list?"

Char's still staring at me. Her lower lip is trembling and

her eyes are filling up again. "Me. I was hurt, East. I'm still hurting," she says softly, her voice cracking.

Again, I'm staring at a stranger—but for a different reason. I can't remember a time—not one—that Char ever uttered a word of self-pity. I guess every relationship can hold only so much of it, and mine filled the quota. I can't remember ever having to pick her up and brush her off when she fell—but a million times it was the other way around. *I'm such an idiot.*

"Oh, Char. I know, Char. You were another victim of all this. You were. I'm so sorry about the—the . . ." I falter and cannot finish.

"The appendectomy?" Char says. There's a hint of a sad smile on her lips and I nod and burst into tears. But Char shakes her head. "It was awful; I was only twelve, and it was like getting a hundred tonsils removed, with no ice cream or anything to coat how raw and sad I felt. But when I say I was damaged too by this, *that's* only part of it."

"Is there yet another secret you're about to tell me?" I say, seesawing between sympathy and fear. Char shakes her head again.

"East, how do you not see? You were never alone in that pit—I've always been right there with you, not only feeling your pain but choking down *my* anger and *my* grief too. I've had to be strong and happy because you were so sad and helpless—I owed that to you and I wanted to be that for you. But that meant that I had to hide the reality and not face how I felt about the—my abortion. I felt it eating me up inside, but being what you needed had to come first. I felt I didn't have a right to heal because of what I did to your family. You know, being what you need whenever you need it has become such a way of life for me, I don't even know who I am—or if I even exist—without you. I know this sounds crazy, but that's how it is for me."

Char studies me for a moment, and then drops her head to study her hands, as if to say *If you don't understand this, I have no words left.* But I do understand, and this doesn't sound crazy to me at all. It's familiar—something I've always recognized in me and in my relationship with Char, but without being able to attach words to it. I feel a strange kind of relief—not happiness, but exhilaration. If truth could *feel* like something, it would feel like this.

"Char. I know what you mean. I *so* know. You've never let me cry alone. Or," I say between sobs, "eat alone."

But Char shakes her head again. "I did, East. For a little bit, after your surgery. I was just so upset about screwing up my own chances for the surgery because of the lie I've been carrying that I didn't have enough energy and I—I guess I just wanted a little something for myself, something that I didn't have to work so hard for in order to feel good about myself again." I'm just nodding. She's talking about Bobby. And, Marcie. And Teenage Waistland.

"Char—God—I'm so sorry about all that too. For screwing everything up for you. With Bobby and Teenage Waistland and everything. But you can still come back and try to work things out—I'll come with you to talk to Betsy," I say. "I know she'll let you back in."

Char widens her eyes and shakes her head forcefully. "East, I could never face those people again. They hate me, especially Bobby. And they totally should. I lied to them, I disrupted the group just to avoid addressing—ugh—everything we've just talked about. Nope—I'm on to the

next chapter in my life," she says. "And that is—ta-da—
Lap-Band surgery in Tijuana, Mexico. Three weeks from
today. Olé!" She dries her face with the back of her hand.
"Oh—I really mean the next chapter in *our* life." She laughs.
"Will you come with?"

30

UNDERLYING ISSUES

Marcie (-16 lbs)

Carlo and I have a running bet that—starting from the time we crossed over the Massachusetts state line into Connecticut a couple of hours ago—I'm going to spew one of my favorite "unladylike" invectives before he breaks down and lights up a cigarette.

"What word is that again, Miss Marcie?" Carlo goads me.

I pull out a pack of Camels from the glove compartment and wave it under his nose. He inhales deeply and I say, "What do you say we just screw the bet and light up one of these delicious death sticks?" But he grabs the pack in his right hand and lowers the window with his left, and out it goes. All without us swerving into oncoming traffic.

"Damn!" I exclaim. Carlo furrows his brow. "I'm still allowed to say that! You're the one quitting cold turkey, not me!"

My vocabulary isn't the only part of me I'm taking out of my butt (along with my head). Take Jill and me, for example. Poor Dad didn't get a word in edgewise all week. I even suggested that we all go away somewhere together over

Christmas break. And maybe even bring Liselle so I don't have to bunk with the cheesy lovebirds. Liselle and I have been texting back and forth constantly, and I miss her. And Mom. And even Ronny, who was such a sweetheart to send Carlo up to Boston to get me although I could have easily taken the train. I'm even sort of looking forward to getting back to Alpine. But first stop is Teenage Waistland, even though Bitsy said I could skip this session if I wanted. If not for Char agreeing to meet East and me for dinner afterward, I'd blow this sucker off in a heartbeat.

o o o o o o

Teenage Waistland is finishing its "round-the-room" confessional where everyone cops to their eating sins—Bitsy calls this the eating behaviors review—when I tiptoe in, but I could've pulled the pin on a hand grenade and gotten the same reaction. *Hey, it's Marcie! Mar-cie! How are you, girlfriend! Oh, so sorry about Jen, Marce!* And Bitsy's not even having an aneurysm over everyone shouting out—actually, she jumps out of her seat before I'm halfway to the circle and hugs me!

"It's good to see you, Marcie. I'm so happy you came. How are you holding up?" she says warmly.

I smile and mumble, "Fine, thanks." And then I feel heat on my cheeks—a blush? WTF?

I quickly take my seat in the circle next to East, and then I stand right up again and ask her to kindly remove her purse from my butt—under my breath for the most part. A couple of chuckles erupt in the circle, but Bitsy just smiles placidly— as if she's got bigger plans for me than a little "shush."

"Marcie," Bitsy starts, "first, again, we are all so sorry—

the group is devastated over Jennifer's death and deeply sorry for the pain and loss you're dealing with. Such a terrible tragedy. She was a smart, lovely, engaging young lady. I'm glad everyone here had the chance to get to know her better at Coco's party." I see Coco and Michelle exchange glances.

"Yeah, well, I guess Jen got to know Jose Cuervo a little more than she did some of you guys. She was awful that night, I know, but she was going through, I don't know . . . some stuff. Really, Jen was an exceptional person," I say. My eyes tear up and East hands me a tissue.

"Can you talk about Jennifer, Marcie? The kinds of 'stuff' she was going through?" Bitsy says. "If it's too soon, I understand—"

"No," I cut in. "I want to talk about her. I miss her and I'm never going to *not* talk about her." The periodic tear is winding its way down my face, and as I glance at East, she shows me her open purse—*wads* of tissues—and gets a clean one ready for me. "Jen's toxicology report came back yesterday. Alcohol poisoning." I stop and let the group do their gasping. I shrug. "Jen has—*had*—been drinking. A lot."

"Since she'd gotten the Lap-Band?" Bitsy says too carefully for me *not* to see where she's going. I feel an unexpected burst of rage.

"She's not your *freaking* group lesson!" I explode. "She was my best friend and I already feel badly enough about what I did to her!" East's ready with the tissue, but I knock it away. Immediately sorry, I gently remove it from her still-outstretched hand with an apologetic smile.

"What do you think you did to Jen, Marcie? When

someone close to us dies, we always think, 'If only I did this,' or, 'If only I didn't do that,' " Bitsy says softly, as if I didn't just go off on her the second before. My hands starts to shake, but I'm going to cop to my horrible deed, here and now, in front of everyone.

"Jen came down to New York to be with me during my surgery—we always did everything together and I was with her when she had hers. Except, she had too much to drink at Coco's party and the next morning—the day before my surgery—she said she felt sick and just wanted to go home. But she didn't go home—she went to hang out with the guy she had met the night before." I don't even look at Coco. It's not her fault and I don't want her to think I blame her in the least. "So I spend the night before surgery alone in my room trying to get Jen on the phone, and my calls are going to voice mail, so I figure she's just home sleeping it off. Except, she calls me after midnight drunk and crying, but all I can hear are the sounds of New York City traffic in the background and all I can think is that my best friend abandoned me *for a guy* at the moment I needed her the most. Except, I didn't realize how much Jen needed *me*. Not only at that moment—when she was alone in the middle of the city at night—but in general. I slammed the phone down on her and turned it off. And that was the last conversation we ever had. But there's not one day that goes by that I don't play back each and every message she left for me that night, crying and begging for me—" I can't finish. It hurts so much, I double over from the pain and howl into my hands. I feel East's hand on my back, and when she strokes my hair, I cry even harder. And then more hands are on my shoulders and back, and when I look up, they're all there—

Teenage Waistland, standing around me, trying to give some comfort.

"Thanks, guys," I manage to say. I try to make eye contact and smile at every one of these wonderful people—even Tia— as they slowly move away and back to their seats. "Jen was drinking and she did show signs of being in trouble, but all I could think about was what I was going through and what she did to me—how she made *me* feel. Everything was about me, and I don't blame Jen for not returning my calls and not accepting my apologies. I've been such a horrible friend that, honestly, when you ask me what 'stuff' Jen was going through, I don't know how much I can even tell you!" I break out into hysterical tears again, and this time, East just passes me a thick wad of tissues. There's another hand on my shoulder, and I see Bitsy's sensible loafers on the floor next to my feet.

"Marcie," she almost whispers. "The way things ended with you and Jen was tragic, but it's important that you don't take the weight of this on yourself. Jen was troubled, but had she not died when she did, she would have forgiven you, I just know it. Please. Try hard not to put this on yourself. She's gone now, and if, in Jen's honor, you can start focusing more on other people, even when you're in pain yourself, it will help you heal from this. I promise. And the next time someone you care about is in pain, you *will* be there for them. That's the only constructive way you can think about this now. Okay?" I nod. Somehow, I even feel comforted. "Marcie, I think you can use Jen's experience to help everyone here. Would you mind if we talked more about her now?"

"Sure," I whimper. "Anything." And that I say in a strong, clear voice.

Bitsy moves away and starts pacing the circle. "Can I ask when you first noticed Jen's problem with alcohol?"

"I'm not sure," I say. "I mean, I first smelled alcohol on her breath the day she came to group, but I'd guess she started telling me about drinking at parties maybe four months ago. That was also when she started feeling good about herself and she became outgoing and sociable. I thought she was happier, if anything."

"What was Jen like before her surgery?" Bitsy says as her pacing picks up speed.

"Jen was mad smart," I say. "Super creative—she wrote a lot of poetry. And sarcastic. She put even me to shame in that depart—"

"Okay, sarcasm is a defense," Bitsy cuts in. "What was she defensive about? Her weight?"

That's an easy one. "Of course. Jen was fat from the day she was born, and taking crap from kids about it. Eventually she developed a tough exterior."

"Marcie, would you agree that Jen turned to food for consolation because it made her feel better—momentarily, anyway?" Bitsy says.

"Of course," I say. "Who doesn't?"

Bitsy nods enthusiastically. "What did Jen need to be consoled *about?*" she says.

"Being a whale, obviously," Tia mutters. Bitsy throws her hands up. "Sorry for interrupting," Tia says more quietly, but Bitsy shakes her head.

"Yes, I understand that Jen's weight affected her physically and socially and therefore made her feel worse—that's the addiction *cycle*. But what bad feelings started the cycle? Why did she turn to food in the first place?"

"Food was obviously Jen's drug of choice," I say.

"What you said wasn't quite as obvious as you think," Bitsy counters. "Why did you call it a drug?"

I shrug—that's just something my mother always says, but then I remember something specific. Shortly before we moved to Alpine, Mom walked in on Dad reading a book, an Entenmann's chocolate cake on his lap—it was resting on his belly, actually—and she snarled, "Why don't you just wind down with a martini like normal people?" My hand shoots up even though I already have the floor.

"In my family, if you feel bad, you head for the fridge, or if someone wants to show their love, they cook something special for you," I say.

"Or give you a lollipop to make you feel better after a vaccination," Lucia cuts in.

"Excellent!" Bitsy says. "Anyone else?"

East hesitantly raises her hand. "I guess it's the same thing as when someone shows their indifference by *not* cooking for you," she says.

"Beautiful, East," Bitsy nearly shouts. "Okay—food is often used as an expression of love, which is why it often translates into a *substitution* for love, or a perceived lack of love. So now, let's go back to Jennifer. Marcie, do you think Jen's eating was an attempt to compensate for something she needed but couldn't get? That she was trying to fill an empty space?" Bitsy returns to her seat.

"Totally," I say. "I mean, aside from not having many close friends and all, her mom was always stressed and her father works for the State Department—he was always out of the country. He was even late to her funeral—he flew in from Shanghai. So she had this whole feminist 'men suck' thing going. But as soon as she got thin, she couldn't get enough of them—older guys, especially!"

Tia snorts. "What girl in this room doesn't have daddy issues?"

"What guy in the room either?" Bobby mumbles, shaking his head. I glance at East, who's got the granddaddy of all daddy issues, but her eyes are clear and wide open.

"*Everyone* has some sort of something," Bitsy says. "And we all try to comfort ourselves in some way, whether it's with food, alcohol, drugs, sex, exercise, et cetera. Sometimes the need for this source of comfort gets so excessive, it becomes an issue in itself. Look at the definition of *addiction*—when the source of comfort has become such a constant necessity that it affects one's mental, physiological, or social well-being, that's when it becomes an addictive behavior. This has been my point from the get-go, guys. There's a reason you all are here, and your weight is only its symptom.

"That's why I have you examining your emotions when you record your food. Observing the connection between psychological need and food intake enables you to recognize the difference between physical hunger and emotional hunger and *that's* what's going to enable you to lose your weight and keep it off. Again, your Lap-Band is only a tool." Bitsy looks around the room triumphantly. Coco's hand shoots up and Bitsy nods at her.

"But if the band *is* only a tool, why was Jen able to lose weight with it?"

"Coco raises an excellent point!" Bitsy says. "Studies have shown that not only does sugar have the same addictive properties as drugs that are considered addictive, but that it can actually serve as a gateway to drug and alcohol abuse."

"Right. From candy canes to cocaine," Tia quips, and Michelle elbows her.

"What I'm getting at is the fact that foods containing sugar go down very easily with the Lap-Band, so we don't see food replaced by another drug very often with Lap-Band patients. The worse thing that typically happens is that they keep eating sugary foods and they don't lose weight. In Jen's case, she probably assumed it was food that was causing her unhappiness, so while she was able to stick to the Lap-Band diet, she probably substituted sugar with alcohol to escape her emotional hunger.

"Jen wasn't in counseling at all, was she, Marcie? For example, a support group like Teenage Waistland?"

"Nope," I say. And there it is again. The cat-that-ate-the-canary expression. This time, on Bitsy's face.

"Okay, people. By a show of hands—who *now* believes that their weight is their only problem?" I scan the circle. Bitsy seems to have gotten to everybody—Bobby looks slightly miserable but he's picking furiously at his fingernail, Alex's eyes are darting back and forth like he's deriving some bold new theorem, and most of the girls are even a little teary.

"We're really getting somewhere now, aren't we?" Bitsy says softly. "See you all next week. And Marcie, here's my cell number. Please call me if you need to talk."

o o o o o o

We're on the elevator heading down and East hasn't uttered a word since we left the room. I'm at a complete loss until Bobby coughs and I realize he's right behind us. *That's* why she's not speaking. Jeez.

I'm toying with the idea of telling Bobby that Char'll be meeting us in the lobby in ten or fifteen minutes, so maybe he'd like to wait with us—Char wanted to make sure Teenage Waistland already cleared out before she arrived, but she's *got* to want to see Bobby. The nanosecond the elevator opens, though, Bobby swiftly maneuvers around East and me and sprints off. Once he's halfway across the lobby and almost at the exits, East finally gets her voice back.

"Sorry. I wasn't ignoring you. I just didn't want—*Holy crap!*" She elbows me sharply and points to the bank of glass doors. Char's coming in the exact same door that Bobby's headed toward. There's a crowd of people going in and out around them, but there's no way they can miss each other. East and I hurry through the lobby for a better view, but there's nothing much to see. Bobby takes one quick look at her and flies out the door. By the time we reach Char, she's standing in front of the doors bewildered and in tears like a child who's lost her mother in a department store, completely oblivious to all the suits and briefcases attempting to detour around her.

East hugs her tightly and rubs her heaving back while I recite, *What a dickhead, what a dickhead,* over and over until she calms down. Then each of us take an arm and lead Char out of the building.

○ ○ ○ ○ ○ ○

Tonight, it's a Greek diner on Seventy-fifth Street—in the opposite direction of Chow Fun House; East mentioned she's in the mood for chicken salad after Char finally stopped sniffling, and Char didn't put up any resistance. We didn't talk much at all on the way over. Once Char instructed me to stop calling Bobby a dickhead, I was pretty much at a loss for something to say, and Char certainly wasn't her usual chatty self. Which left any prospect for conversation in poor hands, since East is where words go to die.

Except, as soon as we're led to our booth, East suggests that Char go to the ladies' room and fix her face. Poor Char's mascara isn't on her eyes anymore, it's under them, and she looks like a raccoon. The second Char's out of earshot, East grabs my arm and hisspers, "We have to talk."

"East—I'm sitting directly across from you and I'm not going anywhere. Unhand me and talk." She's so flustered when she removes her hand that her elbow hits the water glass and I have to catch it to avoid catastrophe.

East leans forward, her eyes darting around to make sure Char hasn't magically left the ladies' room without the door—in our direct view—opening. "Char is going to Tijuana in just over two weeks to get a Lap-Band. Her mother has already booked the flights."

I think this over for exactly 0.3 seconds and holler, "No!" I clamp my hand over my mouth—everyone's staring at us and East is slumping in her seat and primed to crawl under the table. "She didn't tell me anything about this," I whisper. "Am I not supposed to know? Did Char tell you not to tell me?" East shakes her head. "Well, okay," I say in a normal voice. "We'll just have to talk her out of it." East shakes her head again.

"I've already tried. She's set on doing it."

"Even now? Even with Jen? Didn't that send up any warning signs for Char?"

East rolls her eyes. "She broke the news to me at the cemetery!"

"Did Char ever get any professional help whatsoever after that whole abortion thing?"

East flinches. "No, I seriously doubt it. I don't remember her disappearing after school, ever."

"Well, let's just tell her about what happened in group today. How you and I realized that there is something to all that 'dealing with the underlying problem' stuff," I say. "That Jen didn't deal with her issues and look how it turned out for her."

East shakes her head again and gives me a respectable *what kind of freakin' moron are you?* look. "Let's be real, Marcie. Betsy's been trying to explain the same stuff to us for weeks and we didn't get it. You think Char's going to get it just like that?" East says, snapping her fingers. "Trust me. I have thirteen years of experience trying to talk Char out of whatever she's had her heart set on at the time, and it's never happened. Not once."

"Okay—I got it! Let's talk her *into* rejoining Teenage Waistland. Bitsy will make sure Char's dealing with things properly—or is at least willing to—before she clears her for surgery. And we can help her."

But East is shaking her head yet again, and I'm ready to throw the condiments on the table at her, starting with the maple syrup.

"I've suggested that already," East says in a whiny voice, like I'm spouting the obvious and completely useless. "But she said she can't go back—she's too ashamed to face Bobby. And the rest of the group."

I put my head in my hands. "And after today's terrible

run-in with him, she's going to be even more resistant to facing him."

"Unless . . . ," East says, leaning forward.

"Unless what?" I whisper urgently. "Hurry—she'll be coming back any second!"

"Unless we talk to Bobby like you talked to me. Once he understands why Char lied about everything, he'll forgive her. And once *he* forgives her, she'll want to come back!" East says triumphantly.

Now I'm shaking my head. "East, do you really think Char's going to let us explain to Bobby that she had an abortion at age twelve and then *maybe* attempted to kill herself afterward? If so, I agree with you: once he knows those things, he'll understand why Char *had* to hide the reason she wasn't cleared for surgery, which forced her to lie about having had the surgery." I stop to take a breath. "But it's tricky. Once he knows those things, do you think he'll still want to be with her? It's heavy, and their *thang* has only been going on, what, three—"

"She's coming out!" East whispers. She's frantic and rearranging the menus and the napkins as though their disarray will tip Char off that we've been discussing her.

"East, calm yourself and listen carefully! Your job is to talk Char into giving us permission to tell Bobby *everything*." She's nodding nervously like I'm reciting a grocery list and she's supposed to memorize each item. "East, it's *one* thing."

"So what's your job?" East asks as she smiles and waves at Char.

"My *job* is having the stepsister who's going to take us to him, of course." Char's perfume hits my nostrils and I jerk back in my seat and pick up a menu.

"Oh God, you're not really thinking about getting a job this late in the summer, are you, Marcie?" Char says. Her face is clean and she's looking better.

"Nah. I'm just going to sit back and live the good life in old Alpine, New Jersey. There are worse places to be."

31

Football Practice

Bobby (-25 lbs)

I'm knocked flat on my back again for like the fiftieth time today, the latest humiliation courtesy of Freddie LaRocha, who's looking tanned and meaner this year. He's got a good twenty pounds on me these days—I'm down about twenty-five since the surgery. It would've been more, but I've been lifting super heavy the last week or so to make up for lost time. MT offers me his hand.

"Down again, you virgin wussy. What's up with that?" he says as he pulls me to my feet.

"Just rusty," I mumble. I'm sore all over from the squats and bench presses I did this morning *after* my ten-mile run, but lifting after practice would be worse. Dad's home by then, and he'd be on my case over every rep. He kicked my butt so hard this weekend, I'm lucky I can move at all today.

Coach's got his hands on his hips and he's looking at me like I just handed the winning play over to the opposing team in a crucial qualifier. "You're off, Konopka. Quit daydreaming and step it up." He blows his whistle and waves the guys in. Then, as he's leaving the field, Coach calls out, "Tomorrow, ten a.m. Our first preseason game is coming up quickly, and you guys are looking pretty lame."

"Game, lame. You're a real poet, Coach," Craighead says as he sprints in and pulls off his helmet. Then he swings around and whips the helmet into my chest-protected gut— the only place on me that *isn't* hurting. "You owe me twenty bucks, Konopka. I had my money on you, dude, and you let me down."

I yank Craighead forward with his helmet and slip him into a headlock. No matter how tired or pathetic I am, being able to take Craighead is a given.

"That hot-sex-on-a-volcano story is crap," I snap, pulling him in tighter. "What proof does MT have anyway?"

"MT—show him," Craighead yells as he struggles against my grip. MT, over by the bleachers chugging Gatorade, puts the bottle down and strides over all cockylike. Like he's rehearsed this. He reaches into the front of his sweats and rips out a tiny red lace thong. There's more fabric in my sweatband.

"So that's what you're wearing lately, MT?" says Zoo, running over so he doesn't miss any action. I release Craighead and use my freed arm to give Zoo a high five.

"Funny, dick. They're Alicia's. Volcano Girl proof," MT says, twirling the panties around on his finger.

"Nah—they're his mother's," LaRocha chimes in. Benny, Todd, and a few sophomores from the second string head over, and there's now a small crowd gathered to inspect Volcano Girl's thong.

"Like they don't sell those at Walmart, jerk-off," Zoo says. MT's eyebrows are up and he's grinning broadly, still twirling the thong. "Oh, yeah? How about Camp Trivia for a hundred. How do kids keep track of their clothes?"

"People know their own clothes," I mutter. I don't do camp—I'd be the last to know.

MT makes a buzzing sound. "Sorry, Konopka. The correct answer is: What are name labels?" The guys start howling as MT untangles the thong and turns it inside out. "Alicia Conroy!" he announces, thrusting the panties and the name tag into everyone's faces. MT scores and the crowd goes wild. The label looks legit.

"You're smoked," Craighead says.

"The Refrigerator is da freezah. Dude is froze," LaRocha pipes up.

"Brrr," a bunch of guys repeat. "Brrr. Brrr. Brrr."

"So, Bobby—ready to concede defeat? Unless you scored with those—*cough cough*—Manhattan babes of yours?" MT says, still grinning and getting in my face.

"Give my boy space." Zoo pushes him back.

I don't even care anymore about being the last virgin standing—these guys can be such morons. But I'm tired and my muscles ache, and the heckling is pissing me off. Plus, I don't need to explain myself in front of these sophomores. It's none of their business. "Screw off," I mutter, and walk toward my mom's car, the guys cracking up behind me. Then a gorgeous blonde in tiny white shorts walking toward me from the parking lot starts calling my name. I think I must be having heatstroke or that the late-afternoon sun is screwing with my eyes. I pick up my pace—the guys aren't that far behind and I know they're watching.

"Bobby?" this beautiful girl says, and I nod. It's a girl I've never seen before. "I'm Liselle Rescott, and there are some people who need to talk to you." She motions her head toward a silver convertible off by itself in the corner of the parking lot. East and Marcie are sitting inside looking in our direction. Char's not with them.

"Sure," I say. I turn around and hold my helmet up and sort of wave at the guys, hoping they got a good view of her. And also that they take the hint to back off. "See you tomorrow," I yell. Then I turn back toward the parking lot and walk up the hill with Liselle.

"I'm Marcie's stepsister," Liselle says as we approach the car.

"Yeah, I heard that," I say, and immediately regret it. I don't want to be tied to that dildo thing in this girl's mind.

"Marcie and East were afraid you wouldn't talk to them, so they sent me out to find you," she says, ignoring my stupid comment.

"How did you? Find me, I mean," I say. I glance behind me and see that Zoo, MT, and Craighead have lost the rest of the group, but they're still heading my way—*not* in the direction of their parked cars. Crap!

"Oh, that was easy." Liselle laughs. "You're the only Konopka in Syosset, and when we got to your house, your mom sent us here. She's very nice, your mom. She invited us in to wait for you, but we thought we should speak with you alone."

I'm pretty sure I know who this is all about, but I don't see any way of avoiding the conversation—the guys are like twenty seconds behind us. I glance back again and Liselle, maybe sensing I'm about to make a break for it, says, "Hop in the back, Bobby. We'll go get something to drink."

Liselle's ride is sweet—a sleek 2008 BMW M6 convertible.

Damn thing has a V10 engine and 500 horsepower. But I don't have much time to drool over this beauty because Marcie, in the front passenger seat, and East, in the back, are both glaring at me.

"Hi," I say as I climb into the seat next to East. Already I feel like an idiot. Little sports car—the two of us can hardly fit and our legs are riding up against each other. Liselle slams on the gas, propels the car backward, and then zooms off through the parking lot and onto the street.

"Where to?" she asks.

I give her directions to Buetti's deli and immediately realize how fried my brain must be; that's a prime destination for the guys after practice. "Let's make it the Wendy's on Route 25A—just turn left here."

The wind is blowing everyone's hair around like crazy, and East is trying frantically to keep it out of her face. The breeze feels great, and we're going so fast, I'm hoping it's carrying away the smell of my sweat. Marcie's feet are pushed up against the dashboard and she's screaming, "Liselle, you're going to get us killed!" Between the roar of the engine, Marcie screaming, and the wind, it's way too loud to talk, until in two seconds, we whip into the Wendy's parking lot and Liselle cuts the engine.

"I'm going to get us drinks," she says as she hops out of the car and walks toward the restaurant. Her shorts are riding up and it's hard not to watch. Impossible.

East is smoothing her hair and Marcie is cleaning her glasses with her T-shirt. My chest protector is cutting into my hip, and I try to unhook it through my shirt. *Unhooking a frickin' bra.* Not a skill I have.

Marcie notices and says, "That thing working?"

"Yeah," I say. "Great idea you guys had."

Marcie turns around in her seat and locks eyes with me. "No," she says, "not 'guys.' Char. It was *her* idea."

"How's she doing?" I say, like everything's totally fine and we're just a group of normal kids chilling.

"Char's why we're here," Marcie says. "She thinks you hate her."

"Nah," I say, "I don't hate anybody. Why would she think that?"

Marcie looks at me like I'm an idiot. "Because you pretty much ran face-first into her after group on Friday and then bolted without a word."

"This is what you came all the way out here to talk to me about?" I say and push the driver's seat forward to reach the door handle. Marcie locks the door from the controls on her side and I laugh and manually pull up the lock. She locks it again as I go for the door handle.

"This isn't a game," she says. Not a fun one, anyway. "Look. East and I think you need to understand why Char lied about the surgery to everyone." Not everyone. *Me.*

"Maybe if Char thought I should know, she would have told me herself," I say, and then mentally kick myself for sounding like a girl with all their analytical nonsense. I push the front seat forward again, but Marcie crawls over the stick shift and slams it back with the full force of her body. Now she's peering over the driver's-side headrest, her face maybe six inches from mine. I drop back into my seat.

"When we tell you the story, you'll understand why Char couldn't tell you herself," Marcie says. "So please, just hear us out."

I throw up my hands. "Shoot." Marcie glances at East,

who nods back at her. Right. Like East was going to do the talking. Marcie takes a deep breath as if what she's about to tell me is earth shattering. Just girl drama, probably.

"Park Avenue Bariatrics put Char's surgery on hold because they had questions about something in her medical history, something Char *couldn't* own up to and talk about because it—it could have destroyed her friendship with East. I mean, it didn't, but it could have." Marcie stops and looks at East again, but East's head is turned away, like she's finding this big green Dumpster really fascinating.

"Look, Marcie, I gotta hit the shower and head to my dad's store. Is that it?"

Marcie glances again at East, but she's still looking away. "No. When Char was only twelve, she got pregnant and had to have an abortion. She was so freaked out about it that she took some painkillers she wasn't supposed to. That's what's in her hospital records and that's what Char was hiding."

A wave of nausea passes over me. "Man, that's bad," I croak. "I had no idea Char was raped." The car is spinning even with the engine off. I hope I don't throw up.

"Don't be stupid," East blurts. "She wasn't raped. It was an accident." I stare at East for a second, and then look at Marcie.

"Nobody hurt Char or forced her to do anything, don't worry about that," Marcie says. "So you understand why she lied and forgive her, right?" She's studying my face. I know I should be relieved that Char didn't get attacked or anything terrible like that, but apparently I'm *not* her first boyfriend, let alone her first *real* kiss. I'm not her first *anything*. It's not like she had to tell me about every guy who came before me, but she didn't have to carry on about what a big "first" I am for her. I guess that's just her rap—when she's sixty, she'll be kissing some old pharmacist guy, flinging her hair and giggling, "That was my first real kiss."

"Yeah, of course. It's bad, and I get it," I say again.

"Sorry I took so long," Liselle says, placing a tray of beverages on the hood of the car. "I got you guys unsweetened iced tea. How's it going?" It takes her half a nanosecond to see not so well. Marcie is clenching her headrest like it's my neck and East is glaring at me again. Liselle sighs. "That's not your feet on my leather?" she says to Marcie, and Marcie jumps out of the car and brushes off the seat. When she turns to grab her drink, I push the driver's seat forward again and climb out too.

"That's okay, Bobby," Liselle says, handing me my drink. "I'll take you back to the high school."

"Nah, that's okay," I say. "But thanks for the tea." I back away from the car and wave at Marcie and East. "Thanks for coming. I appreciate it, I do," I call out. I suck down the tea, and then turn around and start walking. I'll probably catch up with some of the guys at Buetti's and get a ride from there. I hear a car door slam and then footsteps on my tail.

"You're not going to forgive her, are you?" a voice wails. I spin around. It's East and she's not only *speaking* to me, she's bounding toward me like she's out for blood. I stop and wait anyway.

"Are you?" she says again when she's about two feet away. "Don't you care about Char at all?" She's all teary, but she looks more likely to punch me than burst out crying. I don't know what to say.

"Why can't you just tell her that I understand about why she lied and there are no hard feelings?"

"So, you forgive her?" East says, moving even closer.

"Yeah, sure. No problem. I forgive her," I say. It's a lot to take in. I shrug and take a step back. But East takes another step forward.

"Which means you're going to *call* her, *right?*"

"I—I don't know." I turn away and break into a slow jog. The chest protector straps are biting into my back, and I'm picturing the stockroom again, and how Char looked at me—hell, through me—with her big blue eyes and I told her she was the first girl I ever really kissed, and then she said that I was her first too. My stomach won't stop churning. "Just leave me alone, will you?" I yell over my shoulder. And then I break into a full run.

32

Banding Together

East (-23 lbs); Char (-9 lbs)

"Thanks for saving me the perfect seat, East," Marcie says loudly as she dumps her bag under the chair and slides in next to me. "This way I can stare the jerk down all session long." Bobby's slumped in his chair and he looks deep in thought examining his fingernail, but there's no way he didn't hear her.

I'm such an idiot. I'm good at geometry, and I've got all the formulas for calculating angles and arcs in circles completely memorized. But I didn't know the most important thing about circles until today—when you seat yourself at the furthest possible point from somebody else in the circle, you find yourself sitting directly across from them.

"Lookin' good, girl!" Michelle yells as Lucia enters and lugs herself across the room to the circle. "How'd weigh-in go for you?" Lucia gives her the thumbs-down as she sits. "Down is good, right?" Michelle says. Lucia just hangs her head. Michelle glances at Marcie and me with widened eyes. "Oops," she says.

"How'd your weigh-in go?" I whisper to Marcie.

Marcie shrugs. "Down about eighteen pounds in what—five and a half weeks since the surgery?" she mutters. "No big deal."

"Eighteen pounds is a *very* big deal," Betsy says as she takes the remaining empty seat and crosses her legs. "That's a rate of three pounds a week, and you haven't even had your first fill." She glances at her clipboard. "Most of you have lost between twelve and twenty pounds, even a few over that already. So. Feel any different?" She nods at Alex to her left to kick it off. Alex frowns for a second, then he just flips his arms over so that his palms face upward and shrugs.

"Whoopie?" he says. "I'm not sure what kind of response you're looking for. I'm sure that losing a little weight makes us all feel more optimistic, but a few notches on my belt doesn't exactly change my life."

Betsy smiles. "So does everyone feel the same way—that weight loss of this magnitude isn't momentous enough to feel anything different about?" Pretty much every hand goes up. "Okay, so this is another one of Jen's 'secrets encoded in fat cells' moments for me." She laughs. Nobody's saying anything—or laughing either. Marcie is just staring dully at Betsy. There's no reaction or emotion in her face—it's just like her eyes are resting on Betsy because they have nowhere else to go. Lucia raises her hand and Betsy nods at her, looking relieved. That's something that Char always did here—jump right in and rescue everyone so that they didn't feel stupid in front of each other.

"I'd be happy with ten pounds. I've only lost five, and my band doesn't feel like anything," Lucia says. "I don't understand how everyone was able to lose so much weight."

"Lucia raised an excellent point," Betsy says. "And that's the first thing we're going to talk about today—how your bands feel and how it's affected your eating. But first, Lucia, let me ask you. How well have you been able to stick to your diet?"

Lucia shrugs with one shoulder. "I stuck to it perfectly."

"*Perfectly*, huh?" Betsy says. Lucia shrugs both shoulders and looks away.

"Lucia, if you truly were able to stick to your diet for five weeks without even the smallest slipup, I'm not quite sure why you needed the Lap-Band in the first place."

Lucia slinks down in her chair. "Of course I slipped up. How can I not? My Lap-Band just doesn't feel like anything."

"Excellent, Lucia. Thank you," Betsy says loudly. "I need you guys to talk honestly about your eating behaviors, because if we don't examine them we can't change them. Okay? By a show of hands, how many people feel *any* restriction in their bands?" Everyone is looking at each other trying to figure out what the right answer is. I raise my hand.

"Is East the only person in this room who feels some level of restriction in her band?" Betsy says.

"No," I say. "I don't really feel any restriction, but I'm wondering how we're even *supposed* to feel anything if all we're eating is soft foods that slide right through anyway?"

"Very good, East. That's exactly what I'm getting at," Betsy says. "So, people? Don't be afraid to raise your hands." Michelle's hand flies up.

"Fine, you got me. I was alone in the house with a two-day-old Big Mac sitting in the fridge. For two days, I looked him in the eye every time I opened the door. But I'd grab a water bottle or a bowl of tuna instead. Then, last night, my family went out to dinner without me. They left a note. They figured I couldn't eat anyway, so they didn't wait. And Big Mac was just calling and calling. Does anyone know what a Big Mac tastes like after two days in the fridge?"

"A lot better than two days *not* in the fridge," Marcie says, and immediately clamps her hand to her mouth. "Sorry for interrupting," she squeaks out from behind it.

"A Big Mac that's spent two days in the fridge is hard as a rock," Michelle answers herself. "It's stale. And since it's two-thirds grease, it's congealed—like eating uncooked bacon. I felt the band after my first bite—not the band itself, but the food against the walls of my stomach. It wasn't a big deal—the food got through pretty quickly. The weird thing was *feeling* it go down. And this experience did change my eating behavior. I ate the rest of the Big Mac a lot more slowly." Lucia starts clapping first, and we all join in.

"Beautiful, Michelle," Betsy says. "Anything like *that* happen to anyone else?" Lucia, Jamie, Coco, Alex, and Tia raise their hands. Marcie and I look at each other and Marcie's hand goes up too.

"Did anyone have any trouble getting anything down?" Betsy asks and looks at the cheaters one by one. No one budges. "Well, don't worry. Once we get your bands tightened correctly, getting a whole Big Mac down will cost you half a day. And that's our next topic—we've scheduled your first fills for next week. We've got them all in for Friday afternoon so that you guys can come to group afterward."

Marcie raises her hand and Betsy signals her to hold off.

"Now's the perfect time to discuss what to expect at your fill appointment. Our fills are always done using a fluoro-scope, an X-ray machine that enables us to see the Lap-Band so that we know exactly where the port is located under your skin, and, once you drink a few sips of barium sulfate—a contrast agent—we can watch how quickly fluids pass through the band. After filming your Lap-Band, the doctor will inject one point five ccs of saline solution into the port and then have you swallow more barium to make sure the fill isn't too restrictive."

Marcie starts waving her hand again, and Betsy holds up hers.

"But this is a question," Marcie mutters. "About *this*."

Betsy sighs and nods.

"Jen said that she needed about seven ccs of fluid to get the band tight enough. Why are we only getting one point five ccs for the first fill, and how often can we come back for another?" Marcie says.

Betsy starts to respond, then stops and taps her pen against her arm. After a moment, she starts again.

"Okay, Marcie raised an excellent point, and this is a good thing to talk about here. When Jen was telling us about how her eating behaviors changed after the band, she noted that she tended to favor softer foods. The problem with relying too much on soft foods—or liquids like protein shakes—is that you're developing new eating behaviors that work *against* the band. Meals consisting of softer foods lead to higher caloric intake because you end up eating greater quantities without feeling restriction. And the tighter your band is, the more likely you are to favor soft foods. So please don't focus on how tight your band is—focus on building your diet around solid foods, like meats, salads, fruits, and vegetables. *Capisce?*" Betsy surveys the room. She raises her eyebrows when she comes around to Marcie, who's waving her hand again. "Yes, Marcie. Please. Ask your question."

"It's more of a statement than a question," Marcie says, and Betsy makes an abrupt sweeping motion with her hand.

"Betsy, there's something that you—everybody here—needs to know. It's about Char." Marcie turns from Betsy and throws Bobby a manacing look. Except, he's still just examining his fingernail.

"What about Char, Marcie? Is she okay?" Betsy says, all impatience gone from her voice.

"Char is getting the Lap-Band surgery in exactly ten days. The same clinic in Mexico that Jen went to. East and I have tried everything. We think she needs to come back here." Marcie looks at the floor. "We think what you're—we're—doing here is important."

My eyes fly to Betsy, then to each of the kids, one by one, trying to gauge their reactions. They're not really responding. But Betsy's eyebrows are furrowed and she's tapping her pen against her pursed lips.

"Thank you, Marcie," Betsy says solemnly. "About what you said. I think it's important too—obviously. But I'm not sure what I can do. Char's welcome to return anytime. She wasn't asked to leave the program, it was her choice. But it's my job to insure that our patients are ready, psychologically, before they're approved for surgery, and even if she came back, I couldn't guarantee any—"

"It's not that at all," Marcie cuts her off. "We know all that, even Char. I mean, I don't think that Char understands—not in the way we do—why Teenage Waistland is a really important part of this, uh, journey, but the main reason she won't come back is because she thinks she let everyone down."

"Didn't she?" Tia snaps. "I mean, I couldn't give a crap one way or the other, but isn't this where we're supposed to feel comfortable being honest about ourselves? Char sat here, listened to us spill our guts, and acted like she cared. And the whole time, it was a lie." Marcie shakes her head and looks helplessly to me. I stand up and take a deep breath.

"There was a reason Char lied," I say in a low voice. "I— I think everybody probably would have lied under the same circumstances too." Marcie sighs and I elbow her. What am I supposed to say?

"Why did Char lie?" Alex says.

"Char lied to protect *me*," I try again. "That's all I can say—she's got to tell you herself. But the reason's got nothing to do with any of you—she *does* care, Tia. More than you know. And that's why she thinks she can't come back. That's why she can't face anyone."

"Or even text anyone," Michelle adds. "I've texted her a few times."

"Me too," Coco says.

"Yeah," I say softly. "That's what I mean. She's so ashamed, she can't face anyone."

"*But*," Marcie says, bolting upright in her seat. "Maybe we can face *her*."

"How's that?" I hear Bobby mutter, and I jerk up my head to look at him, to see if I imagined it. He's still slumped in his seat and he's studying his fingernail. But then he raises his eyes to mine and nods his head to let me know I heard right.

33

Heavy Weight

thursday, august 27, 2009

Bobby (-27 lbs)

I'm struggling already—even though I'm still on my first set of bench presses—when I totally freeze mid-grunt to listen. *Crap*—it *is* the hum of the electric garage-door opener I hear. Dad's home. Knew it would be tight today! With my morning run, some stupid glitch in the store's inventory system that I had to deal with, then football practice, I had no choice but to save my chest workout for late afternoon. And I was busting my hump to finish before Dad showed up.

Dad's involvement with my weight training over the years has helped me move some serious iron—he's kept track of my progress, designed my training routines, and taught me how to break through plateaus. And just having him here in the basement with me has always been great motivation. Now, though, when Coach has been complaining about my performance and I've been benching the same wussy weight for two weeks straight, the last thing I need is Dad in my face.

"What do you mean you can't finish three sets at two ten?

We were at two sixty only two months ago." "It's the running, kid. You're burning through all your muscle." "For God's sake, buddy—what, are you growing a *vagina?*"

Footsteps in the kitchen above me, the slam of the refrigerator door, and then—my stomach churns—creaking on the basement steps.

"Hey, buddy. How's it going?"

I push with everything I've got and manage to set the barbell back on the rack before he comes into view. My face is dripping with sweat and I still have another half hour before I'm done.

"Your last set?" he says.

"Nah—two more to go," I answer, and mentally kick myself in the groin. Should've said yes.

"Great," he says as he gets behind me. "Ready for more weight?" I can push myself to the limit when Dad's spotting me because he's there to grab the barbell if I burn out. But the weight I've got is already a bitch.

"Nah—I'm good," I say, still breathing hard from the last set, and then brace myself for some grief. Instead of giving me any, though, Dad strides over to the mini-fridge and tosses me an ice-cold bottle of water. And then, instead of getting behind me again, he plops down in the old recliner and takes a long swig of root beer. Our favorite.

"Dawson wants the store," he says. I grab my towel, wipe my face, and sit up on the bench. The water bottle feels God-like against my forehead. "He's offered me two million for it." Damn. I unscrew the top and suck the whole thing down in one gulp.

"But the building and the real estate's worth more than twice that!" I say. Dad shakes his head.

"Two mil just for the business itself. He wants a twenty-year lease." My adrenaline shoots back up. "I got to admit," he continues, "it's a good offer. Especially with the housing slump. We could cover the mortgage and live comfortably on the rent alone. Crazy to pass up, b—"

"Totally crazy," I practically shout.

"*But*—as I was saying—it's your legacy, kid. You're the next Konopka in line for it. And the minute Dawson puts his name on the sign, that's fifty years of our family's heritage gone forever. So, obviously, I had to turn him down."

I bury my face in my towel. From total elation to total devastation in less than a minute. I try hard to keep my back from shaking. The last time he caught me crying—I was nine and the football we were tossing hit me in the face and gave me a bloody nose—he said, "Hey, buddy—what, you get your period or something?" But Dad's not saying a word. And then I feel him lower his weight on the bench next to me. I shove over to make room.

"Talk to me, kid. It's been rough for you, I know. You're off to a rocky start in football, and your mother just told me about that friend of yours who died and how depressed you've seemed about it." I know Dad's trying to comfort me and all, but now I'm pressing the towel into my eyes to crush out the tears. We sit like this for a couple of minutes. Finally, I whip the towel across the room and turn to look him straight in the eye. I don't give a crap if he sees me crying—keeping the truth from him would be much worse.

"Dad, I know how important all this—this stuff is to you, and I don't want to let you down, but I—I just don't feel the same way about it anymore."

"What's 'all this stuff,' buddy?" Instead of the icy look he's given me the few times I've challenged him on something, though, Dad looks away and then starts examining the freckle under his nail. I take a deep breath, and then another. *Grow a pair!*

"All your 'legacy' stuff, Dad. I'm sorry, but . . . I don't want to be stuck in the same town for the rest of my life running a lumberyard. Maybe I'll go into computers or engineering or something. And—and"—*grow a pair!*—"and I don't want to be a—a fat—a lineman anymore." I did it. I just broke the old man's heart. Dad's just staring at his fingernail. But I'm breathing easier now. And I feel a ton lighter. Like it's all finally off my soft titty chest.

I'm examining my fingernail now. The two of us Big Bobby All-State Lineman Konopkas crammed up next to each other on a weight bench examining our fingernails. Dad sits up suddenly and raises his arm. For a split second, I think he's going to slam me in the face with his elbow and my heart starts pounding. But his arm goes over my head and around me. He even pulls my head against his.

"I want you to know how proud I am of you, son," he says, almost like he's whispering. Almost like *he's* crying! I can't see, though—the side of my head's leaning against his temple. "You made your own decision to have that surgery. Even when you knew I didn't want it for you. And then with enormous discipline I've never thought you capable of, you've been up every morning with your running. Up with the bloody *sun!* Just so you could get it in *before* work. Past summers, I had to come into your room and kick you out of bed to get you over to the store. And now, not only are you logging, what, ten miles at the crack of dawn, but you always show up on time, and, without any prompting from me, decide we need to automate the business, and then spend weeks with a stack of manuals and install it for us. *Your* contribution to the business played a role in Dawson's generous offer." That's when I jerk my head away and look at Dad. His eyes are a little red but he's smiling and nodding at me. "The deal Dawson's proposed includes *you* installing that RFID system of yours. In all his stores."

There's this amazing runner's high—a feeling of pure happiness and power and freedom that flows through every inch of your entire body and makes you feel like you can do anything. Like you can run forever. That's nothing compared to the way I feel at this moment—when Dad's proud of me not for what he's wanted for me, but for what I've accomplished on my own. Nothing in the world can beat this feeling. Until Dad rises from the bench and says, "I'd better call Dawson before he changes his mind." I'm absolutely flying—until I realize that there's only one person in the world I want to share all this with, and she's in trouble. But when I pick up the phone, I dial Marcie instead.

34

Avoiding Plan B

East (-26 lbs.); (Char -8)

Mom and I are just getting back from our morning walk when Liselle flies by going at least double the speed limit, then screeches to a stop at the curb. Her right front tire is on the curb, actually. *Great*, I'm thinking, *the whole plan's done for.* There's no way Mom's letting me anywhere near that car, let alone drive fifty miles to Long Island in it. Before she has a chance to say a word, I run into the house to get my bag, praying to myself the whole time. And when I get outside again, it's like a miracle. There's Mom standing in the street *chatting* with Marcie and Liselle. I give her a big kiss on the cheek and say, "I'll call you when we get there." Then I get into the backseat and whisper, "Slowly, please, or you'll freak her out," as we pull away, all of us smiling at my mom and waving.

"East, listen up," Marcie starts in as soon as Mom's out of view. "You play it exactly like we discussed, like this is no big deal."

"I don't know—"

"You were able to talk her into letting us tell Bobby everything. If she can handle that, she can handle this." Liselle glances at Marcie and Marcie ignores her. "All I know is we can't let her go to Tijuana tomorrow. Char's got a lot of heavy stuff she hasn't even started to deal with, and the best place for her to do it is in group."

"I know," I say. "But it's one thing to let us tell Bobby and another to come face to face with him with no advance warning. Imagine how upset Char could be when she discovers what we've got planned for her. . . ." Marcie shapes her fingers into a gun and pretends to blow her brains out.

"East, you need to focus on the big picture. If Char gets her surgery in Mexico like Jen and isn't forced to tackle her 'underlying issues,' she'll have much bigger problems than being confronted by people who want to help her. Besides, Char *will* be psyched to see Bobby, especially since this was his idea in the first place."

"No, Marcie. This was *our* idea. You're the one who said that if Char wasn't going to come to Teenage Waistland, then TW should go to her."

"But it was Bobby's idea to meet up at his football game, and it's the perfect setting for this—this—"

"Ambush?" suggests Liselle. Marcie turns her imaginary gun on Liselle. "Nooo—I'm driving!" She laughs, and then Marcie turns back to me.

"*Intervention*, East. The word is intervention. That's where a group of concerned family and friends confront someone in trouble and get them to seek help. That's what this is," Marcie says. She turns her finger gun back to Liselle. "Right?" Liselle nods and laughs again.

I shake my head. "She's not going to like this." Marcie is

closing her eyes and shaking her head, like not only does she strongly disagree with me, but my concern over Char's reaction is too dumb to waste ear function on. "Seriously. I mean Bobby is like this football hero, and to have a bunch of fat kids show up at his football game? He couldn't get us out of there fast enough when we visited him at practice."

"East, you raise an excellent point," Marcie says, mocking Betsy. "It's a *ginormous* deal that this football hero invited a bunch of fat kids to his big game. If he didn't care about Char—or everyone in TW, for that matter—he'd never have done it."

"But Marcie," I say, "he never even texted her after all the horrible things we told him, and it's been like almost two weeks. What if he gets freaked out in front of his hotshot football buddies and acts like he doesn't know her again— like that time in the lobby?"

"East, stop catastrophizing and compose yourself," Marcie shrieks. "This isn't about Bobby anyway—this is about Char's life, and it's our only foolproof chance to stop her from going to Mexico!" Marcie stares at me from over her headrest, but I don't look away.

"It's *not* foolproof, Marcie, it's fool*ish*," I say. "Dangerous, even. Char says she can't face anyone from TW ever again, but even if everyone else makes her believe how wanted she is and how necessary she is to the group, I know her. *Bobby* rejecting her could break her. He's too much of a wild card in this plan."

Marcie pulls out her finger gun. "Look, East, we're about there, so just clam up and put your best foot forward. Remember—if this fails, we'll have no choice but to move to plan B."

"Plan B?" I almost shout in relief.

"Yeah, but in plan B, Liselle has to total her car with all of us in it. People in traction find travel difficult." I watch as Marcie and Liselle crack up and high-five each other. Then Liselle swerves into Char's driveway and honks the horn.

Char peers out from her bedroom window, and two seconds later, she flings opens the front door and comes running out in a pale yellow blouse, white flowy skirt, and flip-flops. Perfect. She looks really nice. Even her hair is all blown out.

Her hair. I tap Liselle's shoulder. "Can you put the top up for Char so her hair's not a wreck when we get there? Getting her out of the car is going to be hard enough," I whisper frantically.

Liselle clamps her hand to her mouth and then moans, "I'm such an idiot. The top's home in the garage!" Already things are going badly.

"So, does this work for my surprise?" Char's calling as she spins around in front of the car.

"Absofreakinglutely stupendously," Marcie yells. "Now get in this car!" Char gets in next to me and we're off.

"So, now you guys can tell me. Where are we going?"

Liselle says something in hushed tones to Marcie, and Marcie pulls the scarf we planned to use as Char's blindfold out of the glove compartment.

"Put this on—it'll keep your hair from flying all over the place. It's a bit of a ride," Marcie says to Char.

"Okay. Enough. I don't like surprises—" Char starts, but Liselle immediately launches into this rambling tale of how she mixed this green-mud facial-mask stuff for herself and Marcie last night, but read the directions wrong. After it hardened, they had to chip the mask off their faces with butter knives.

"Like freaking concrete!"

And then I'm telling the story of how once Char and I were making our own play dough but we didn't have cream of tartar, so we idiotically substituted tartar *sauce* instead. We ended up burning my countertop with the hot blob of relish-y doughy junk.

"Shroud and I still get sick when we smell anything related to pickles," Char laughs.

"Well, we're not going to any sloppy burger joint, so no worries," Marcie says.

As we near the exit, Marcie's pointing at the road signs and mouthing, *Do something* to me. After a moment of panic, I start blathering on to Char about this birthmark on my arm that I'm afraid might be turning cancerous. She examines it closely and then pulls out her cell phone to Google "skin cancer." While she's tapping away, Marcie grins at me and shakes her head mouthing, *She's so predictable.* But that's not entirely true. None of us can predict how Char's going to react when she looks up from her research and realizes we just pulled into the Syosset High School parking lot.

○ ○ ○ ○ ○ ○

"Oh no!" Char wails. "You have got to be kidding me!" She slumps in her seat. "Please, Liselle, get us out of here quickly!" As a carload of rowdy guys pulls into the parking spot next to us, she ducks down even lower. Marcie gives me the nod.

"Char, Bobby called Marcie and invited us all to his

game," I say. "Told her you should come. Great surprise, right?" Char gasps and looks me straight in the eye. I look at Marcie. Marcie just opens her car door and gets out.

"He knows I'm coming?" Char asks quietly, like she's afraid of the answer.

Marcie rolls her eyes impatiently. "Of course! And you're not just 'coming,' you're the reason we're all here."

Char looks at both of us like she doesn't quite believe, but she yanks off the scarf and starts brushing her hair and checking her lipstick. I get out of the car and walk around to Marcie.

"We should tell her that it's only a TW group thing so she doesn't get her hopes up about Bobby just to have them shattered."

"Football is a group activity by definition, East. We don't need to get so specific. We know how Char feels about Bobby, but we don't know how she's going to feel about facing the others," Marcie whispers. "So please just chill before Char changes her mind about going in. This will turn out great, you'll see."

But as Char chucks her compact back into her bag and almost levitates out of the car she's so happy, I can't help worrying that *this* could turn out the exact opposite.

35

INTERVENING FACTORS

Bobby (-29 lbs.)

It's only the third down in the second quarter of our first game of the season, we're up against Massapequa—our biggest rival—and the crowd's already chanting, "Refrigerator! Refrigerator!" But that's only because I'm laying flat on my back on the thirty-yard line seeing stars. Tony Litella on Massapequa's defensive line is ridiculously massive this year. He came in hard and low and that's the last I remember.

"Konopka finally got laid," I hear MT shout. Even though I'm still trying to piece together what day it is, the thought of flattening that dickhead is enough to get me up. But as I'm on my feet and the crowd starts clapping, Craighead runs over and says, "Tough break, bro—Coach's waving you in." When I approach the sideline, Coach, without saying a word or even looking in my direction, points me to the bench.

I can't remember the last time I watched a game from the sidelines, but I'm lucky I got to play at all today—let alone ever again for Syosset. Coach looked totally stunned when I stayed after practice yesterday to tell him about my surgery—like I just plugged the whistle hanging from his neck into an electrical socket or something. His eyes and his mouth opened wide for a second, and then he looked away and spit on the field. Finally he said, "Selfish move, Konopka, for not giving me more notice to work on this year's roster. Thought you were a team player."

"I know it," I said, nodding. I wanted to explain about trying to keep up my strength while losing weight, but the idea that I ever could have pulled that off seems idiotic. Coach watched me study the ground with nothing to say for a few minutes. Then he said less angrily, "I'm with you on the weight, though. College linemen are getting bigger and fatter every year to stay competitive, and many of 'em wind up sick and hobbling around on destroyed joints when their football days are over. Still, wouldn't have thought this of you, Konopka, not from the family you come from," he said, walking away. Without even turning around.

o o o o o o

I'm cheering the team on harder than ever, waving my towel and keeping up the best game face I can. The funny thing is, the thought of the TW gang—of Char, mostly— thinking I'm a loser is bothering me more than the idea of my buddies coming face to face with my group of merry band-sters. And way more than losing this game.

Massapequa is totally kicking the crap out of us. Brad Dwyer, our first-string running back, hasn't been able to take three yards in one play from these guys, and Zoo and the others just can't keep the defense off him. As the second quarter ends, we're down 13–0.

Third quarter, fourth down. Syosset's behind 32–7 and Massapequa has the ball. The crowd is quieter—lots of people are taking off. There's so little hope for a comeback that Coach pulls Dwyer before he gets completely mauled. He's putting in Lou Farrell from the second string, but this guy's pretty easy to get to, so things can't get too much better. I look at the stands, and they're now half empty. I spot Mr. Dawson sitting a couple of rows back, and he toasts me with his Gatorade and a shrug. I smile and raise my helmet.

We're in the fourth, and finally have possession of the ball. But the offensive line is totally dejected, and Farrell is taking more heat than he ought to, thanks to me. He's already been at the bottom of three pileups and he looked like he might have been limping after the last one. There are three more seconds on the clock when Coach calls a time-out and waves Farrell in. He *is* limping.

I'm thinking Coach's going to put Connelly in, but that douche bag has been more unreliable during practice than even me. Then, out of the corner of my eye, I see Mr. Dawson hop down to the field and pull Coach aside. And then they're both looking at me. *There's no way they do this.* But Coach motions me over.

"Konopka, I'm putting you in as running back for the last play. Our asses have already been handed to us, so just try to run down the clock without any fatalities." Then he throws Dawson a quick glance over his shoulder, turns back to me with a half shrug, and adds, "Guess it's your lucky day."

Lucky? I glance over at Dwyer and Farrell, and they're both slumped over on the bench nursing multiple ice packs. My stomach is churning, and I'm kicking myself for telling Dawson about wanting to try out for the position in college—

there's no way I'm ready for this now. As ridiculous as this is and as scared shitless as I am, though, there's no way I'm turning down this opportunity.

I turn to the stands to signal Mom and Dad to leave. I'd feel better if they weren't around to see me get destroyed, or worse, laughed off the field. But they're not in their regular seats, and as I scan the emptying bleachers, I spot Char. She's standing in the middle of the aisle halfway up the stands looking right at me—and she's surrounded by a smiling Teenage Waistland: Marcie, Liselle (honorary member, I guess), East, Alex, and Coco in two rows on one side of the aisle, and Tia, Michelle, Lucia, and Jamie on the other.

Char can't see my eyes because my helmet's on, and she can't see if I'm smiling because I've already got my mouth guard in. She knows that I know about that horrible stuff in her past—and that, like a pussy, I couldn't face her. Or even text her. But there she is—with her hair flying all free and that crazy big grin of hers—beaming right at me anyway. And I'm standing here taking her in—that crazy runner's high surging through my veins again.

As I jog onto the field and get behind Zoo and LaRocha at the scrimmage line rather than take my usual spot next to them, the crowd's chatter level rises. I shut my eyes for a moment to make them disappear. Once they're gone, it's my mental voice I hear. *This is crazy, you can't do this*, it's saying, over and over. The voice of defeat, Dad calls it. Everyone hears it at one point or another—the people who end up on top are the ones who can turn it off. It's my big chance to prove to myself that fat lineman isn't my only position on this field or anywhere. I really can choose what and who I am. But I just can't turn the voice off! I'm ready to bolt from the field when it hits me: *Don't have to turn off the voice in your head. Just change it.* And, two seconds before the play is about to begin, I do it. I play the voice I want to hear.

It's the final down at the fifty-yard line, three seconds to go. Syosset doesn't have a prayer, but in a surprise move, in comes Bobby Konopka, all-state lineman turned running back. He can't save the game, but can he save his team from total humiliation? The ball is hiked, and Tino rolls right, then tosses the ball to Konopka. Konopka stiff-arms Litella and puts him on his back in a big reversal of their earlier encounter. It's his size and speed, and he's plowing through another of Massapequa's finest. He's on the forty-yard line, and then the thirtieth, then—splat—he's tackled. But there it is, folks—first-time running back Bobby Konopka at three hundred pounds took twenty yards before annihilation— pretty amazing!

"Bobby! Bobby!" *the crowd is roaring, and his teammates, the cheerleaders—everyone's in a frenzy. As Konopka pulls himself up and makes his way toward the sideline, Coach is shaking his head in disbelief.*

Suddenly the broadcast happening in my mind dissolves and I look up and hear the real noise, see the real crowd. This isn't a fantasy! There's Mom and Dad and Mr. Dawson. And the crowd's closing in, Zoo, MT, and Craighead leading the rush. I toss my helmet and mouthpiece onto the field, plow right through the crowd on the sideline as they're cheering and pounding my back, and take the bleachers two at a time. Char's waiting for me smiling. I don't care how sweaty and smelly my pits are or how many idiot guys she's ever kissed. I wrap my arms around her and kiss her. Then Char's face ex- plodes into that grin again and she throws her arms around my neck. We kiss again, a longer one this time. Now everyone's gone quiet—even MT, and it's just the two of us, back in the stockroom closet.

I pull away from Char to wipe my sweaty forehead with my arm, and that's when I see MT, Craighead, Zoo, and, hell, all of Syosset, at the base of the bleachers gaping up at us, and even though their mouths are open, nothing's coming out. I slide my arm right back around Char and pull her in close.

"Guys," I bellow into the silence, "this is Charlotte. But she prefers 'Char.' "

As Char wraps her arm around me, Zoo finally yells, "Great to meet you, Char! We've all heard so much about you!"

36

teenage waistland redux

friday, september 4, 2009

Char (-10 lbs)

Bobby's got his arm around my shoulder, and I have East on the other side, holding my hand. Marcie's got my back—literally. She's rubbing my neck like I'm a prizefighter entering the ring. We walk into the room, and all the kids abandon the circle and are around me hugging and laughing. Betsy stands and says, "Welcome back, Char!" and gives me a hug too. We return to the circle and everyone sits down, but Betsy gives me the signal and I remain standing. "Hi, everybody, I'm Char Newman, and I'm fifteen."

"Hi, Char!" Everyone cheers, and I take a deep breath.

"I've been eating heavily for three years now, and it started—" East is smiling and nodding and Bobby's squeezing my arm.

I take another deep breath. And then I tell them everything.

the fat ladies sing

East (-132 lbs.); Char (-84.7 lbs)

"Mom?" I'm in the doorway of her bedroom, but her bed is neatly made, and she's not in there. "Mom?" I call louder down the stairs. She could be right in the next room and not hear me through the din. It's been like this for weeks—first plumbers, painters, carpenters, masons, and landscapers; now florists and catering people, all scurrying around and working on something that they have to bang on, drill through, knock down, or some other noisy thing. She practically redid the entire backyard just for the event—a lush sod lawn has replaced the brown weedy grass; the plant beds have been cleaned, pruned, and packed with white lilies, pink hollyhocks, and lavender; and an elegant bluestone patio now sits where the rotting wood deck used to be. "Moooooom," I'm forced to scream at my lungs' capacity. Finally, Mom pops her head out of the kitchen.

"What is it, East? I'm on the phone. Crystal says to tell you that they'll be picking you up in about half an hour."

"Why so soon? I'm not close to being ready!" I say, panic rising.

She comes to the foot of the stairs. "Calm down, and tell me what you need. If it's your hair dryer, it's in my bathroom—mine's been overheating, and I keep forgetting to pick up a new one while I'm out," she says. Crystal is on hold on the phone in the kitchen and Mom is waiting at the foot of the steps to see if I need anything. If I *need anything*. The thought of this simple stupid thing chokes me up. Almost everything does these days.

Mom's ear to ear with smiles, even with all the work and chaos. That Julius is coming home to help deal with all his last-minute wedding details has put her—us—in a ridiculously happy state of anticipation. It'll be the three of us alone for an entire week—and then his fiancée, Karina, and her family will descend, and we'll finally have a huge extended family. Before that, though, I plan to have a long talk with Julius about Char. I was in the same pain he was, so how could I ever be angry or not understand what he was going through? But his guilt over what happened is probably what's been keeping him so distant from me, and I need to be close to my brother again. The idea of having such an honest conversation would have terrified me once, but now that I've finally opened up to my mom, not only have I helped her with her issues but she's helped me with mine.

Mom's bedroom gets the midafternoon sun, especially with the new curtains open. And with the new off-white-on-white color scheme, her room is so bright, it almost hurts. I head into her bathroom and spot my blow-dryer, its cord neatly wrapped around the handle, on top of the wicker hamper. But what really catches my eye is the digital scale on the floor next to it—Mom must have gotten it yesterday, immediately after I mentioned that I weighed a quarter pound less on the Park Avenue Bariatrics scale fully dressed than I did on our old scale naked. Mom and I have been doing weekly weigh-ins together since she started dieting with me last fall, and they still make me laugh out loud. Mom starts off by gently nudging the scale back and forth with her toe to get it into the exact right position. Then she mounts it like a surfboard, shifting her weight from one foot to the other to find the lowest reading. Another one of Jen's *universal rules encoded in fat cells*: every ounce on the scale matters. Even when they're the difference between 248.6 pounds and 247.8.

I grab the blow-dryer and try to leave, but the lure of the new scale is too powerful to resist and it stops me at the doorway. I put the dryer back down, nudge the scale to where the floor's most level with my big toe, and remove my bathrobe—it's a light summer cotton, but 2.4 pounds is 2.4 pounds. I take a deep breath and step onto the scale gently so as not to wake the higher numbers. The digits race back and forth as I take my hand off the sink and slowly release my full weight.

"Holy Mother of Shroudness!" Char shrieks from over my shoulder. She grabs my arm to steady me as I almost go flying off the scale.

"Char! Don't sneak up on me like that! And I thought you weren't picking me up for another half hour." I pull my bathrobe in front of me even though I've got panties and a bra on.

"Who's sneaking? Your mom and I both called up to you—what's making such a racket outside?"

I shrug. My mind has been acclimated to hearing *one* sound in this house—it's still learning to parse aggregate noise. "C'mon back to your room and get dressed," Char orders. "I got you a surprise."

"You've surprised me enough for one day," I mumble as I put on my robe and trot after her.

There's a box wrapped in Sak's signature paper on my bed, and Char plops herself down next to it. "Go on, open," she says.

"Char—what is that? Why'd you get me a gift?"

"Because it's your very special day."

"It's *our* special day, and I didn't get you anything. Let me do my hair first before it dries funny." I glance at Char in the mirror as I blow out my hair. She's only lost about eighty-five pounds since her surgery last October, but she's tall enough to carry the sixty extra pounds she's got left and looks drop-dead gorgeous. Not gorgeous for a fat girl. Gorgeous for any girl—any woman. Of course, today, she and her cleavage are at full volume in a strapless close-fitting yellow sundress. I run the flat iron over my hair one final time—it's silky and shiny, and finally reaches my lower back, but it's jet black and covers almost half my body—a shroud indeed. I apply a bit of the anti-frizz smoothing serum Mom bought and turn to Char.

"Maybe I should wear it in a ponytail?"

"You've always got it in a ponytail or a bun. Leave it down today—it looks beautiful—and open the box," she says, motioning toward it impatiently.

"Just one more minute," I beg as I flip frantically through my closet. "Where are my new black jeans?"

"You're so not wearing jeans today," Char says—not as an order or a question, but as a statement of fact. "Now, if you don't open this damn box pronto, you'll have to get your own ride into the city." She watches me pick at the knot in the gold string for a few moments before she yanks the box out of my hand, rips through the string with her teeth, and tears off the wrapping.

"Now," she says, and hands the box back to me. I remove the top and peel off the layers of white tissue paper one by one in slow motion just to annoy her. "You've got exactly one second to—" she starts, but I just laugh and whip out the small neatly folded pile of silky black cloth.

"It's *so* my color—how'd you know?" I giggle. "What is it—a shirt?" Char helps me unfold it and lay it out on my bed. It's a little black dress with cap sleeves and a scoop neck—just like the one Jen showed up at Coco's *quince* party in—and almost as tiny. I look up at Char. She's smiling with tears in her eyes.

"*This* is what you're wearing today."

"Yeah, right. Funny." I laugh. Char frowns and I realize she's not kidding. "Look, Char. It's beautiful, and it's so sweet of you to get this for me, but this dress is *sizes* too small. I won't fit into it for months—maybe never!"

Char just shakes her head. "You're still wearing baggy clothes several *sizes* too big, and for months I've let you get away with it. No matter how fat your head thinks you are, scales and tape measures don't lie and I'm not going to let you catastrophize yourself any longer."

I reach over and hug her. "You're such a good friend to me, Char, and none of this would have happened if not for you. But you're certifiably insane, and the reality is, this dress can't possibly fit me."

Char wriggles out of my grasp. "Listen, Ms. I'm-So-Normal-and-Char's-the-Crazy-One—I *embrace* my craziness and you try to hide yours, my friend. That's the only differ-ence between us, and I bought you this dress *in the right size* to prove it. So just try the freaking thing on and let's see once and for all who's the bigger mental case."

"It's a deal," I laugh, and toss off my bathrobe. "Give it."

Bobby (–131 lbs)

We're stuck in traffic outside the Midtown tunnel tollbooths, and Dad is tapping his fingers on the dashboard. "I told you we'd be better off taking the Queensboro Bridge," he mutters, "but you had to have it your way."

"Sorry. I didn't know the inbound tunnel was going to be down to one lane," I mutter back.

"It's Friday rush hour, for God's sakes. Three lanes coming out, one lane going in." He raps his fingers harder and I take a quick swerve into the next lane before the bearded stoner in the Subaru tries to cut me off. This lane's crawling a lot faster through the tolls and I'm feeling pretty good about my big move, so it takes a moment for me to notice Dad pointing at a big purple E-ZPass sign right in front of me.

"Crap!" I say, and pound my fist into the dashboard. I don't have a damn E-ZPass, so now I've got to wait for someone to let me back into the cash-only lane while Subaru and the sixty million E-ZPass holders behind him lean on their horns.

Having Dad in the passenger seat is not exactly a boon to my visibility, and he won't look over his shoulder to help me out, so I lower his window and lean forward to make eye contact with a driver who might let me in. I figure that some mom with her own kid at home will show some pity, and it's a pretty redhead in a yellow Volkswagen convertible who finally waves me in. Now we're back in the same lane we

started in, but something like fifty cars that were once behind us have since sailed through the toll. Dad doesn't say a
word, about that or the redhead. He's just chewing on the
inside of his mouth—a nervous habit of his—and shaking
his head.

"I'm sorry!" I finally snap. "I usually take the train in. I
didn't know. You should have just insisted that I take the
Queensboro exit." I turn up the air conditioner and fiddle
with the vents to get air to my face. It's hot as hell.

Dad lets out a deep sigh and hits the button on his arm-
rest to close his window. "This might help cool things down
a little."

"Why are we even doing this, Dad?" I fume. "Why was it
so important that we drive in together?"

"You've got something in the city tonight, I've got something in the city tonight, and I thought, 'Wouldn't it be nice
to spend a little quality time with my kid,'" he says with a
shrug. "You haven't been around much."

"Yeah, I know," I mumble, feeling bad about making Dad
say it. And also feeling bad about how much things have
changed between us. It's not like we had a fight or anything.
We were just busy doing our own thing—or maybe more
accurately, my thing and his thing weren't the same thing
anymore.

With my running and stuff, I was losing about twenty
pounds a month through the fall, so by the middle of November, Coach practically stopped playing me altogether. If
I didn't have that huge automation project for Dawson Depot
on my head, I would have been okay hanging at football
practice every day after school, even if I was spending most
games on the bench. But I talked it out with Coach, and

after he couldn't commit to putting me in more regularly as halfback, we agreed that staying with the team wasn't the best use of my time. Dad was upset that I didn't talk to him about it first—he didn't understand that there wasn't any decision to make. As far as college football went, I was in no-man's-land. No longer a suitable lineman, and too overweight to be seriously considered for a halfback position. With that gone, it seemed my focus had to be Dawson's inventory system project—and finishing Park Avenue Bariatric's online Patient Eating Behaviors (PEB) database I was getting paid to set up. It didn't help that I was spending long hours at Dawson Depot and Dad didn't have a Konopka & Sons Lumber to go to anymore.

Then there was Char. Every free moment—and there weren't a lot of those—I spent with her. Still, she ragged on me that I was always busy, always talking about colleges. She couldn't see how hard it was to go from being a football hero to a nothing, which was the second mistake I made: not spending Super Bowl Sunday with Dad and taking Char to MT's party instead. Char got all flirty with my friends and I wound up in a shoving match with MT. I acted like an idiot to him and to Char. She broke up with me on MT's front porch and refused to let me even wait with her for her ride. I walked home, and found Dad snoring on the couch, TV still blaring, and Chinese food boxes stacked on the coffee table. Luckily, he sucks at ordering for just one, and I dove happily into an unopened container of fried rice. But I faithfully signed in to my PEB account and made my fried rice entry (*feeling bad so wtf*) and tagged another five miles onto my run the next morning as penance.

"So this franchise seminar sounds cool, Dad. Are you

really considering opening a Gold's Gym? There's nothing you don't know about bodybuilding," I say.

"And nothing I *do* know about the gym business. There'll be a lot of different franchises for me to look at tonight, buddy. I don't know. I'm just going to get some ideas . . . ," Dad says. We're finally in the tunnel, but he's just staring out the window watching the grimy yellow tiles go by.

"Dad?" I say. "Isn't there anything you always wanted to do that you couldn't because of the store and all? Maybe you can do that now."

"Yeah?" he says, turning to look at me. "I wanted to play college football. Maybe even go pro."

There's a light at the end of the tunnel, but it's only the Midtown tunnel—Dad's just never going to let this go. I put on the radio and flick through the stations, not really even hearing anything.

"Buddy?"

I keep flicking. Dad puts his hand on mine and pulls it gently away from the console.

"Bobby. Listen. I shouldn't have said that. That was about me, not you—my life, not yours."

I take my hand back and turn the radio off. "Dad, it's hard for me too. I love football and I've lost a lot of who I am— or was—when I gave it up. But I don't regret it."

"Don't. Not ever. Look at what you've done. You bucked the tide, you got yourself into California Polytech—"

"Which has one of the worst teams in college football history," I add.

"Yeah, but so what? It's one of the top engineering schools in the country, and it was your brain—your RFID inventory gizmo—that did it. Plus, you've got a shot at their football team anyway. If you want it, that is. To tell you the truth, I'd have killed to play running back over lineman." He pats his stomach. "Heart attack waiting to happen. Maybe it's your turn to coach me—*here*, buddy, pull over. There, in front of that cab. You just head uptown and I'll walk the rest of the way."

"Thanks, Dad. I'll try to meet you at the Sheraton, maybe check the franchises out with you a little—I think my thing will break up pretty early tonight."

o o o o o o

There's an open spot on the street, but I pull my new Prius into the overpriced parking garage anyway—no point risking getting it stolen. Yeah, that "RFID inventory gizmo" *has* been good to me. All of this has. And, as I turn to walk into Coco Rosa, it keeps getting better. There, in front of me in line, is a beautiful girl with long flowing black hair in a tight short black dress. I hear Char's voice in the crowd calling, "Shroud, where are you?" and then it hits me. *That's* East.

Marcie (-113 lbs)

Marcie Mandlebaum here: seventeen years old, five feet four, 175 pounds, and reluctantly—albeit *fabulously*—sporting a pair of $300 black formal Dolce & Gabbana trousers and a $135 cap-sleeve Dolce & Gabbana T-shirt, both in size 14, and both courtesy of my mama, the big spender. As it turns out, I'll need to drop a few more sizes to fit into their $325 denim jeans, but Mom winked and said I looked spectacular and we can go jeans shopping in a few months.

We're seated at a large round table for ten in the private dining room of Coco Rosa beneath a large banner that reads BON VOYAGE, TEENAGE WAISTLAND, and I'm not the least bit tempted to point out that the sign is tacky, childish, and, most important, patently incorrect—that we've already embarked on our journey, exactly one year ago today. After all, whoever thought of it and took the time to make it—Coco, undoubtedly—meant the very best.

East and Bobby are the last to enter, though East arrived twenty minutes ago with Char, and it was the same funny routine with the two of them—East pulling on her freaking *tiny* dress and saying, "Why did I even wear this, I'm like popping out of it," and Char saying, "You look so amazing, stop adjusting." Finally, East had to teeter to the ladies' room— Char lent her a pair of mad high pumps to go with the dress—for some last-minute reassurance from the mirror that she wasn't popping out of *anything,* and Char rose to follow her and then sat down again. "My Shroudette's all grown up," Char said, leaning into me, and when I saw she really had tears in her eyes, I put my arms around her. "You done good."

Bobby pulls the chair next to Char out for East and waits for her to be seated. I get the urge to bellow, "Remove your eyes from my friend's backside, buddy," but don't. I *was* born with a flap between my mind and my mouth—it's just another muscle that needed to be developed.

As Bobby seats himself on the other side of the table between Alex and Tia, Betsy takes the floor and shoos the waiter away as he approaches with water pitchers. But she doesn't have to clap for attention—there's no taking our eyes off her. She's as big as a house, a week overdue, and if she makes it through our Teenage Waistland grand finale before that baby pops, it'll be a miracle. Not so bitsy anymore—and not all of it baby.

"Everyone," Bitsy announces, waving a stack of printouts, "the results of your final weigh-ins are online, but if you haven't seen them yet, I have them here." I snort and everyone else laughs. Betsy tosses the papers on her chair and laughs too. "Right. Of course you've seen them."

Bobby clears his throat. "My—*the* Eating Behaviors application automatically e-mails each patient when their weigh-in results are posted," he offers.

"A round of applause, everyone, for Bobby, our technology expert. The online food diary, weight charts, and other tools will help you stay on track. Speaking of which, Bobby, you certainly look like you've been on track—the running track, that is," Betsy quips painfully. The clapping and hooting cover some groans, and then Char leads us into chanting, "Bobby, Bobby, he's the man, if he can't do it, no one can," until Betsy signals for us to simmer down.

"I want to tell you how proud of all of you I am, and how beautifully you've all done. Keep in mind that teen weight loss with the Lap-Band typically averages between one and two pounds a week and everyone has come in above the low end of the range, so I'm very impressed." We break out into a spontaneous round of applause. For ourselves, for what Bitsy's taught us to do for ourselves, and for the grilled cilantro shrimp appetizer being set down on the table.

"I was hoping that Michelle would be able to join us so that we could all be together as a full group one more time, but she had a scheduling conflict and sends her regrets," Bitsy says.

Char elbows me under the table. "Michelle told me she

couldn't help cheating the band and couldn't lose enough weight with it, so she's scheduled for gastric bypass surgery next week—if they can't bring her weight down quickly, she'll need to go on insulin for her diabetes," she whispers—a little too loudly.

"Yes, Char, that's true, unfortunately." Betsy sighs. "While the band is the safer surgical weight loss alternative, it isn't the fastest, and it only works for patients truly willing to modify their eating behaviors. When people like Michelle have health problems like diabetes and heart disease caused by obesity, the gastric bypass guarantees the fastest weight loss up front. By the way, Char, that was another disruption. See me after group." Betsy pauses. "Just kidding." Char nods her head fake-dejectedly, which garners more laughs than Bitsy's original quip. You don't mess with the Char-iff. "Seriously, Char. You created the name Teenage Waistland, but more important, you were a big part of making it the warm supportive family it is. A big round for Char, everyone." We all clap and Char bows and then Betsy continues.

"Now a big thank-you to Coco, who has so generously hosted this final group session," Betsy says.

"Yay, Coco!" Char shrieks, and we start banging the table in unison. "Yay, Coco! Yay, Coco!"

"Okay, gang—I mean it. If I go into labor, we're not going to fin—"

"Tia!" Char shrieks. "What happened to your rings?" Tia eyes Char with her usual suspicion, and then I notice it too. Tia has lost her lip and nose rings!

"You look really pretty," Jamie offers, but the truth is the truth. Tia no longer looks scary and dangerous. In fact, she's quite ordinary.

"I had them removed," Tia mutters.

"Why?" says Char. "They were cool."

"The kids were going to call me something, and I preferred 'Ringed Freak' to 'Goodyear Blimp,' " Tia says matter-of-factly, but it's about the most personal thing she's ever said about herself, and another round of spontaneous clapping erupts.

"Actually, they started calling me 'Saturn, the ringed planet,' " Tia grumbles, but there's a full-blown smile on her face—another first.

"Group—one more quick callout before we eat," Bitsy roars to cut through the chatter, and has to steady herself again. "East Itou, you deserve a standing ovation, but I'm sure you'll understand if I take my seat." Betsy clears her throat. "East, in the very beginning, you made me a promise. You promised that you would be the very best teen Bandster we ever had, and, East, you kept that promise. You've lost an amazing one hundred thirty-two pounds this past year—the best performance not only in this group, but the best of all the teen patients we've ever had! Congratulations, East!"

Char and I scream in unison and jump to our feet. Char is whooping and pounding East on the back, and Coco tosses a shredded napkin in the air that flies like confetti, and Bobby follows suit by flinging a handful of tortilla chips in the air. East is grinning wildly, but tears are streaming down her cheeks and she looks like she's going to vomit. Or, at the very least, put forth a productive burp. East hangs her head.

"Shroudness, what's going on?" Char says softly. "Are you okay?" East takes a napkin and dabs at her eyes. She looks up at Char questioningly, and Char whispers, "You're good—no mascara running."

East turns to face Bitsy. "Betsy, you've been so kind to me, and being in Teenage Waistland is the best thing that's ever happened to me. But I have something to tell you. All of you. My Lap-Band never had enough restriction. I've had the fills, and it just never got tight. Everything kept going straight down. I'm not a Lap-Band success at all."

Bitsy shakes her head numbly. "East, why didn't you tell us? It's rare, but sometimes, during surgery, the band gets nicked by a scalpel or a needle and it springs a leak. Or, the needle can miss the port and puncture the tubing during a fill. If you've never had restriction after so many fills, that's what it probably was, East. A leak. But I just don't understand why you didn't say something." East is still studying her plate.

"There was something more important I had to do, and the failure of my band gave me the excuse to do it," East mumbles.

"Shroud, whatever are you talking about?" Char says, pretending to pound her on the head. East brushes Char's hand away and looks up at Betsy.

"The thing is, as soon as I made the connection between the bad feelings I had inside and my eating, I found that I was able to control my eating and the weight kept coming off—even before the surgery. I knew I had to help my mother with her weight, and she was too terrified to even think about getting the surgery for herself. So I made her copies of the eating behaviors food diaries and we dieted and exercised together. I thought if I could do it without restriction, then she'd be able to also. And she did! She's lost almost a hundred pounds since November!"

My God. Could anyone be that selfless? I burst into tears!

Right in front of everyone! "East, you are so *fucking beautiful*," I blubber. East tears up and now Char, East, and I are combo laughing and blubbering, and there's not a dry eye in the house.

"Do you know what this means, East?" Bitsy chokes out. East shakes her head again. "I guess it means you're kicking me out?"

"Well, yes. I'm kicking all of you out." Bitsy smiles. "But this means that you lost this weight with absolutely no assistance whatsoever. It is absolutely remarkable."

"No," East says. "That's not true. I had all the assistance I needed. I had my mom, and I had Char and Marcie, and all of you. I had Teenage Waistland."

o o o o o o

I'm out on the sidewalk with East and Char as we wait for East's mom to pick them up, and the three of us are singing, "It's only Teenage Waist-land," and bobbing our much-diminished hips back and forth. East breaks into a Char-strut/Char-shimmy combo, her heels clicking smartly on the pavement.

Suddenly, Char freezes, leaving me hip-bumping the wind. "Oh, Marcie! I can't wait to see what Liselle is going to give you for graduation at your party tomorrow night!" she shrieks. "You're going to open your presents in front of everyone, aren't you?"

"In front of whom? It's not exactly a big crowd. My parents, Ronny, Liselle, a few friends of hers, a couple of friends of mine from Tenafly High, you guys, and whoever else from Teenage Waistland shows," I say. "Besides, Liselle already gave me her gift." I smile mysteriously and wait for them to beg me to tell them what it is.

Char and East close in on me fake-menacingly. "Spill," Char says.

"Yeah, spill, Marcie."

"Yeah, the dynamic duo—I'm scared. Okay, I'll just show you. A picture being worth a thousand words and all." I open my purse and fish around for my key ring, and then whip it out for them. "Ta-da," I say.

East doubles up with laughter while Char yanks it out of my hand.

"Liselle got you a *gold penis key chain?*" she screams, then clamps her hand to her mouth as passersby turn to look.

"It's a dildo, actually—see the tiny battery slot on the bottom? She had it custom made for me," I say proudly. "But the best part of her gift is what's on the key chain."

Char gasps. "She gave you her BEEMER CONVERT-IBLE?" I grab it back and point to a newly cut metal key.

"Nah, this is better than a car key. It's the key to Liselle's *apartment* in Boston. Where we'll both be going to school next year." Char shakes her head.

"Okay, Liselle getting into Harvard is just a tad more ridiculous than East losing a hundred and thirty pounds with a leaky LapBand."

"Astronomically more ridiculous," I correct. "I'm going to be at Harvard in Cambridge, and she's going to be right across the Charles River in Boston. She'll be a sophomore at Northeastern."

Char throws her arms around me. "That's so nice for you, Marcie. You'll be neighbors!" I peel her off and shake my head.

"No, you guys. Even better. We're going to be *sistahs*. Just like the three of us."

"Whoa, too sappy!" Char shrieks. "Shroud-e-licious will start crying again." But it's not just East whose eyes are brimming. It's all of us, and we unite into this super-tight, cheesy group hug that only East's mom's beeping can break apart.

AFTERWORD

Teenage obesity is a huge problem.

Research conducted by the National Institutes of Health (NIH) and the Centers for Disease Control shows a dramatic increase in obesity rates in children, adolescents, and adults over the past twenty years. What's going on?

The answer seems simple: Obese people consume more calories and burn fewer of them than nonobese people. Most of the food we in the United States consume is calorie dense, meaning that we take in a lot of calories without necessarily eating a lot of food. And Americans don't exercise as much as they used to. School physical education programs and after-school sports activities get cut in cities and communities where budgets are tight. Almost every teenager has access to electronic or computer games, which allow them to experience the excitement of combat or sports without getting any physical exercise. Too many calories in, too few calories spent.

Yet we all know skinny people who seem to be able to eat anything and never gain weight. They never seem to watch what they're eating, and they don't seem to exercise much. So maybe the answer *isn't* so simple.

In fact, obesity is a very complex subject. For the most part, genetic factors determine how quickly and efficiently our bodies burn fuel. But hormones also play a part in determining our weight: some hormones make us feel hungry; others make us feel full. A host of factors influence how well our bodies absorb what we eat, how quickly food travels through our gastrointestinal tract, and how our hormones (particularly insulin) function. Metabolic factors go hand in hand with many eating disorders, some of which are associated with excessive weight gain (and some with excessive weight loss).

Most obese teenagers have an adult in the family who is also obese. That person may have heart disease or diabetes, trouble breathing, or less apparent problems like high cholesterol or fatty liver. Adults who are obese may first begin to address their weight problem seriously only when their health is in real jeopardy. Obese teenagers in the program at Columbia University Medical Center whom we have surveyed state that they, too, are concerned about their own health.

No doubt that's true. But that's not why most adolescents really want to lose weight.

Most obese adolescents who try to lose weight do so because their obesity is having a serious impact on their social lives. For many, being fat means being made fun of. Their choice of clothes is limited. It may be difficult or even impossible to sit in a movie theater, or even in a desk at school. Trying to squeeze onto public transportation is embarrassing. They may feel that their weight is keeping them from getting dates, never mind steady boyfriends or girlfriends. They find it hard to exercise because they run out of breath quickly and their knees and ankles hurt. They become depressed. In short, obese adolescents have a tough time trying to lead the kind of lives their nonobese peers do.

There are many ways people try to lose weight. Most try to eat less and give up sweets or other "fattening" food while doing some exercise. Some try hypnosis, acupuncture, or meditation. Some join a gym or a school sports team or hire a personal trainer. Most people can lose ten to fifteen pounds, maybe even more, with these changes. Well-advertised diet programs can have similar results. Sleep-away camps for overweight kids often go further; kids who attend may lose thirty to fifty pounds or more. The end of camp, though, means less control over their environment, less structured support, and less physical activity; within a few months of returning home, many kids will regain some or even all of the weight. Indeed, the weight loss industry is huge and keeps growing. People can buy almost anything to supposedly help them lose weight, from dietary supplements to workout equipment to belts. Few of these products and services are regulated by the FDA, and their effectiveness is mainly anecdotal.

A few medications have been approved by the FDA to help obese people lose weight, often by interfering with food absorption or by making the body burn more fuel. These medications can have side effects that range from unpleasant to intolerable. Recent studies suggest that people with underlying heart disease may be increasing the risk of a heart attack by using some of these medications. And remember: genetic factors heavily influence how easily a person can lose weight, with or without the use of medication. Bottom line: losing more than fifty pounds is *really* hard to do.

Surgery becomes a consideration when a person is morbidly obese and has not successfully lost weight in spite of a prolonged and concerted effort. The goal of obesity surgery is not to remove the fat (as is the goal of liposuction, which gets rid of some external body fat tissues but does not cure obesity) but to limit the number of calories that the body has available to absorb. Most such operations are categorized as *restrictive* or *malabsorptive*, though some use both mechanisms.

Gastric bypass is the most common operation used to treat obesity in the United States. During this operation the stomach is divided, leaving only a small pouch into which food passes from the esophagus. The intestine is also divided, and one end is attached to the little stomach pouch. The result: the small stomach pouch limits the amount of food the person can eat (restriction), and the intestine bypasses the area where breakdown of that food normally takes place, so that less of it actually gets absorbed (malabsorption). People who have this operation can lose a lot of weight in a relatively short time, but they don't absorb vitamins and minerals well and need to take nutritional supplements to avoid vitamin deficiencies. The operation itself is technically challenging and is best done by someone with considerable experience.

Gastric banding is an operation that has been used more in Europe, Australia, and South America than in the United States, in part because the bands have only been approved since 2001. Gastric bands have still not been approved by the FDA for use in the United States for anyone under the age of eighteen. As of this writing, just four centers in the United States are permitted to perform gastric band surgery, provided they follow an FDA-approved protocol. Banding is a purely restrictive procedure; by narrowing the inlet to the stomach, the band converts the stomach into an hourglass-like configuration. Food reaching the uppermost part of the stomach is held up, making the person feel full or "restricted" soon after starting to eat; the food then gradually passes into the stomach and then into the intestine, where it is digested in the normal way. There is no malabsorption. To benefit from gastric banding, though, a patient needs to learn how to eat in such a way that the band will help him or her lose weight. High-calorie juices or drinks like milk shakes will zip right through, and all of those calories will be absorbed. Eating too much or too fast will cause food to get stuck, making the patient throw up—not the best way to lose weight. By using the gastric band to eat less, the patient can reduce the number of calories taken in without feeling hungry. Fewer calories, more weight loss.

Other operations for obesity, such as gastric sleeve resection and the duodenal switch, have been used successfully in a few teenagers. Regardless of the procedure, many teenagers who undergo weight-loss surgery are able to improve or correct their obesity. Anyone—teen or adult—who is considering such surgery needs to learn as much as possible about it. Information is available online, and high-volume obesity surgery programs are good resources for researching the procedures.

Weight-loss surgery is an option for teens who have been severely obese for many years; it is not intended for overweight individuals who want to lose a few pounds, nor is it an alternative to dieting and exercise. Surgery is really only for morbidly obese adolescents who have tried to lose weight other ways and have been unable to do so. Not every obese person will be a candidate for a surgical weight-loss procedure; criteria are available online at the NIH website.

Teenage candidates who enter a surgical weight-loss program undergo extensive screening by a multispecialty team. Specialists in endocrinology, gastroenterology, and adolescent medicine are often members of the team, and consultants in pulmonary medicine, cardiology, and kidney disease may be asked to see the potential patient. A nutritionist's evaluation is essential, especially if eating behavior may have a significant impact on a successful weight-loss procedure. A psychiatrist and/or a psychologist sees every candidate. After extensive testing and repeated evaluations, the team determines whether or not a candidate is likely to benefit from surgery, then discusses that assessment with the candidate and his or her family. Some teenagers have family members who have already undergone weight-loss surgery, providing some degree of experience and support. Other families have members who may be indifferent or even hostile to the teenager's plans. In the best situation, the patient has lots of support and feels little pressure from family and friends, but ultimately the patient himself or herself needs to be motivated to lose the weight and to follow through with the changes necessary to keep the weight off.

In our program at Columbia University Medical Center, the teenager interested in gastric band surgery comes with at least one parent for an interview and to learn about the program. If they would like to enter and meet protocol-specific criteria, the teen and the parent sign a voluntary consent to participate. Over the next several weeks the patient is screened by a nutritionist, a pediatric endocrinologist, and a psychologist. Lab tests and imaging studies are obtained. Each patient is given an individualized diet and exercise program. Over the next three to six months the patient is reevaluated to determine how well he or she is making changes and whether there are any problems. At the end of that period, the patient is offered surgery if (1) no significant weight loss has occurred, (2) the patient has followed instructions, and (3) no psychiatric or medical problems have emerged or worsened that would make surgery ill-advised. After the operation, we follow patients for five years, making band adjustments as necessary. We then move the patients into our adult weight-loss surgery program for long-term follow-up.

How much weight can you lose with surgery? How much weight *should* you lose? A doctor can calculate your ideal weight based on growth charts and give you an estimate of your excess weight (the percentage of excess weight lost is used as a measure of success in practice), but whether you want to lose forty pounds or more than a hundred, you must work to lose enough weight to allow you to lead the life you want to lead.

Weight-loss surgery does not guarantee weight loss. Individuals who have restrictive procedures often have to change how they eat to lose weight; some have great difficulty making these changes. Almost all patients who undergo bypass procedures lose weight for several years, but the loss may be insufficient for their goals, or they may regain some of the weight. Additional surgical procedures may be an option.

Most teenagers who undergo weight-loss surgery will lose weight, but results vary. In our program, the average person loses about a third of the excess body weight by the end of the first year after the operation. Some lose more in that year, and some gain weight. The patient and his or her team must work together to be sure that he or she has every chance for an excellent long-term outcome. For the right patient, weight-loss surgery may be the key to overcoming obesity.

—Jeffrey L. Zitsman, MD
Director, Center for Adolescent Bariatric Surgery
Morgan Stanley Children's Hospital
of New York Presbyterian
Columbia University Medical Center

About the Authors

LYNN BIEDERMAN is the coauthor of the acclaimed young adult novel *Unraveling*, available from Laurel-Leaf. She has worked as a librarian and as a lawyer and has enjoyed intermittent periods of being a professional time waster (which rises to a profession when one excels at it as she does). Currently, Lynn is back in the field of law and, during free play, vacillating between two obsessions—tennis and cooking.

Among her many incarnations, **LISA PAZER** has been an economist and editor, a Wall Street analyst and market commentator, a consultant and lecturer, an inventor and entrepreneur. With *Teenage Waistland*, Lisa has finally come home to her first love—fiction.

Visit the authors at teenage-waistland.com.